C000314778

THE PET SHOP

K D GRACE

Published by Xcite Books Ltd – 2011

ISBN 9781908006790

Copyright © K D Grace 2011

The right of K D Grace to be identified as the author of this
work has been asserted by her in accordance with the
Copyright, Designs and Patents Act 1988.

The story contained within this book is a work of fiction.
Names and characters are the product of the author's
imagination and any resemblance to actual persons, living or
dead, is entirely coincidental.

All rights reserved. No part of this book may be reproduced,
stored in a retrieval system, or transmitted in any form or by
any means, electronic, electrostatic, magnetic tape, mechanical,
photocopying, recording or otherwise, without the written
permission of the publishers: Xcite Books, Suite 11769, 2nd
Floor, 145-157 St John Street, London EC1V 4PY

Printed and bound by CPI Group (UK) Ltd, Croydon, CR0 4YY

Cover design by
Madamadari

The Pet Shop is dedicated to the animal in all of us and the exquisitely beautiful world of which we're a part. May we love it more and live in it more consciously.

Thank you with all my heart!

Renee and Jo and all the lovely Ladiez at Sh! who never cease to inspire and encourage me. Lovelies, as always, you're a fountain of information, fun and friendship! You're the best.

The multi-talented Miranda Forbes, to the tireless Hazel Cushion, and to all of the fabulous people at Xcite for making *The Pet Shop* a reality.

Lucy Felthouse for keeping me on the PR straight and narrow, and for cracking the whip when necessary. You rock!

The indomitable Kay Jaybee for friendship and encouragement and commiseration as needed, and it was very much needed.

To Raymond, for easing the journey and believing in me and being proud of me. Volim te mnogo!

Prologue

'YOU CAN'T BE SERIOUS,' O'Kelly said, nearly dropping the phone. 'You can't really mean to give Stella James Tino for the whole weekend. Wouldn't a nice gift voucher from Selfridges be more appropriate?'

The Boss offered her a tolerant chuckle on the other end of the phone. 'Didn't she tell you she thought an occasional shag wasn't too much to ask for doing such a demanding job?'

'Yes, but she was joking. I'm sure she never expected–'

'Well, she's right. It isn't too much to ask, is it? She's a very dedicated employee, and we've always done our best to reward dedicated employees, especially one with such promise, one that we have such plans for.'

'Yes but–'

'Hasn't she met and surpassed our expectations since she's joined Strigida, and didn't we both agree she's exactly what we're looking for?'

'Yes, but–'

'She's not in a relationship, right?'

She rolled her eyes and glanced down at her watch. He was on a roll. Nothing for it now but to hear him out.

'No relationship, no family. Stella can afford to live in London because she has no life outside of work, all factors we took into account when we hired her. There's no arguing she doesn't have time for sex.' He paused long enough for a quick breath. 'Sorry to say that's the way of the world these days. All work and no play. Very sad. Very sad indeed.'

'Yes, sir. It is sad, but, sir, Tino?'

'Yes. Tino.'

'OK, maybe for a couple of hours, *maybe*. But surely not for

1

the whole weekend.'

'Yes, for the whole weekend, O'Kelly, from Friday night till Sunday evening. Every last second of it.'

O'Kelly rubbed her forehead impatiently then rolled her shoulders to loosen the knots, which she could always count on the Boss to tighten. 'It's not that the woman doesn't deserve a weekend of blow-your-brains-out sex. God knows she does, but ...'

'But what, O'Kelly? Get to the point.'

O'Kelly squirmed uncomfortably in her seat. She found the whole thing a bit embarrassing, actually. 'Well, sir, she's just so ...'

'So what?'

'She's just so tight laced, so prim and proper. I don't know – all business. I can't help but wonder if we've made a mistake, and even if we haven't, a weekend with Tino is just so hardcore at this stage, don't you think?' She straightened in her chair and brushed her skirt free of the few remaining crumbs from the sandwich she had wolfed for lunch. 'I can't picture her being the kind who could appreciate or even be able to handle a weekend with Tino.'

'Prim and proper? Really? You just told me she was joking about the company providing sex as a fringe benefit for its overworked employees. Doesn't sound very prim and proper to me. In fact she sounds like exactly the woman we've been looking for.'

'Yes, sir, I know we both agreed about that before we approached her, but Tino? You know how–'

'How out of control and undisciplined he can be? Of course I know. And I think you underestimate our Stella. I think she's exactly the one to handle Tino. Just make sure she has a copy of the Pet minder's manual, and I'm certain she'll do just fine. Besides, Tino can behave himself when he has to.' His voice drifted off as though he were lost in thought, then he returned his attention to O'Kelly. 'My mind is made up on this. You have Tino's schedule, and you know our dedicated Stella never has weekend plans. Work it out. And make sure she gets Tino for the whole weekend.'

'Yes, sir.'

'And O'Kelly. Don't allow her to back out.' She could almost hear the smile in his voice. 'It'll be good for her. Good for both of them. Now, if you'll excuse me, I have a flight to catch.'

For a long moment, O'Kelly listened to the buzz of the dial tone in her ear, then she hung up and sat in front of her laptop contemplating her conversation with the Boss. There would be hell to pay. It was obvious. It was too soon to test Stella out on such a grand scale. How could he not see that?

She gritted her teeth and pulled up the Pet Shop website. She entered her password, then scrolled down till she found the list of Pet profiles and clicked on to Tino's.

It wasn't easy to book a weekend with Tino, and O'Kelly was half hoping that his schedule would be as maddeningly full as it usually was. She was surprised to find there was one opening. Next weekend. She grumbled under her breath. No doubt this was the Boss's doing. She couldn't see any good coming out of this on any level, but he was right. Stella had practically set herself up for it. Though any fool could see the woman was just joking.

She wished now she had kept her mouth shut. She never imagined the Boss would send in the big guns this early in their search. If this little ploy backfired they could lose her, then they'd be back to square one. But if hot sex with Tino was to be a part of the test then she'd do her best to make sure that's exactly what would happen. She was in on this little charade to the bitter end, and she had way too much at stake not to make every effort to see that it all worked out.

Chapter One

'THIS IS TINO.' ANNE placed a hand under the man's chin and lifted his head so Stella could see his lovely stubbled face, blushing as though she had just caught him masturbating behind the sofa.

He offered half a shy smile then quickly lowered his head again, dark eyes disappearing behind a fringe of unruly auburn hair.

'Tino's uncomfortable around new people.' Anne dropped the blue rucksack she'd been carrying by the door, and the two followed Stella into the lounge. 'Don't worry. He'll get used to you.'

The way-too-freely offered stories of Anne O'Kelly's love life had provided Stella with endless entertainment since the two had met when Stella started working for Strigida. In spite of their total lack of anything in common, the two had become fast friends. It was times like this when Stella wondered why that was. No doubt this Tino character was one of Anne's nutters, ready to provide kinky sex for the weekend in Bath. Even Stella had to admit, a whole lot of neurotic could be overlooked in exchange for a hot weekend with someone that tall, and that hot.

Stella knew Anne had planned to drop in this evening on her way to Bath, but she hadn't expected her quite so late, nor had she expected her to bring a friend. She said she had a surprise for her, a little token from Strigida for a job well done. Stella figured it was probably a gift voucher or maybe theatre tickets, which she would never find time to use. She'd given away mountains of them in her previous job to less deserving fellow employees simply because there was never time. A few

5

extra quid in her paycheque would have been a lot more appreciated, though she never had time to spend that either.

In the lounge, Anne made herself comfy in the leather recliner then turned her attention to Tino. 'Sit,' she commanded.

The man dropped onto the floor next to her, and she ran her hand absently over his dark hair, caressing the back of his neck.

Still wondering what was going on, Stella sat down across from the two. She couldn't help noticing, as Tino shifted to rest his head on Anne's knee, that he was sporting an impressive erection beneath thin summer trousers.

She quickly averted her eyes, but not before her pussy got the message and warmed to the thought. These days Stella didn't see too many hard cocks.

Anne chuckled softly and rearranged herself in the chair so Tino could nestle against her leg. 'He's always got a hard-on, and he loves to show it off.' Then she added nonchalantly, 'How about a G&T? I'm gasping.'

Stella clamoured to her feet, trying to keep her eyes on Tino's face. 'And what about you? What would you like?'

The man only buried his head against Anne's leg like a shy child.

'Tino doesn't drink, and he's already been fed.'

'Already been fed?'

Anne disengaged Tino's arms from around her leg and stood. 'Stay here, Tino, mistresses need to talk.'

'Mistresses? What the fuck's going on?'

'Shshsh!' Anne grabbed Stella's arm and hustled her off to the kitchen. 'He's very sensitive to other people's emotions. He's nervous enough just being in a strange place.' She helped herself to a glass and found the gin. 'Remember I told you my therapist said that with my relationship issues, before I got involved with a man, I should start with a plant?'

Stella nodded, 'And if you didn't kill the plant, work your way up to a goldfish then maybe a cat or dog. Yeah, I remember. So?'

Anne plopped an ice cube in her glass. 'What if I don't like

6

goldfish? And maybe I'm allergic to cats and I'm afraid of dogs. Well ...' She nodded toward the lounge where Tino was.

'What? Is the RSPCA adopting out men these days?'

'Even better.' Anne moved closer to Stella and spoke softly around a wicked smile. 'There's a site called the Pet Shop. They set people up with Pets, and I'm not talking cats and dogs here, Stel. It's temporary, only for a night, a weekend at the most.'

'You're kidding, right?'

'Hon, I wouldn't joke about something as yummy as Tino.' She offered a naughty giggle. 'Anyway, if I had to venture a guess, I'd say having a Pet occasionally would probably suit people like us much better than having a relationship. Our conversation the other day made me think a Pet might be exactly what you need. You certainly seem to be responding well to Tino.' She gave Stella's tits a passing stroke with her free hand. 'I'd say your nips approve.'

Stella slapped her away. She had lamented to Anne that with the demands of her job, she had no time for a relationship, but someone working as hard as she did surely deserve a good shag once in a while. They had been walking along the Serpentine at the time. Anne had laughed around the mango ice lolly she had practically been fellating. Stella had assumed that meant she realised it was a joke.

She grabbed the gin bottle and poured herself a double.

'Tino's very low maintenance, well behaved – at least most of the time anyway, clean, quiet.'

'Jesus, Annie, this is a bloke you're talking about, not a stray cat.'

'Come on,' Anne grabbed Stella's hand and led her back toward the lounge. 'If he's left alone too long, he gets bored and sometimes gets in trouble.'

'What the hell's he going to do, piss on the carpet?'

'Don't be daft. He's house-broken, but unlike most blokes, he always remembers to put the toilet seat back down.'

'I don't believe we're having this conversation. How did–' Stella stopped in her tracks sending a cascade of gin over the rim of her glass onto the carpet.

There on the floor, exactly where they left him, was Tino, head thrown back, eyes closed, enthusiastically thrusting the thick cock he'd extricated from his trousers in and out of his fisted hand.

'Tino! Bad boy! You know better than to play with your thing without permission.' Anne shoved past Stella and slapped his hands away from his penis.

Stella watched in fascination as the pouting Pet let Anne push his trousers down far enough to bare his exquisite bum. There were no underpants. Then, on hands and knees, he presented his arse to Anne, who gave him a resounding thwack on each cheek. Stella's pussy practically gushed as Anne spanked him again, and his muscular buttocks clenched and relaxed, beautifully displaying the dark pucker of his anus. Stella wondered how the hell one connected up with a place like the Pet Shop and someone like Tino.

'I hate to punish you, darling, but you must behave. What will Mistress Stella think of you being so ill-mannered? Here, let's get you out of those clothes. I know you're uncomfortable. You don't mind, do you, Stel? Pets only wear clothes in public. They're much more comfortable naked.' She didn't wait for Stella's response.

Tino sat back on the floor and lifted his arse while Anne stripped him. The spanking had done nothing to diminish his huge erection. His heavy balls bounced against his thighs with Anne's efforts.

From the dark blue rucksack by the door, Anne produced a black leather collar studded with heavy silver riveting and a D-ring. 'There's a leash in the bag too if he needs it,' she said, as she buckled the collar around Tino's throat. 'Pet Shop Pets are all very well trained, but a collar and a leash make people feel good, you know, like they really do own the Pet. It's kink in disguise, really.' She spoke over her shoulder to Stella. 'You can still have leather and PVC if you want, but most of the Pet Shop's clientele take pleasure in the subtlety of no one else knowing what they're up to. But the collar does give you a bit more control if he should get out of hand, or if you just want to play a little rough.' Once Anne had him completely naked, except for the collar, she stuffed his clothes into the rucksack and turned her attention to Stella. 'Sit there in the chair. Let him get used to you.'

Stella couldn't believe she was participating in this circus, but with her heart pounding in her chest and her pussy twitching in rhythm, she did as she was told. She was painfully aware of the weighty fullness of her breasts, feeling like they were mostly nipple and areola at the moment. She felt as naked as Tino, who watched her with wide-eyed curiosity.

Anne was saying something about the twat in IT, who didn't know his arse from his iPhone, but Stella wasn't listening. How could she when Tino had crawled across the floor, erection still bouncing at full attention, and now he sat only inches from her, looking up at her with those deep dark eyes.

Anne smiled her approval. 'You can touch him. He won't bite, not unless you tell him to.'

Stella reached out her hand, and he slid closer until her fingers rested in his hair just above his left ear. At her touch, his erection surged, and he moved forward to lower his head onto her thigh.

'There. You see, he likes you.' Anne knocked back her drink and tinkled the ice around the glass. 'I need another one of these.' She padded off to the kitchen, leaving Stella alone with the Pet.

As she stroked his hair and the nape of his neck around the collar, Tino rubbed his face against her thigh in much the same way her grandmother's cat had when she was a little girl. Marking territory, her gran had informed her. Was this man marking her as his territory?

He scooted still closer, making a sound at the back of his throat that wasn't completely unlike a cat's purr. He continued to nuzzle and rub his face and nose against her thigh, moving in feline stretches, insinuating his way into the space on the floor between her legs. Once there, he rose on his haunches and nestled and stroked until his face rested on her upper thigh. Then with another throaty moan, he nuzzled in, nose first, against her crotch.

9

She gave a little yelp and grabbed the arms of the chair, a move that he took for an invitation, and snuggled in until she could feel his hot breath through her trousers. 'Oh God! Tino, I ... Ah!' She bit off the words in a gasp, as Tino began to lick her crotch with long wet strokes of his tongue. His warm saliva made the fabric cling to the contours of her vulva, now moist inside and out. Curling her fingers in his hair, she opened her legs and shifted her hips. It was as though her mind had completely disengaged from anything other than the pleasure of his exquisite tongue. He pulled her closer to his face, sniffing, inhaling, sampling her scent. She thrust her pussy against his nose with a rush of heat forgetting that this sort of behaviour wasn't normally tolerated in polite company.

By that delicious smell of cunt, mammals recognise when a female is ready to be mounted. And males do whatever it takes to stimulate them to readiness. Humans were no different. She knew her own smell, when her vulva was slick with her juices and aching to be fucked. And Tino was sniffing her, testing her, familiarising himself with that intimate scent. Male dogs in the wild were always horny. They lived to copulate, and here was Tino with a hard-on almost from the moment he met her. He really was like an animal!

'Tino! Bad boy! Get back.' Anne stormed into the room and grabbed the man by the collar, pulling him away from Stella's cunt.

'What the fuck are you doing?' Stella gasped, using every ounce of her control to keep from dragging him back to her.

Tino wrapped both arms around Anne's leg until his full cock rubbed against her calf; then he began to hump.

'Bad boy!' She shoved him off. 'You know you don't lick someone's pussy unless they ask you, and you don't hump my leg.'

She turned her attention to Stella who was still struggling to catch her breath. 'I'm sorry about that, but he's so uncomfortable. Look how full his balls are. The Pet Shop keeps its Pets horny to heighten the pleasure for their keepers, but that's no excuse for his bad behaviour. He can't go bashing about like a randy baboon.

10

'Bend over, Tino, take your spanking.'

To Stella's surprise, Tino turned his lovely buttocks to her. Bracing with his arms against the coffee table, his arse was practically in her face, his little back-hole clenching nervously. Both intrigued and aroused, she brought her hand down with a stinging smack against his pale bottom. His cock twitched, her wet pussy got wetter. As she spanked him again, he grunted and humped air.

Anne chuckled. 'Poor thing. He's so horny. He's not used to waiting this long before he comes, and it's pretty clear he's got your scent.' She nodded to the wet spot between Stella's legs.

Before Stella could explain, Anne took Tino's face in her hands and kissed him. The Pet responded enthusiastically, and the delicious tongue that had laved Stella's cunt only minutes before now ate Anne's mouth as though she were his favourite kind of chocolate. She reached down and cupped his balls, kneading them until he whimpered. Then she turned to Stella. 'I'd say he's definitely primed and ready. Whatever you want him to do, just ask.' She looked down at her watch and heaved a sigh. 'I'd love to stay for the fun, but I'm off to Bath for the weekend. I've left the Pet Shop instruction manual in the kitchen on the counter, and anything else Tino might need is in the rucksack. If you have any questions just text.'

'What?' Stella grabbed her friend by the arm as she headed for the door and jerked her back. 'He isn't going with you? I thought he was your Pet?'

'Don't I wish, hon, but Tino is way out of my budget. He's all yours, compliments of Strigida for a job well done.'

Stella was sure she was sinking claws into her friend's arm, but she didn't care. 'You can't leave me. I don't know what to do.'

'Oh come on, Stel, it hasn't been that long. He's yours until Sunday evening, and I can tell you if I were in your shoes, I'd enjoy every second of him.' She sauntered to the door and let herself out.

Chapter Two

SURE ENOUGH ON THE kitchen table was an instruction manual from the Pet Shop entitled, *On Keeping Pets*.

She opened it to the first chapter and read.

Get to know your Pet

Your experience will be more enjoyable if you take time to get to know each other, to get comfortable with each other before you initiate sexual contact. Pets, like people, have different personalities. Some may be shy and in need of some gentle coaxing before they get comfortable with their keeper. If your Pet is shy, do make sure he or she is comfortably acquainted with you before you initiate sexual contact.

If, however, your Pet is not shy, he or she may try to initiate sexual contact. DO NOT ALLOW THIS. It is the keeper who must choose when sex takes place. Your Pet must never be led to believe she or he is the alpha in the relationship. You must maintain control. No matter how aroused and uncomfortable your Pet may appear to be, do not allow even masturbation without your explicit permission. Your Pet is there for your pleasure. Even if your pleasures are voyeuristic, you must always be the initiator of the sex act. Permission is yours to grant or deny.

All Pets arrive at their keeper's highly aroused and ready for sex play – the males with erections, the females well lubricated and ready to accommodate a penis or a dildo. But they are also well-trained to control themselves. Make sure that they do. This will enhance your pleasure as well as theirs.

Pets experience the world through their sense of smell, and they will get to know their keepers through that sense. Do not

*be nervous. Assume a relaxed position, preferably in a chair or
on a sofa, with your legs open.*

Note: This should be done fully clothed.

*Command your pet to sit on the floor next to you then allow
her or him to sniff you and touch you. Some pets will also want
to lick and taste you. Remember, this contact is essential for
your Pet to get to know you as PETS DO NOT TALK. Keep the
mood light. Do not allow anything more than this initial
contact until you and your Pet feel comfortable with each
other. Only after this occurs should your interaction be of a
sexual nature.*

Stella felt something warm and wet against her hand and
looked down to see Tino kneeling next to her, his tongue
flicking over her fingertips, his eyes locked on her face.

'I'm sorry, Tino. It's just I've never had a Pet before.' She
reached out and stroked his head.

Still holding her gaze, he stood and led her back to the
lounge. When she sat in the recliner, he sat on the floor in front
of her, watching her expectantly, shifting uncomfortably
around the weight of his distended penis, clenching his
buttocks and rocking his hips. She couldn't take her eyes off
such blatant, insinuating sexuality. With a little gasp of
surprise, she realised her own hips were rocking, rubbing her
swollen cunt against the chair.

'I'm sorry, Tino,' she shoved to her feet, tearing her gaze
away from the gorgeously horny man sitting on the floor by her
chair. 'But I just can't do this. If I had known what Anne –
what Strigida – had planned for me, I would have never
consented, surely Anne knew that. Anyway, I feel really bad
that I've wasted your time, but this is just not something I can
do.'

The pet only looked up at her with adoring and expectant
eyes.

'I'll gladly give you taxi fare home, of course. I mean that's
the least I can do. None of this is your fault, after all. Anne told
me that you were a gift, so I assume you've already been paid.'
She raced through the last sentence breathlessly, her face

burning at the very thought that the company had paid for a prostitute for her.

Did they really think she was that desperate? And never mind how desperate she was, surely she had worked at Strigida long enough for them to realise this was not the gift for her. And she was bloody well certain Anne knew that. There would definitely be words when she returned from Bath. 'Is that all right, if we do that? If we just call it even and I get you a cab home?'

Tino made no response. Instead, he rubbed his cheek affectionately against her leg and moved to sit back on his haunches, a position that made his erection look even more enormous, bulging heavily against his thigh. At the sight, her stomach muscles tensed low and tight and her pussy clenched and half convulsed.

'I forgot,' she looked down at the manual still gripped in one hand, 'Pets don't talk. But since I really don't want a Pet, couldn't you break the rules just this once?'

He brushed her leg again with his cheek, then with his lips, making delicious shivers run up her spine.

'Guess not. OK. Well, I realise this is an awkward situation, Tino, and I'm really sorry about that. I know you're expected to stay here. I appreciate your position. Really I do. I'm sure we'll get through this if we work together.' She nodded down the hall. 'I have a guestroom. You're welcome to sleep there. It's small but comfortable.' He followed her on silent feet, and looked on as she showed him the guestroom.

'The closet's there.' She pointed. 'Though I guess you won't need that. Extra toiletries are on the dressing table there. Those you might need. And the remote for the telly, well it's a little tetchy. Here let me show you.' Suddenly she realised he wasn't paying any attention. His gaze was locked on her – more specifically on her crotch. She blushed hard and forced a smile. 'Never mind. I imagine you can figure it out if you decide you want to watch telly. Anyway, make yourself at home. Are you hungry? Can I get you something to drink?'

Again, he plopped down on the floor. This time he wrapped his arms around her leg and began to rub his cheek against her thigh.

'Tino, really. I don't think I can ...'

He made little grunting sounds and shifted his hips forward and back. If anything, his erection seemed still bigger. She suddenly remembered the manual said the Pet Shop kept their Pets horny. Hadn't Anne said he usually didn't have to wait this long before he came?

She found herself blushing again at the sight of his heavy hard-on. 'I'm sorry. I didn't think about how ... uncomfortable you must be. I know you're not allowed to touch yourself unless your keeper gives you permission, and, well, since we can't, since we're not going to ...' She nodded to his cock. 'It's all right with me if you do what you need to do. You know, for some relief.' She felt like her face would burst into flames.

For a long moment he looked up at her with his bottomless cinnamon eyes, as though he couldn't quite comprehend what she wanted of him. Then, slowly, carefully, holding her gaze, he laid a hand against his cock and ran a curled palm up the length of it. A shudder ascended his spine. He threw back his head and released a trembling breath that ended in a deep animal groan at the back of his throat.

Almost before she realised it, she replied with a little whimper of her own that slipped between her lips. Her nipples pearled through the thin silk of her blouse, and her pussy felt slick and giddy. She closed her eyes only for a split second, but the next thing she knew, Tino was standing beside her, so close that her hand, resting low against her belly brushed his cock, and they both gasped at the feel of it. Before she could do more than marvel at the velvety softness that felt like it sheathed granite, he pushed in closer, and his large hand engulfed hers easing it gently against his cock with just enough pressure to encourage her fingers to wrap around the girth of him.

She should have stepped back, she should have commanded him to stay in the room and do what he needed to do and not come out until he was done. But she didn't. Instead she curled her fingers around him and felt his hand tighten over hers. She expected him to hump like a dog, but he only stepped closer, engulfing her in a feral scent not unlike cat fur on a sunny day.

The shifting of his hips was almost invisible but for the tensing of the muscles low in his hard belly, tightening and lifting until his soft pubic curls just grazed the inside of her wrist. Instead of the blatant sexuality she expected, he simply laid his head on her shoulder, his warm breath raising the fine hair along the back of her neck. His heart hammered a heavy drumbeat that matched her own, and her nipples seemed to be pressing ever forward to get nearer to it.

His free arm encircled her, resting just above her hip, where his hand moved in a gentle caress up and down her ribs, almost tickling. The sensation of it all accumulated warm and heavy just below her belly. The heat of his lips rested close to the pulse of her neck. They were slightly parted, his breath coming in fast little puffs.

She knew she should be pushing him away, making him bend over for the spanking a misbehaving Pet deserved. She hadn't asked him to touch her, and she hadn't volunteered her services. 'You're a very naughty Pet, Tino.' She barely managed to gasp before he tensed, and a strangled groan escaped his throat just as his cock twitched and she felt the silky slick heat of his come spill over both of their hands and against his bare belly. Then his whole body convulsed, and involuntarily he pulled her tight against him, an act which sent her into her own convulsions. She let out a startled cry. She hadn't expected to come. She hadn't intended to come, and yet there she stood quivering out her pleasure against the Pet, who held her in a powerful, sex-stimulated bear-hug.

It was only when her own body had calmed to after-shocks and tremors that her brain began to reassert itself, and she pulled away and gasped. 'Bad Tino! Bad Pet!' She grabbed the guest towel from the foot of the bed, wiped her hands and offered it to Tino, but he only stood there, hand, belly and cock pearlescent with his come. She groaned a frustrated sigh, moved forward and began to wipe him briskly. 'You're a very bad boy. That wasn't what I asked you to do. Do you have any idea how uncomfortable this all is for me?'

The Pet hung his head, turned his back to her and braced himself bent over the bed, bottom up.

'No! I don't want to spank you! That would only make matters worse, damn it!' She shook the manual she still held in one hand. 'And they're already bad enough.' She paced the floor, her heart racing in her chest, still unable to believe what had just happened. Tino was a glorified prostitute, she reminded herself. Jesus, had she gotten so desperate? She forced herself to calm down as Tino turned a questioning gaze to her over his shoulder. 'The bathroom is down the hall to your left if you want to clean up.' Then she turned on her heels and quickly fled to her own room, shutting the door soundly behind her.

The whole weekend yawned before her like an abyss. The power of her own desires frightened her almost as much as having Tino's naked sexuality ever present, almost as much as the fact that they had no way of communicating other than her giving orders and spanking his lovely bottom when he disobeyed.

Use only your open palm to punish your Pet, and only on his or her presented bare buttocks. You will also find a special leather spanker in the rucksack that arrived with your Pet. You may safely use this, but only on buttocks and upper thighs. If your Pet is female, you may use this and your hands to produce a gentle sting on your Pet's breasts. Alternatively, for punishment, you may use a rolled-up newspaper on other areas of the body. Never use anything else unless special dispensation has been granted by the Pet Shop.

If special dispensation is granted for rough play, you must remember that your Pet has a safe word. It is the only word any Pet will ever utter in the presence of his or her keeper, and only then when play is too rough for her or him. It is of interest to note that in the Pet Shop's history, no Pet has ever had to use the safe word.

If, on the other hand, a keeper chooses a Pet who likes to play rough, it is important the keeper let the Pet know her or his safe word at the beginning of the visit. The safety of Pets and keepers is paramount in rough play.

***

She blushed at the thought of punishing Tino properly for his transgression, a thought there was no denying her pussy was fond of. She reminded herself again that she didn't need to resort to sex with prostitutes. She knew how to use a vibrator. Sex for one was a good thing, the perfect tool for busy women, for women in control of their own lives. God, why was maintaining control in the presence of a man pretending to be an animal so difficult?

It could have something to do with the fact that he was running around her flat gorgeously naked with a huge hard-on, she reminded herself.

She cleaned her teeth, took off her make-up, and changed into her tracksuit. She always had work to do, since she took the position at Strigida, but her laptop was in the lounge. The thought of being in the same room with Tino made her heart race and her hands shake.

She sat down on the bench in front of her vanity and stared at her face in the mirror. Her cheeks were still flushed and her dark hair was coming loose from the knot in which she'd worn it all day. She tried to remember the last time she'd had any kind of interaction with a male she didn't work with. It was better that way, she reminded herself. Her working skills were always a lot better than her social skills.

She supposed it must be obvious, even at Strigida. Why else would they offer her a prostitute? She took out the clip and shook her hair free around her shoulders. She wondered if Tino would like her hair down. Furious at herself, she forced the thought out of her head. She stood and paced back and forth at the foot of the bed. What difference did it make what Tino thought? And why was she letting this situation get to her? She didn't ask for it. Her behaviour wasn't in question here.

She squared her shoulders and blew out a nervous breath. Tomorrow she would take him down town and check him into a hotel. He could wait it out there. She didn't have to allow this. Gift or not. Plus, surely it must be illegal. First thing tomorrow that's what she would do. In the meantime, she'd get her laptop and tell Tino she had work to do and ... She opened the door a crack to find him sitting on the floor in front of her.

He looked up at her, eyes bright, questioning.

'Um, I'm really tired,' she blurted. 'I'm going to sleep now. Make yourself at home in the guestroom. Good night.' She jerked the door shut between them and leant back against it, heart racing, ignoring the gnaw of guilt below her sternum at being so rude. It didn't matter, she told herself. He'd get paid anyway, and he wouldn't even have to work for his money. She undressed and plopped into bed. It was a little past ten, and thanks also to Strigida, she was always under-slept. This would give her a chance to catch up on some much-needed rest.

Two hours later she was still tossing amid the tangle of sheets absolutely refusing to masturbate, though she desperately needed to. She told herself it was the principle of the thing, but in reality she was afraid that Tino might somehow magically know she was masturbating and ... And what? His feelings would be hurt because he didn't get to service her? He'd smell it on her in the morning and lick her crotch. Oh God, she so didn't need to think about that right now.

She was just about to drift off with the pillow settled in the crook of her arm when the gnaw of guilt returned. If Tino really did have to stay in character the whole weekend he must be dying of thirst. She was always thirsty after sex. But it hadn't been sex, she reminded herself again. Not real sex. Still, she had helped herself to all the water she wanted from the en-suite sink, while poor Tino had none. And what if he was hungry? Anne said he'd been fed, but that was ages ago. Come to think of it, she was a bit peckish herself. But then again, he might have just settled in to watch the footie and fallen asleep in front of the telly, without giving a second thought to what had happened. Surely he would be happy for an unexpected night off, right? If that were the case, then the coast would be clear. She could get her laptop and bring it back to the room without him even knowing.

She got out of bed and carefully slipped into her blue satin robe, tying the sash loosely around her waist. Then she tiptoed to the door holding her breath. Somewhere deep in the city a siren wailed, but the flat was silent. Slowly, carefully, she opened the door, and her breath caught in her throat.

There on the floor in front of her lay Tino, curled around himself in a foetal position, his breathing the deep even breathing of sleep. She couldn't resist the urge to stare down at him, to take in the sheer wild maleness of him lying there bathed in silver moonlight, sleeping in nothing but a leather collar.

She had just lifted her foot to step over him when suddenly he woke and sat up with a start causing her to yelp in surprise. She lost her balance and would have tumbled backward if he hadn't caught her by the hand and pulled her forward to land against the hard rise and fall of his chest.

'Tino, I'm sorry,' she gasped. 'I tried not to wake you. Did I hurt you? Oh God, I hope you're OK.' Too late she realised her robe had fallen open, and the Pet's gaze was locked on her breasts, his naked cock jutting like a velvet-sheathed knife against the inside of her bare thigh. They both sat frozen against each other, holding their breath.

Chapter Three

SHE MADE A SCRAMBLING effort to get up and stepped on the sash of her robe, which sent her sprawling again. This time right on top of him. The robe ripped completely open revealing her nakedness beneath.

A deep growl erupted from Tino's throat, a growl that had nothing to do with pain, but everything to do with his tightening grip around her and the insistence of his stiff penis against the inside of her thigh.

A frisson of fear rippled up her spine and, for a split second, she thought he would take her by force. She braced herself. Instead, he just held her there, his whole body bristling with need. And Jesus, the feel of him, the feel of his naked skin against hers! Her own skin suddenly felt like every pore was open wide, aching to soak up his touch. With each breath, the expansion of his chest pressed against her, and with it, his cock gouged upward toward her gaping pussy.

And yet he didn't move. The physical sensation of his body surrounding hers had so overwhelmed her that she hadn't noticed his gaze locked on her face, questioning, longing, achingly tender.

She let out a slow, even breath. 'You're an obedient Pet, Tino, aren't you?'

His only response was to rub the slight scratch of his stubbled cheek against hers and sigh a lingering breath onto her earlobe.

'Such a good Pet, the best Pet,' she crooned softly.

He nuzzled in still closer, bathing her throat and nape in warm humidity that moved on ticklish little feet down over her breasts and belly, causing her pussy to grasp and tremble. She

21

whimpered and curled her fingers in his hair. 'Tino, I need you. Oh God,' she half sobbed, then the words tumbled out. 'Tino, I need you to ... I need you to take care of me. Like a good Pet.'

For an agonizing moment he held her there, his cock stretched against the inside of her upper thigh almost but not quite in position for her to wriggle down onto.

She brushed her lips against his, half expecting him to lap at her with his tongue. Instead his response was feather soft, more breath than mouth, but it was enough to encourage her. This time as she pressed her mouth to his, he nipped her lower lip with his front teeth, following the resulting gasp with the darting of his tongue, quick and playful.

And she was completely undone. She took his mouth with all the pent-up passion she didn't know she had, and he responded in kind.

With a sinuous shifting of his hips, he moved just enough to make contact. There, he remained, rubbing the head of his cock between her labia, just at the point of pressure, pushing just enough to open her, but not quite enough to penetrate. There, he held her, preventing her from settling down onto him, preventing her from taking by force what she so desperately needed.

'Tino,' she breathed, 'be a good Pet. I need you to put it in me, now.'

Instead, he pulled out just enough to rub the tip of his cock, now well lubricated with her slickness, against her clit, which was already distended nearly to the point of pain in its arousal. She squirmed and wriggled in a frenzied effort to push onto him, but he was too strong.

'Tino,' she hissed, 'you're a bad Pet. I said put it in me. You're supposed to obey me.' She grabbed him by the hair and held him tight. 'Damn it! Obey me. Now!'

With one more subtle shift followed by an upward thrust, he did just that. And in spite of how wet she was she felt as though he had ripped her in two, leaving her breathless and gasping. She knew he was substantial, but she hadn't counted on her own tenderness. Apparently Tino had. He held very still, waiting for her to get used to him. All the while, his large right hand gently stroked her flank.

At first it was just a subtle rhythmic rocking beneath her, like ripples on a pond. But she found herself mirroring each movement of his body. When he was certain she could accommodate him, he scooped her into his arms and rolled with her until she was beneath him. Then he pulled out and manoeuvred her onto her stomach. One strong arm around her waist hoisted her bottom into the air.

Suddenly Tino was every inch the animal he was pretending to be. And she found herself responding like an animal, like a cat on heat. She lifted her arse up high and opened her legs for his perusal. He took time to sniff her, took time to give her creamy pussy a delicious lapping with his tongue, before he covered her with his body. She was amazed at how large he seemed, how diminutive she felt as he shoved into her, so deep and so hard that he left her breathless again.

He growled and bit her shoulder, then her neck, just hard enough to feel possessive, to feel feline. In the dim light, she could see the outline of their joined bodies in the full-length hall mirror. He thrust with the animal movements she would have expected of a big cat, muscles rippling in waves, the pistoning of his hips driving his cock with a force that might have been painful if it hadn't felt so damn good. One hand gripped her hip, kneading her hard with each thrust. His other arm still encircled her waist, but his hand migrated over her mons to flick and tweak her clit until it was raw and swollen way beyond the protection of its hood.

It took her sex-crazed brain a few seconds to realise the guttural animal howl vibrating off the hallway walls was not Tino's but her own. Before she could dwell on it, the orgasm that had been building exploded through her like a hurricane, and she would have collapsed beneath him if he hadn't been supporting her weight.

Then his whole body convulsed and he threw both arms around her, driving his cock deep and hard. She could feel his penis shudder again and again inside her as he emptied a load that clearly his earlier masturbation had done little to diminish. At last he wriggled and scooted just enough to maintain their

23

connection while curling her into a spoon position against the heat of his body as they caught their breath.

Then, Tino's stomach growled.

'Oh you poor thing. You must be starving and thirsty too. I know I am.' She reached over her shoulder and ran a hand through his damp hair, hair that smelt like her, and he rubbed his face against her palm. She sat up and tried to pull on her robe, but he nuzzled it away, then took the hem of it between his teeth and shook it playfully, with a low growl.

She laughed. 'All right, you naughty boy. You win. I guess there's no law against scrambling eggs starkers, is there?' She stood and slid her index finger into the D-ring of his collar to pull him to her, though Tino really didn't need any coercion to follow.

Be sure to keep your Pet well hydrated. Do not give your Pet anything to drink but water. The Pet will happily drink tap or bottled. Just fill a bowl with cool water and keep it in a place where your Pet has easy access. Refresh it several times a day. This is especially important after your Pet has sex.

Note: Do not give Pets fizzy water, as it tickles their noses.

She followed the instructions, and watched as Tino lapped thirstily until the water was nearly gone. When she had refilled the bowl, she turned to find him standing, shifting from foot to foot, cupping his penis and balls. She understood exactly what he needed.

Pets may be allowed to relieve themselves outside if the Pet keeper has a secluded garden, and is so inclined to properly attend the Pet. In cases where this isn't possible, or desirable by the Pet keeper, simply escort the Pet to the toilet, shut the door behind, and leave him or her to attend to needs in private.

Note: Most Pet keepers are more comfortable with the latter.

Stella lived in a flat, and she wasn't about to take Tino out for a piss in the park. She trotted him down the hall to the loo, shut the door behind him, and hurried back to the kitchen to make eggs.

What started out as just scrambled eggs quickly turned into a full fry-up. The way Tino behaved, she figured surely he was a carnivore and he must be at least as ravenous as she was.

Pets don't like to eat alone. They prefer to sit on the floor by the table next to their keeper's chair, where they enjoy being hand-fed. If this is not possible, place food in a bowl next to the water dish. Make sure meat is always cut into bite-sized chunks.

Note: The former is preferable, as most Pets and Pet keepers find sharing a meal in this fashion very enjoyable and a part of their bonding experience.

The manual was right. Once she got the hang of offering Tino choice morsels in her open hand, the laving of his velvety wet tongue, the slight nipping of teeth and curling of lips was lovely. He sat on his haunches, once again fully erect, resting his head on her naked thigh in between bites. If she hadn't been ravenous, she would have never been able to concentrate on eating. He was as happy to nibble the mushrooms and tomatoes as he was the bacon and eggs. The toast with honey forced him to lick the sweet stickiness off the tips of her fingers, even occasionally off her thigh when her efforts were clumsy with the excitement of having such an exquisite creature eating from her hand.

She'd had a similar sense of excitement the first time a horse had taken a sugar lump from her hand. That something so powerful, something potentially wild and dangerous had allowed itself to be fed by her was an exhilarating experience. At present, the magnificent beast on the floor insinuated himself a little closer to her with each bite, and she was pretty sure this wild animal had more than food in mind.

Tino scooted and wriggled himself until, at last, he sat between her legs, his humid breath warming her mons. With each morsel of food, he insinuated his waiting face a little closer to her pussy until her open palm with its offered tidbit was practically resting against her pubis. When a particularly sticky morsel of toast ended up on the chair between her legs, he carefully licked up every bit from the chair, and then he continued lapping his way right on up between her legs.

She caught her breath with a little whimper and a jerk. The bite of toast she was about to offer slipped from her hand onto her belly. Tino wasn't bothered. He simply squeezed in between the table and her body, forcing her chair back just enough that he could nibble and lick the toast and honey from her tightening abdominal muscles. That done, he picked up where he'd left off, nibbling and licking between her pouting labia.

Fascinated and aroused by his eating habits, she grabbed a handful of egg and wiped it across her breasts and down her stomach, licking the remains from her fingers, feeling a bit animal herself. He raised his head again and worked his way up her belly nibbling scrambled eggs as he went, pushing her chair back farther and farther from the table.

She gave up on any semblance of proper table etiquette and slid onto the floor next to him. She grabbed the plate from the table on her way down, shoving a handful of egg into her own mouth before smearing more egg and a bit of tomato across her breasts and belly. Lying back she let Tino nibble and lap his breakfast off her body until she was writhing and grinding on the floor beneath his enthusiastic tongue.

He surprised her by taking a rasher of bacon from the plate and offering it to her, mouth to mouth. It was almost like a porn version of *Lady and the Tramp* as they gnawed and nibbled their way to each other's mouth, tongues lapping and lips smacking the salty savoury taste of the meat.

She plucked a nice plump mushroom from the plate. It reminded her of the tip of a cock as she eased it between her slippery folds far enough that Tino had to work to get it out.

But Tino didn't mind working for his breakfast. And by the time he had extricated the mushroom, she was completely convinced his tongue was prehensile. His face glistening with her juices, the mushroom pressed daintily between his lips, he slid up her sticky body and offered her the morsel with its unique sauce of their lovemaking. Together they gulped down the tangy fungus between gasps for breath, breath which seemed to be harder and harder to get as their meal continued.

She gulped a bite of toast then wiped the honey and butter from the remains of it in circular motions around her nipples. Tino watched wide-eyed, his cock standing at full attention, his balls resting heavily on his thigh. She could see the silky droplets of precome now seeping from the domed tip of his erection. As he lunged forward to suckle her honeyed nipples, she ran a thumb over the slick tip of his penis. A shudder climbed up through him, and a deep-throated moan vibrated against her areola. 'You poor thing. You're so uncomfortable, aren't you?' she crooned. 'You really need to come, don't you, darling? Let me help you then. Let me make you feel better.'

The suckling pressure of his lips against her nipple became almost painful. She opened her thighs and lifted her hips. He eased into her like his cock had a built-in homing device and her pussy was home. Just as he did, she dumped the remaining eggs and tomatoes onto her stomach and wiped them up over her breasts. If he were shocked, he gave no indication. He simply lowered his head to lick a trail of tomato juice from between her breasts as he pushed into her with a satisfied grunt.

Their bodies squished and slurped and humped against the banquet spread over her belly. Occasionally he came up from the press of her for a nibble or for a tidbit to offer her, mouth to mouth.

In the strange erotic mix of eating and feeding and slippery, slidey fucking, she came in trembling shockwaves, and his tightening grip told her he was about to do the same.

'Tino,' she breathed, 'I want you to come on my stomach. I want to see you unload. Do it!' Her command surprised her in its forcefulness. But she needn't have worried that he wouldn't obey. He withdrew from her and straddled her belly, offering a harsh groan just before a vicious spurt of semen arched over her stomach and breasts followed by another and another and another.

Then she pulled him back down onto her. Caught off-guard, he slipped and slid across her belly catching his breath in heavy gasps. She pushed him off onto the floor, knelt next to him, and began to lick the slippery mix of breakfast and come from his belly. She felt a primitive sense of power and hunger that made her skin tingle all over, made her raise her arse and wriggle it as though she were ready to be mounted again.

Tino responded by growling and curling his fingers in her hair, pulling her down into an animal rough and tumble on the floor, licking and tasting and rubbing and stroking until they were both slippery with egg and come and sweat, and shiny with butter and oil and heat. Tino had taken her so far beyond what she had ever felt in sex before that she hardly recognised herself or her response. The feeling of animalness was so far removed from anything she had ever experienced that she felt like tossing her head back and howling.

He sniffed her and licked her and rubbed against her. She imitated his actions, wondering if such exhilaration was what their primate ancestors had felt. When a female was in full season, a male's whole reason for being was to couple with her, to do it as often and as hard as he could until they were both too exhausted from their endless, obsessive copulating to do anything but collapse next to each other and sleep. She smiled at the thought and wondered why it had taken her so damn long to give in to her own animal lust.

Chapter Four

STELLA COULD BARELY GET out of bed Monday morning. But in spite of the sex-crazed weekend that should have left her sated and exhausted, she was wide awake and buzzing with energy. Once she managed to pull her aching bones out from under the duvet, she quickly discovered the tension between her legs was stubbornly unsympathetic to the soreness in the rest of her body.

It started in the shower with memories of giving Tino's lovely bottom a thorough scrubbing, memories of feeling his soapy cock press insistently against her stomach and thighs. His lapping droplets of water off her breasts and neck made it impossible for her to concentrate until at last she relented and gave him what he so clearly needed, what she so clearly needed.

It was delicious self-torture not to give in and scratch the itch. She was anxious to get to the office before Anne did. She knew Anne would be full of questions, and she just wanted to bask in the afterglow for a while longer before she had to endure Anne's sexual inquisition. Reading *On Keeping Pets* during the bus commute did nothing to ease the need below her belly. With its innocuous dark blue cover, the manual was respectably bound and perfect for reading on public transport.

You may feel free to take your Pet into public places. She or he is provided with proper clothing for that purpose. If you plan to take your Pet to a more formal event, or an event that requires special clothing, you must let the Pet Shop know in advance and appropriate attire will be provided. The Pet Shop does not recommended formal events for Pet/keeper bonding, however, as such events are not the proper place for Pets, and appropriate behaviour cannot be guaranteed in formal settings. Pets prefer outings in parks and outdoor events. Pets also enjoy going to the cinema, but not if it is crowded, as crowds make Pets nervous.

Note: Rules for Pet Interaction with any form of media or technology apply when taking a Pet to the cinema or watching a DVD at home.

Note: On an outing where sexually segregated public toilets are present, toilet rules for Pets do not apply. Rest assured your Pet may be relied upon fully to tend to his or her own needs in a publicly acceptable way.

When taking your Pet on an outing, you must keep in mind that Pets are not comfortable in clothing and, if the outing is a long one, at some point the Pet's need for sexual release may override his or her good behaviour. This could be embarrassing to the keeper, as Pets aren't too concerned about where they pleasure themselves or how. To prevent this from happening on a long outing, take frequent privacy breaks to relieve your Pet's needs and see to her or his comfort. These breaks are also opportunities for the pleasure and relief of Pet keepers as well, and usually a very enjoyable part of any outing for both Pet and keeper.

Looking to all casual observers like the paragon of perfect posture, Stella took full advantage of the thrumming of the bus engine vibrating up through her seat. It sent yummy shockwaves of pleasure over her lady bits while she read the Pet keeper's manual and fantasising about sexy outings with Tino. All the while she adjusted her hips with subtle shifting to keep the buzz right where she needed it.

She exited the bus and endured the delicious torture of vulval friction caused by walking the six blocks to the Strigida offices in French-cut knickers that rubbed and stroked with every step. Upon her arrival, she made a mad dash to the loo to finish off the job. There she sat on the throne, skirt hoisted high, panties hugging her ankles, legs splayed wide at the knees. She rubbed and pinched her clit. Her fingers darted in and out of her drenched quim swirling and thrusting as though she were planning to dive in up to her elbow. When she came, she nearly catapulted herself off the commode bumping one knee painfully on the toilet roll dispenser and jerking until several vertebrae in her spine popped and cracked in protest.

'Password? You didn't say anything about giving her a password. Are you sure that's a good idea?' O'Kelly's grip on the receiver clenched. 'I mean I thought Stella having Tino was a one-off, a gift?'

'It was a gift,' the Boss replied. 'Of course it was a gift, but that doesn't mean it has to be a one-off, does it? Besides, you've always known this was a part of the plan. Why are you suddenly so squeamish?'

Anne was silent for a long second. 'She won't accept it.'

'Then don't tell her it's a gift. Just give her the password to the website. Let her think she's paying for it.'

'What I mean is ... I had a heck of a time getting her to take Tino in the first place. I had to practically slam the door behind me and make a run for it.'

There was a warm chuckle on the other end of the receiver. 'But she kept him, didn't she? She kept him for the whole weekend and got him back late, if I understand right.'

Anne caught her breath. 'I hadn't heard that.'

'Hadn't you? I would have thought the two of you would have shared all the steamy details by now.' She could hear him tisk-tisking into the phone. 'Don't tell me she was late for work this morning after the rigors of her weekend?'

'She was early actually. She was hard at work when I got in at eight.'

'You were in at eight? O'Kelly I think *you* need a Pet.'

'I have one, sir, whenever I want.'

'Of course you do. And see what a great employee you are, having access to all those lovely Pets.'

She bristled. 'I'm not an employee.' She knew he was only winding her up, but she was a little short on temper today.

'If we ever want our plans to come to fruition, O'Kelly, then you know as well as I do she needs a password. That's the first step.'

Anne's shoulders rose and fell in a frustrated sigh. 'I understand that, of course I do. But I don't know. I ...'

'What is it, O'Kelly? What's bothering you?'

She hated it when he used his patient voice on her. She hated it because it usually meant she had to come clean. And what was troubling her was usually something she couldn't quite name, but her gut told her she should be able to. She let out a slow breath. 'I'm just not convinced she's the right one, that's all.'

'I think she is. But giving her the password will help us confirm it one way or another.' She could almost hear the smile break in his voice. 'And if she isn't, well then you can happily say you told me so, and I shall be humbled before your superior intuition.'

'No you won't. You never are.'

'That's because I'm never wrong. If I ever am you'll see just how humble I can be.'

She offered a forced smile that no one saw. It pained her to admit it, but he *was* always right. She was the careful one, the pessimist, the voice of reason. It had been that way since they were at uni together. He said that's what made her the perfect business partner. Not that he seemed to need her voice of reason. Every time he was reckless, every time he threw caution to the wind he was right. You'd think she would have learnt by now. The man had more than intuition, he had instincts. It was uncanny.

'O'Kelly? You still there?'

'I'm here, yes.'

'This is still what you want, isn't it? It's a hell of an inconvenience for me, mind you. And no one would be happier than I if you changed your mind. But there's no denying you've earned it.'

'Yes. Yes, it's what I want.' When he talked to her like that, it shook her resolve, but this was what she wanted, she reassured herself. It wasn't just what she wanted, it was also what she needed, and even if he couldn't admit it, surely he knew. Anyway, he'd just have to deal with it, wouldn't he?

He released his own breath, and it sounded like a strong breeze over the phone. 'Then you have to trust me, O'Kelly. I promise you won't regret it.'

'I know. I know I won't.' She didn't really believe it just yet, but then she never did.

'Good. Now I want you to make a lunch date with Stella. Find out what happened. I'll wager she'll ask how she can have Tino again at her own expense. Then give her the password.'

In the afternoon, there was a conference call to Portland, Oregon, with possible recipients of grants from Strigida. It had been positively embarrassing. Well not for anyone else. The Boss and the people from the Vanguard Nature Trust were completely unaware that Stella was participating in an important conversation about preserving wetlands wearing damp knickers. It added a whole new dimension to dressing for the occasion.

She sat doing the isometric squeeze with her thigh muscles while engaging in a discussion about hides and observation decks and reclamation of derelict land. Just as arrangements were being made for a face-to-face meeting, Stella pushed herself over the edge into an orgasm that nearly shook her out of her ergonomically designed chair. It was the silent but powerful fireworks to celebrate the deal.

Terrified, and ashamed that she might have missed something important, she checked and rechecked the recorded minutes of the meeting, but strangely enough, she had missed nothing. Her comments, her responses, her suggestions were all sharp, even bordering on genius at times.

Later that day, the Boss phoned her. From the background noise and flights being called over the intercom, she knew he was at the airport. In Chicago, if she remembered right. He often hopped from city to city, from country to country several times during the course of a day checking out nature reserves and reclamation sites, helping find legal ways to preserve tracts of threatened woodland and championing any number of environmental causes by spreading Strigida funds wherever they could do the most good. The man seldom rested. In fact she hadn't seen him more than half a dozen times since she took the job.

'Stella, you were brilliant in the conference today. How'd you know that there'd been a lumber mill on the site? The idea of using the reclaimed lumber to build the hides is genius, both economically and environmentally.'

'Thank you, sir. I just did my research.'

'Brilliant, as I said.' She could almost hear him smiling. 'This sort of research is why you have no life outside of Strigida.' It wasn't a question.

'You told me the job would demand a lot of me.'

'Yes, I did, didn't I? Now, O'Kelly tells me you worked right through your lunch break. I've given her specific instructions to order a nice takeaway. Chinese, I think she said you like. If I'm not mistaken it should be arriving about now. Go meet her in the break room and eat something. I know you'll be burning the midnight oil, but I won't have you do it on an empty stomach. Now go. That's an order. And good job, Stella.'

There had been no mention of the "gift" Strigida had so thoughtfully provided, and though Stella felt like she should at least say thank you, it didn't seem appropriate to do it on company time. But then again there was nothing appropriate about the gift in the first place, was there?

'You walk like you've been in the saddle too long,' Anne said as she watched Stella sit at the table in the break room. 'Bit sore today, are we?'

Stella couldn't hold back a smile and a blush as she thought of Tino waking her Sunday morning with his tongue. He was such a naughty Pet. She did spank him for it afterward, but that only served to make him more fuckable and her more horny.

She dragged her attention back to Anne who was busy riffling through the Chinese takeaway bag for the fortune cookies at the bottom. 'Understandable, really. Tino wields a sizable meat whistle.'

'Shshsh!' Stella gave a quick glance around to make sure no one was listening.

34

'Oh would you relax. No one will hear us, Stel. Everyone else has gone home for the day, and the only reason I'm still here is because I'm dying to know how you got on with Tino.' She leant over the table. 'I hear he got back to the Pet Shop late.'

Stella dropped a wooden chopstick and it clattered across the table in a spatter of soy sauce. 'Who told you that?'

Anne wiped at the table with her napkin and ignored the question. 'Tino will always hold out for one last fuck if he can get away with it, and who's gonna discipline him for that? So tell me,' she leant so far over the table that her head was practically touching Stella's. 'Was it as good as I said it would be?'

Stella felt the uncontrollable smile split her face, the one that had been taking all facial muscles by storm ever since she first made love with Tino. 'Better, actually. Tino's amazing.'

Anne giggled. 'Tino is a very naughty boy, that's what Tino is.'

There was the staccato burst laughter not unlike misbehaving schoolchildren scheming something forbidden, then the room fell uncomfortably silent as they both concentrated on their hot and sour soup.

Stella laid down her spoon and wiped her mouth on the napkin. 'After Tino left, I looked up the Pet Shop website.'

Anne didn't seem surprised.

'I was curious, as you can imagine. But I couldn't get access.' She scrunched her napkin in her lap and shrugged. It was more than curious, she thought. It was frightening just how bereft she had felt after Tino left. It bordered on desperation. Her stomach knotted at the thought.

'You have to have a password to get to the good stuff. That is what you were looking for, isn't it? Good stuff about Tino?'

'I spent the whole weekend ... making love with the man. I'd just like to know a bit more about him. He can speak, right? I mean not talking is just a Pet thing, isn't it? Like it says in the manual.'

Anne laid down her spoon and held Stella in a scrutinizing gaze. 'Why? Would you have preferred he speak?'

Stella shook her head and looked down into her soup. 'No. It was nice not having to make witty conversation. And besides, Tino really didn't need to speak to express himself.' She found herself blushing again, and her pussy quivered at thoughts of just how well Tino had expressed himself. She looked back up at Anne, who was still watching her as though she were expecting a confession. 'Still, it would be nice to know a little bit about him.'

Anne held her gaze until Stella squirmed and looked away, then she spoke. 'You want him again. Don't you?'

Stella nodded, and felt a strange tightening in her throat. It was insane, but she missed him. How stupid was that? He had been paid to fuck her for a weekend. That was all it was. How could she miss him?

'May I make a suggestion,' Anne said, still studying Stella.

Stella knew she would, no matter what her response was.

'Try a different Pet next time.' She forced an unconvincing smile. 'Variety is the spice of life, after all. If you liked Tino, who knows, you might like some of the other Pets even better.'

'It's a moot point, isn't it?' Stella ran the spoon around the edge of her soup bowl. 'I don't have access to any of them.' She could feel Anne's steely gaze boring into the top of her head.

'Eat your soup, Stella. I know for a fact the Boss gave you lots of homework, and you have an early day tomorrow. You'll need your strength.'

For some ridiculous reason, Stella found herself fighting back tears.

Neither of them ate. Stella toyed with her soup spoon and Anne stared at the top of Stella's head. At last Anne released a heavy breath. 'When you get home tonight, check your personal emails. You'll find an email marked simply "ps". There'll be a link. Follow that link and you'll be able to retrieve a password. Then once you're into the website with access to the Pets, you'll receive further instructions.'

'Thanks, Anne. You're a star!' Stella felt as though her chest would burst with the relief of knowing she would see Tino again. Suddenly she was ravenous.

'You will consider my advice.' Anne held her gaze. 'About trying a different Pet.'

'Don't get the wrong idea. I don't expect the Pet Shop to become a habit or anything. It's just that I've had so little sex for so long that one weekend just wasn't enough, you know.' She offered a shaky smile. 'Guess I didn't know how much I was missing it. I'm sure one more weekend will do it for me.'

'Then a bit of variety should be just the ticket to get your libido all sorted, don't you think? Besides, I should warn you that Tino isn't easy to get.'

Her stomach knotted again. Tino had to be available. He just had to be. 'Of course, variety's nice.' She avoided Anne's gaze and shovelled the now tepid soup into her mouth. No doubt variety was good, but it was Tino she wanted. She wouldn't even bother with anyone else. Just one more hot weekend with him then she'd be content to fall back into her old routine, a good fantasy and an occasional encounter with her vibe when there was time.

Chapter Five

IT WAS LATE BEFORE Stella got home. She kicked off her shoes, poured herself a glass of wine, and sat down with her laptop. Just as Anne said, there was an email marked "ps". She opened it to find nothing but a link, which led her to a password. She copied it quickly to her BlackBerry then entered it.

That was it. She was in.

The design of the site could not have been more simple. It had the look of a daguerreotype photograph with a clean san serif font. The only image was a lifelike pen and ink drawing of a leopard lounging in a relaxed sprawl which curved around the bottom right-hand corner of the screen. Beneath that was some small copperplate writing that barely registered to Stella. Only one urgent matter concerned her. With fingers that were ridiculously shaky, she followed the prompt to Pet Diaries. She scrolled down through the alphabetical list of Pet names, holding her breath until at last she came to Tino's diary. She clicked on it.

Anne was right. Tino only had one opening for the next three months, and that was because of a cancellation in two weeks. Even though she could find no price list on the site, Stella took the cancellation and scheduled the Pet for the whole weekend. She barely felt the knot that tightened in her stomach at letting go of some unknown chunk of money that would definitely not be small. Strigida paid her extremely well for the life that now pretty much belonged to them, and she was not without her own resources if she needed them. She figured she could afford one last blow-out weekend with Tino. She'd ask Anne about the price tomorrow.

It was when confirmation of her weekend with Tino appeared on her email that she realised not only had there been no listing of prices, but there had been no mechanism set in place for payment. She left a query on the "contact us" space and wiped unusually sweaty palms on her trousers. She would check with Anne in the morning. But surely the confirmation was enough.

That done, she clicked back on to Tino's profile, hungry for any bits of information she could glean about him. Strangely there were no photos of any of the Pets. His Pet Shop bio said only that his full name was Valentino. That didn't surprise her. Nor did the fact that his keepers chose to call him Tino. There was nothing formal about Tino, rather everything playful and relaxed. Height, 6'1", weight 190 pounds. Most of that solid muscle, she knew from experience. Hair auburn. And outrageously soft and unmanageable, she thought. Eyes brown. And expressive. Deep enough to drown in, she recalled.

Then the bio got personal. At least physically personal. It contained a detailed listing of his physical attributes right down to size of his circumcised penis – diameter, and length, erect and flaccid. She didn't think she had ever seen him totally flaccid, and she found herself smiling at the problem that must have presented for the measurers. By the time she got to the description of the half-domed globes of his bottom, the ever so slight curve to the right where the cleft between his buttocks met the small of his back, her hand was in her knickers. She parted her labia to find the slippery place in between, which had been moist and quivery most of the day. Her fingers plunged and tweaked as she recalled the physicality of each of those attributes and how they had affected her. She squirmed and wriggled free of her blouse and unclasped her front-loader bra to thumb her nipples and cup and caress the weighty swell of her breasts.

Next to the list of physical attributes was a brief personality profile stating that Tino was headstrong, independent in nature, and though very affectionate and responsive, with considerable stamina, he had a tendency toward misbehaving. Not a Pet recommended for first-timers.

Stella came at that point. She shuddered and jerked her orgasm while the words on the screen blurred in front of her eyes. As she slid down in the chair like butter melting on toast she wondered who had chosen Tino for her. Had they somehow understood that she would have sent a less forceful, better behaved Pet home with cab fare before the weekend had even begun? That had been her intention. The aftershocks of her orgasm spread upward to a butterfly dance in her stomach. Maybe it was that they saw in her the ability to handle Tino in a way the Pet would understand and best respond to. She liked that idea even if it was just wishful thinking.

There was a long list of testimonials from Tino's previous keepers. They were all rave reviews. Suddenly Stella didn't feel so special any more. This was the rude reminder that she was just one more satisfied customer. That made her pretty pathetic she supposed.

Still, she couldn't stop thinking about him. She thought about Tino nibbling smoked salmon from her hand, Tino curling up on the floor by the bed waiting patiently until she invited him to join her, until she told him how she wanted him to touch her, to taste her – what she wanted him to do with his cock. Tino so obedient in such delicious ways. Tino so disobedient in even more delicious ways. No matter how ridiculous it was, she missed him. She missed the way he listened to her, the way he seemed to hang on her every word, the way he looked at her with those adoring eyes, the way he stretched and moaned and offered himself to her when she caressed his perpetually heavy penis.

He had only been with her for a weekend, she reminded herself angrily. And what was he anyway but a glorified prostitute? Yet how would she endure being without him for two long weeks?

Before she shuffled off to bed in the wee hours, Stella explored every area of the website multiple times. It hadn't taken long, especially since she had no interest in any of the other Pets. There were profiles of a dozen-and-a-half active Pets, including Tino, along with a dozen more who were inactive or available only upon special request. A quick glance showed that, as with Tino, there were no photos. Instead each Pet's physical attributes were expounded upon in detail, all guaranteed to be exactly as per description.

There was an extensive system of tagging and cross referencing to best take into account all tastes, fetishes and preferences, from erect penis size to sizes and shape preferences for breasts, nipples and areolae. Pets were classified according to height, muscle mass, curviness, roundness of bottoms, hair and eye colour, body hair, even size of feet and hands. Their personality profiles ranged from very shy and submissive to Pets who played rough and bit hard and everything in between.

There was a wealth of information presented with the understanding that anyone accessing the Pet Shop site would be willing to take the time and effort to do the research involved in choosing their perfect Pet. And from the testimonials, whatever the Pet Shop was doing seemed to be working very well indeed. There were several areas on the site reserved for VIP members. Stella had no idea what that meant and no way of finding out.

Before she headed off to bed she checked the news feeds as she always did, especially now that her job depended so much on her keeping abreast of any situation at any time. She was about to shut down when an article on one of the more obscure environmental sites caused her to do a double take, and she quickly brought the link back up, her heart pounding in her chest.

The caption read: *Vincent Evanston does it again.* But it was the photo that caught her attention. In spite of the poor quality of the image, which was labelled as an archive photo, the man standing at a podium with an arm raised in some grand victory gesture looked just like Tino – a little younger perhaps, and the hair was a little shorter. She squinted hard and readjusted the reading light. She enlarged the image, but that only made it worse. When her eyes began to water from her efforts, she turned her attention to the short blurb underneath.

Reclusive philanthropist, Vincent Evanston's, crack team of lawyers and investigators have found discrepancies in the contracts that would have allowed the Bear Grass Corridor to be ploughed under and replaced by a luxury apartment complex by Collins Development. The Bear Grass Corridor is a habitat for several endangered species of invertebrates and insects. Though the stay of execution is temporary, a spokesman for Evanston says it will buy much-needed time to find other legal routes to save the corridor.

The article said the Bear Grass Corridor was someplace outside Portland, Oregon, someplace a very long way from London. Evanston couldn't possibly be Tino, though there was no denying that he looked enough like Tino to make her heart beat fast and her pussy tighten. Stella gave the image one last long squint, then as an afterthought, she saved the article to her Favourites folder.

As she shut down the computer for what was left of the night, she wondered what Tino did when he wasn't being a Pet. What did he like? What music did he listen to? What did he believe in? What was important to him? A photo of Tino, she thought to herself as she cleaned her teeth. That's what she needed. She'd be sure to get one next time he was here. In the meantime a Tino lookalike would have to do.

Chapter Six

'SHE CHOSE TINO AGAIN.' O'Kelly drummed her fingers on the desk and stared at the phone which was now on speaker.

'Oh really?'

'You don't sound surprised.'

'Should I be? Tino's one of the most popular Pets for good reason.'

'That's just my point.' She gestured wildly to the phone as though it were actually the Boss sitting there across from her. 'Tino's next to impossible to schedule a weekend with. And yet, here he is with two cancellations in three weeks. Doesn't that strike you as a bit odd?'

'Well, I for one am glad Stella was able to get Tino again. Knowing Stella, and knowing Tino, I think they'll do each other a world of good.'

'That's not the point. You know as well as I do that if we offer her the position, if she takes it, she'll have to be able to maintain objectivity.'

He offered her his usual don't-take-life-so-seriously chuckle. 'O'Kelly, she doesn't know that, does she? Just a few weeks ago you were convinced she wouldn't even accept Tino. I'm not stupid. I knew that it would be a big leap for her, a frightening leap for someone of her restraint. But she took that leap, didn't she? She feels safe with Tino, that's all. Most people are only willing to nosedive into the unknown when absolutely necessary, and for Stella, this time it isn't necessary. Let her enjoy Tino. She's earned it. And stop worrying.'

'Yes, sir.' It was a lie, of course. She never stopped worrying. It was a part of her job.

'Oh, and O'Kelly, I think I'll send Stella to meet with the

Vanguard folks over in Portland.'

'Really? Seems a strange thing to do under the circumstances, don't you think?'

'It's time we let our little bird fly. And there's no place nicer for her maiden flight than the American North West. I was going myself, but the more I think about it, the more convinced I am that Stella should handle Vanguard. Most of the best suggestions are hers anyway.'

'If you're sure, then I'll make the arrangements,' O'Kelly said, feeling the tension beneath her sternum. That little edge of mystery in the Boss's voice when he changed plans in the middle always put O'Kelly on her guard. He was up to something. The question was what, and how many sleepless nights would she spend worrying about it?

If Stella hadn't worked for Strigida, the days would have dragged waiting for her weekend with Tino. But the Boss made sure she had little time to dwell on her upcoming hot weekend. Anne had reassured her that the Pet Shop would see to the proper billing for Tino's services. And though Stella was relieved that her weekend with the Pet would not be cancelled for lack of payment, the niggle was there in the pit of her stomach that she was, in essence, paying for a glorified prostitute.

In spite of the long hours and the super-human schedule, the Boss dismissed her promptly at five on Friday. The disembodied voice she had now grown used to communing with on the speakerphone ordered her to go home and enjoy the weekend. She'd earned a break. She'd worked long enough at Strigida to learn that if she didn't follow orders, he'd know. He always knew. Strange that it should be more difficult to manage anything sneaky behind the back of a boss she seldom saw in person. Even stranger that most of her sneakiness had involved doing more work rather than less, a testament to how little life she actually had even when she had a life. None of that mattered though, not with Tino coming in just a few hours. When he dismissed her the Boss didn't mention Tino, but she suspected that he knew.

She'd had time to stock the cupboards and fridge with yummy morsels, all tidbits she thought it would be fun to feed Tino. She had bought several exotic shower gels, along with oils and lotions and a soft-bristled body brush that she was dying to try on him.

She couldn't decide whether to wear clothes with easy access or to wear clothes that Tino would have to nibble and tug to get off her. She settled for a bit of both. She wore a loose-fitting summer dress that flounced around her body to mid thigh. It was a soft jersey print patterned in tiny mauve and melon flowers. If she moved just right, her braless breasts played peek-a-boo at the easy-access plunge of the front. She was sure Tino would have fun with that. Beneath it she wore French-cut knickers of ivory satin that she figured he could sink his teeth into.

When the doorbell rang, she gave her make-up and hair one last check in the hall mirror, willed the butterflies rampaging in her ribcage to settle and opened the door.

A Pet handler in an immaculate black suit offered her a businesslike smile. 'Are you Stella James?' Once Tino caught sight of her, the man had to strong-arm him into standing quietly.

'I am, yes.'

He handed her the official Pet Shop rucksack and his smile broadened. 'Based on this big boy's reaction, I thought you must be.' Then he released Tino, who practically catapulted over the threshold, taking an immediate position on the floor at her feet. He wrapped both arms around her leg and commenced with a deliciously ticklish tongue bath over her right kneecap, working his way to the inside of her leg where the sensation was far more than just ticklish.

The man in the suit smiled down at him as Stella ran her fingers through his hair and placed a heavy hand on his head to temporarily slow the progress, at least until the door was shut. 'Yep. I'd say he's definitely glad to see you.' He looked down at his watch. 'I'll be back for him the same time Sunday evening.' He gave her a stern glance. 'This time try not to keep me waiting.' Then he offered another smile, turned briskly on his heels and was gone.

By the time she managed to shut the door, Tino was already shoving at the hem of her dress, his hands moving up to cup her arse cheeks beneath the fabric. His enormous erection was fully visible through his trousers.

'Tino. Tino! Behave.' She couldn't keep the smile out of her voice. 'At least let me get you out of these clothes before you maul me.' She joined him on the floor, but instead of sitting quietly while she undressed him as he had for Anne, he sprang. He pulled her into a rough and tumble across the floor of the lounge, biting and nipping and raking his fully clothed cock hard against her every time there was contact.

'Tino. Tino! You're a bad boy!' Her voice was breathless, accentuated by the hammering of her heart threatening to jump out of her throat. Fear, hunger, loss of control, animal lust all jumbled together inside her and so much more. 'Tino, am I going to have to spank you first thing?' The slight tremor in her voice was now clearly evident.

But before fear could dominate the cocktail of emotions Tino pinned her splay-legged beneath him. Her dress had ridden up around her hips in the romp on the floor. Fully clothed, he insinuated his body so that the erection threatening the integrity of his fly rubbed shockingly against the satin gusset of her knickers. Then he began to rock and shift and rub against her, his barely restrained penis pressing the damp crotch of her panties into the deepening trough between her swelling labia. 'Oh God, Tino. You're so, so naughty,' she managed to gasp before he took her mouth. His tongue ravaged hers and danced across her teeth and hard pallet, and her body found his rhythm very pleasing. She matched the rocking and shifting of his hips, intensifying the sensation by wrapping her legs around him and lifting to meet his thrusts as his enthusiasm grew.

'Tino,' she gasped, as his tongue forsook her mouth for the soft hollow of her throat, nipping the tender flesh just hard enough to make her suck in a harsh breath, which caused everything to tense. 'I'll have to punish you. You know that?' Her words ended in a little shudder as he nuzzled aside the fabric to expose her left breast, which felt like it was mostly nipple as he took it into his mouth and suckled like he would draw the very heart of her up through it and into himself.

She was riding the edge, unable to concentrate on anything but the liquid heat between her legs. Tino was a Pet, she reminded herself, her Pet, and it was way too soon to give over the reins. But any thought of controlling her Pet was completely lost when he lifted himself onto his hands in a modified push-up position, which gave him more driving force against her grasping cunt. The shifting of his hips became a delicious battering. She could smell the seashore scent of her arousal, wet and demanding, and the smell of animal heat not masked by deodorant or soap radiated off him in an olfactory feast that made her hungry all over. Whatever was human in her took a holiday. She responded to his grunts and growls with growls and mewlings of her own.

Then all sound stopped, all breathing stopped. Only the hard friction of cloth raking against cloth broke the silence. Tino's pupils dilated with desire, his gaze locked like a homing beacon on hers. His face was dark and drawn tight around the intensity of his need. The hard mechanics of animal desperation hammered them against each other, each grasping, each straining until joints popped and muscles ached.

Then Tino came. His face shattering into a grimace that could have been pleasure or pain, and the growl that burst from his lungs offered no evidence as to which. But the convulsing of his cock through his trousers told the true story, and it was a story that sent Stella growling and clawing into her own wild release. She pulled him down to her in a hard bear hug, her orgasm raging through her pelvic girdle and up over her belly with him still thrusting and trembling all over before collapsing on top of her, his face and arms sheened in the sharp sweat of animal heat.

'Bad Tino,' she managed to gasp before he covered her mouth in a playful rain of kisses. 'You're such ...' kiss, kiss, nip. 'A naughty ...' Nip, kiss. 'Pet ...' Kiss, kiss, lick. 'You should have at least let me take your clothes off.'

As previously stated, Pets prefer to be naked. It is best to
remove clothing as quickly as possible once your Pet arrives.
The Pet will, naturally, be very excited to see you, and since
your Pet is already aroused upon arrival, occasionally an
overly stimulated Pet will break control and come in her or his
clothing before the keeper is able to remove them. Though this
doesn't happen often, the Pet Shop has provided for such
incidents, along with a Pet's natural disregard for clothing and
tendency toward untidiness. In the official Pet Shop rucksack,
you will find a complete change of clothes in addition to those
in which your Pet arrived.

Note: You should only need clothing for your Pet if you take
her or him into public places and when you return him or her
to the Pet Shop handler at the end of your Pet's stay with you.

Suddenly Tino was the perfectly behaved Pet. He rolled off her
and lay very still while she peeled off his damp shirt. The he
lifted his arse so she could pull off his trousers, wet with the
combined results of his ejaculation and the rub of her sopping
cunt.' The piquant musky scent of sex and sweat filled her
nostrils and she was hungry for him all over again. As usual,
his cock was still erect, sticky and shiny with his ejaculate, a
situation that didn't seem to bother him in the least. When he
was completely naked, and even more exquisite than she
remembered him to be, he held her gaze for a brief moment,
then rolled over onto his hands and knees and presented his
bottom to her, an act that made her pussy tense and caused a
strange mix of emotion to fill her chest.

'I suppose I do have to punish you, don't I? After all no
matter how nice the end result, you still broke the rules. She
brought her hand down hard enough to sting on his left buttock.
His cock surged. His anus clenched, and the smell of body heat
and sex bloomed, filling her brain, making her ache with deep
needs, ancestral needs, need that had been around long before
humans walked the Earth. She spanked him again and again
until his arse cheeks each bore the blurred pink print of her
hand, and his erection looked as though it would burst.

Suddenly she no longer cared about him taking off her

48

clothes. She shoved the dress off over her head and yanked at her knickers. 'I need you to fuck me, Tino. Be a good Pet and take care of me.'

This time, he took her from behind in true Pet fashion, mounting her doggie style. This time her cunt was ready for the breadth and the depth of him as he hammered her, cupping her tits and raking her clit, bathing her neck in hot animal grunts accompanied by the occasional possessive nip. She had already come twice more when he convulsed into her, and they collapsed in a heap on the floor.

When the shuddering finally subsided, Tino pulled free from her pussy, unselfconsciously dribbling her inner thigh with warm come. As though he were unaware of the embarrassment or the mess, he manoeuvred her onto her back, then licked and suckled his way over the curve of her hip down to the juicy flood between her legs.

Blushing hard, she tried to push him away, but once his mouth made contact with her drenched slit, she was lost. He pushed her knees open and licked and slurped while she ground her bottom, shifting and rocking against his face. He suckled and lapped and tongued her, not stopping until he licked up every last drop of their combined pleasure – at least what was on her legs. She reckoned that, if anything, he'd made her pussy even wetter. All that remained of their coupling was what slicked his cock and dried on his thighs. That bit, he happily wore.

She had come again during his efforts to clean her. He was well and truly hard once more and very aromatic with the combined scent of their heat and the tangy smell of hot perspiring flesh. It made her want him again. She had seen her share of nature programmes. She knew how it was. Often mammals in the wild let their body fluids dry on them, creating a feral cologne unique to each individual and designed to drive the opposite sex mad by advertising animal virility, in pungent pheromonal blasts.

When at last there was the energy to move, she stood and offered him her hand. 'You need a bath, Tino, and so do I.'

Pet Hygiene – Bathing: Be sure to bathe your Pet regularly, as Pets cannot bathe themselves, and they tend to be rather messy. All Pets enjoy frequent bathing. The Pet Shop recommends twice a day unless activities demand more. Most Pet keepers, as well as their Pets usually find the experience enjoyable.

Note: Pets are especially fond of bathing with their keepers, and they love fluffy towels and vigorous rub-downs.

Note: You will find oils and lotions specifically formulated for your Pet's needs in the accompanying rucksack.

Chapter Seven

UNDER NO CIRCUMSTANCES ARE Pets allowed to handle books, magazines, newspapers computers, mobile phones or any other information device or print media. Pets do not read, and do not engage with the media in any way unless they are in the company of their keeper and have their keeper's express consent. Any engagement with any sort of media must absolutely be with the consent and full supervision of the keeper.

Without express permission, a Pet is never to browse, look through or disturb in any way any of the personal belongings of her or his keeper.

Both of the above offences are to be punished severely.

Stella didn't think Tino had seen any of the film. She had seen damn little of it herself. Not only had she figured there might be some distractions, but she had counted on it. That being the case, she had picked something older and something she would never have gone to see without ulterior motives. Other than a few stragglers, they had the place to themselves. She found seats isolated in the centre of the cinema, a task not too difficult since everyone else seemed to be seeking out their own isolation.

Tino sat quietly in his seat through the adverts and trailers then he lowered himself onto the floor and rested his head on her thigh. She fed him popcorn and bottled water. The popcorn, he loved, but he preferred to pull back just as she tipped the bottle to his lips so that the water ended up soaking her thigh. Then he lapped the dribbles from her leg. The minute he had repositioned himself on the floor, he nuzzled her skirt up, so the fabric did not interfere with the thirsty lavings of his tongue. It was a bit of a shock at first, but she quickly discovered the feel of cool water licked from her bare thigh by a warm tongue did amazing things to her pussy.

Tino quickly lost interest in the popcorn and the water and found his way to his favourite thing to eat. She made little effort to dissuade him, grinding her arse deep into the plush seat, sliding down until she could open her legs enough to give her Pet unhindered access. He nuzzled and nibbled the minuscule crotch of her thong out of the way until she was bare and gaping for the long sensuous explorations of his tongue and the suckling and nibbling of the path up to her straining clit. She curled her fingers in his hair and held him to her with one hand while the other worked its way into her blouse, into her bra to play with her tits.

After she came, she commanded him back into the seat next to her. Then she opened his trousers and teased out his heavy erection. There was no easy way she could take him in her mouth without getting onto the floor herself, so she licked her palm until it was slick with her saliva and took him in her fisted hand. She loved the way his body tensed, the way his hips shifted and rotated to get the best benefit from her tightening grip. She loved the way he closed his hand around hers lightly as though he feared she might stop pleasuring him. He was amazingly quiet in his thrustings. She wondered at times if he was holding his breath. She slid one hand into her bag to find a handkerchief as he drew near his release, but her timing was off, and with a convulsive jerk he shot his wad against the back of the empty seat in front of him. It was an act that made them both snigger quietly behind their hands, an act that made her hot all over again.

'You should have used the loo in the cinema,' she whispered next to his ear. 'The manual said you would. It specifically said that you were OK to use public toilets when we're on an outing.' When she had gone to the ladies after the film, he had refused the gents, and now, just a few blocks down the street, he was holding himself rather rudely. Though the street was fairly deserted, it still was a bit embarrassing.

She looked around, frantic to find a private corner where he could relieve himself. She wasn't 100 per cent sure that if he got desperate enough, or mischievous enough, he might not just whip it out and have a pee right there on the street like some sodding drunk. 'There. That's a good place.' Between a sandwich shop and a shoe repair, both closed for the night, she pointed to an alley cluttered with dumpsters. 'Go on. Do it there. I'll wait here.'

Still holding himself, shifting from foot to foot, he held her gaze expectantly for a few seconds as though he wanted her to go with him. But when she folded her arms across her chest and huffed at him, he trotted off between the dumpsters to get on with it.

She had always been a little shy about toilet protocol, even though he clearly was not. It was one part of the total Pet experience that she was quite happy not to share with him. She concentrated on the surroundings, taking in the night sounds, any of the night sounds that didn't involve her Pet peeing behind a dumpster. She watched a hen party complete with sparkly headbands and fake feather boas trundle into the off-licence across the street laughing drunkenly. The bride, in a flimsy gauze veil, stumbled and nearly fell off her nose-bleed heels as one of her girlfriends shoved a shiny pink dildo in her face. They all laughed hysterically.

Stella was so caught up in the antics of the hen party that she didn't hear the man approach until he spoke.

'You all by yourself, luv?' The words came only seconds before an arm snaked around her waist and jerked her back against a thick body that smelt of stale curry and lack of soap. His fetid breath came in hot little whooshes against her neck. The light from the off licence across the street caught the glint of metal in his hand.

She froze. Her stomach lurched threateningly. 'I'm not alone.' She forced the words up through her tight throat, amazed that she could actually speak at all. 'I'm with my boyfriend.'

'Oh right. Watshe, then, the invisible man?' The thug

tightened his grip and slid his other hand inside her bag, which was still unzipped after her efforts to clean Tino and herself before they left the cinema. 'Whacha got for me, hon? It better be good, or you'll havta pay me some ovver way.' He thrust against her lewdly. 'Fact, I'm feeling a bit frisky tonight. I might just 'ave ... gaak!' He finished his sentence with a choking rasp microseconds before his body heaved violently backward, releasing her with an involuntary shove as the knife skittered on the cobbles to land next to the nearest dumpster.

She yelped and scrambled to regain her balance. Through the electric buzz of fear still hammering her ears, she heard the scuffle, the flurry of grunts and hard breathing. Then suddenly Tino stood bathed in the diminished light towering over the thug he now held expertly in a choke hold. He cranked his grip until the man stopped struggling and went limp against Tino's body. Then he shoved him to the ground.

Stella's stomach threatened to rebel. 'Oh dear God, Tino! You didn't ... He isn't ...' But to her relief, she could already hear the man choking and sputtering as he regained consciousness. Working silently and with steady hands, Tino took off the man's shoes and socks and tossed them hard in opposite directions then he did the same with the knife the thug had been sporting. That finished, he grabbed the man by the throat in a grip that could have easily crushed his trachea. He put just enough pressure on to leave the man breath to whimper. Then he shook a finger from side to side as though he were disciplining a misbehaving child. The man whimpered again, raised both hands palm up and shook his head, at least as much as Tino's grip would allow.

Tino gave him a debilitating belly punch and a hard shove. Then he bounded to Stella's side, encircled her in a strong arm and half dragged, half carried her away from the alley. He had her safely settled into a cab headed back to her flat before it hit her that in the midst of all the chaos Tino hadn't uttered a single word.

Then the shakes took over. She tightened her grip around him and buried her face against his chest relishing the strong steady beat of his heart next to her cheek. He laid a warm kiss on the top of her head and pulled her closer.

The ride home didn't take long. There wasn't much traffic. Tino held her possessively as they climbed the stairs. Not entirely sure her shaky legs would hold her upright, she was thankful for his support. Inside the flat she made straight for the kitchen and a G&T, then decided to skip the T. She filled Tino's bowl with fresh water, but he only sat listlessly on the floor staring into it.

'Darling, you should drink something. You'll get dehydrated, and I can't have that.' She plopped down on the floor next to him, slopping her gin. He licked the droplets from her fingers, and his eyes locked on her. 'You need something stronger than water too, after tonight, don't you, sweetheart?' He continued to lick her fingers then flicked his tongue up the edge of the glass still holding her gaze. She pressed it to his lips, tipped, and he drank. He drank until it was gone.

She stood long enough to grab the bottle off the counter and refill the glass then dropped down next to him, sipping, and alternately holding the drink for him. 'I know it's against the rules. But I think our little outing calls for an exception to those rules. Just this once, don't you? She sat the glass down and pulled him close until his large body curled around her. 'I'm so sorry for what happened, Tino. But I'm so thankful you were there for me. I can't even think of what might have happened if you hadn't been.' He took one last sip from the glass, then helped her to her feet and led her into the bathroom, where he planted himself in front of the shower.

He stood unmoving while she undressed him. He was erect as always, and she lingered to caress his balls and run a cupped palm over his thickness. The hard muscles just above his pubic curls tightened at her touch.

He watched while she undressed. His gaze on her made her feel sexy. It felt like a healing salve for what had happened. She took her time, loving the way his serious dark eyes locked on her breasts, her pubis, her face. Then she reached out her hand and pulled him into the shower.

She put her full concentration into bathing Tino, and somehow that made her feel immensely better. She soaped every crook, every exquisite crevice of her Pet's delicious body. Tino was well-behaved except for the occasional shudder of delight or a growl or a nuzzle against her breast or bottom as she soaped and scrubbed.

His penis, very much at full attention, bobbed gently in front of her. She wondered how one man could possibly have so much stamina. He let her wash his hair and sculpt his dark pubic curls into soapy white mounds around his erection. He let her soap down the inside of his thighs past his knees to caress his calves and ankles as though she were rubbing down a fine stud. That was exactly what she was doing, she thought, soaping down the stud who had probably saved her life.

While she was kneeling, he pushed forward until his cock pressed against her cheek. Chuckling softly, she ran a soapy finger down his crack and slipped it into his anus, an act which made his cock surge. She took him into her hand and gently stroked the length of him lingering to kiss the helmeted tip. When she stood to scrub herself, she enjoyed the hungry way he watched as she soaped her breasts and her belly. Then she ran her fingers down over her mons and opened her pussy lips, pushing her hips forward to give him a good view while she washed herself.

Afterwards they both stood dripping on the mat while she towelled him dry, and he lapped droplets of water from her shoulders and breast and belly, working his way downward to her centre until she gave up and threw the towel on the edge of the tub.

'Come to bed with me, Tino,' she breathed. 'I want you next to me tonight.'

She led him to the bedroom, then pulled back the duvet and settled in, the thirsty fabric of the sheets lapping up the last of the droplets from her back and butt. She patted the space next to her. He slipped in beside her then covered her with his body. He entered her without foreplay, with a gentle upward thrust. She sheathed him with amazingly little effort. Her body had become accustomed to the size of him, the shape of him, as though her pussy had somehow been remoulded, reformed so that it fit him perfectly. He barely moved, and yet each little shifting of his pelvis, each little rocking of his hips sent warm, trembling heat up through her body.

She lifted her legs and wrapped them around his waist in an effort to get closer to him. He was insider her. He couldn't get any closer. She was overwhelmed by just how far insider her he really was. He shifted his weight to his knees and lifted his body just enough to run splayed hands up over her ribcage onto the swell of her breasts, caressing her nipples between thumbs and forefingers. Then he slid his hands up under her armpits and onto her biceps lifting her arms over her head. He held her wrists in one large hand while the other returned to caress her face, thumb moving across the flutter of her eyelid, down her cheek, over her parted lips.

The orgasm took them both by surprise. It came out of their lazy, sleepy, tender joining and shook both of them to their core. Stella watched Tino's ecstatic face through misted eyes and wondered how anything could possibly feel this good.

Chapter Eight

'THIS IS ABSOLUTELY NOT acceptable!' O'Kelly paced the floor of her office, then turned and half shouted at the speaker phone. 'What was he thinking?'

'Calm down, O'Kelly.' The Boss's voice sounded so matter-of-fact that she would have slapped him if he'd been there in person. 'It was a mugger. It wasn't anybody's fault. You can't blame Tino for that. In fact, I'd say it was a damn good thing he was there. I shudder to think what might have befallen Stella if he hadn't been. Why are you so upset about this?'

'The handler said when he came for him, Tino wouldn't leave, and Stella had to keep reassuring him that she was all right. Even then she practically had to force him out the door. It took ages to get Tino away from her. The handler was not happy.'

'Dogs are protective of their masters, O'Kelly. Possessive of their pack, as it were. Tino's behaviour was not un-pet-like at all really. As for the handler, well, Pets can misbehave. He was told that when he took the position. But just to smooth things over, give him a nice little something in his next envelope.'

'And what if that thug had had a gun? What if he had been stronger than Tino?' She swallowed hard and felt an icy knot tighten in her gut as she contemplated what might have been.

'But the thug didn't have a gun, and we knew Tino was that sort of a bloke when we hired him. He's cavalier, reckless, he's headstrong, and has a very powerful sense of fair play. I think those were the words you used, weren't they?'

'And you hired him anyway.' O'Kelly recalled the

argument they'd had over Tino. An argument that, not surprisingly, she had lost. The very first sight of the Pet had caused her heart to beat a little faster and the muscles below her belly to clench. It wasn't that Tino was good-looking, oh he was good-looking enough, but she worked with good-looking Pets all the time. It was the ease of the man, his totally unassuming comfort at being in his own skin. Somehow, just shaking his hand had made her want to have that skin he was so comfortable in up against hers with nothing in between.

She had always maintained a certain distance with Pets, and even when she did take a Pet for her own pleasure, it was only for pleasure. Never anything else. But Tino was different. Tino invaded not just her fantasies, but her dreams. She was in charge, though. She knew what was going on. She knew how to handle it. She had kept away from him. She had never taken him for a Pet. She suspected what might happen, even if she took him for only a couple of hours. But poor Stella was broadsided. How could the Boss have not seen this coming?

Then there was the unconventional way Tino had approached the Pet Shop. He just went right into the website and announced that he wanted to be a Pet. The Boss had promised to take care of it. He had reassured her it was probably just some rich nutter wanting to reverse the Pet experience and be the one in the collar for a while. And then, all of a sudden, the Boss was Tino's biggest advocate.

'O'Kelly? I know you've grown attached to Tino, but he's safe now. And so is Stella.'

His words jerked her back from her ruminations, and made her feel like she'd been caught in the act. There were times when his intuition, the way he read her, was almost frightening. 'Of course I'm attached to him. He's our most popular Pet. We'd lose a fortune if anything happened to him.' She fought back an irritating tremor with the last words.

'If you're only concerned about our investment then you can relax. Tino's fine. You said so yourself. Not a scratch on him.'

O'Kelly huffed an exasperated sigh and plopped down into her chair. 'Did you not hear me? The handler could barely get

Tino away from Stella. If Tino had not obeyed Stella, then what? And here's the real rub, Stella has scheduled Tino again in two weeks. He's made room for her in his schedule by cancelling paying customers.'

'What do you mean, he made room for her? He's a Pet, O'Kelly. Pets have no say in who we schedule them with.'

She squared her shoulders and sat up straight. 'That's right. Pets don't, but someone clearly does, and it certainly wasn't me.'

'If you're accusing me of something, you'd best come out with it. You usually have no trouble accusing me of all sorts.'

'Sir, Tino's falling for Stella, and Stella for him, can't you see that?'

This time the pause was so long that O'Kelly feared they'd lost their connection. 'Sir?'

There was a heavy release of breath. 'Really? You really think so?'

She frowned at the phone. 'Isn't it obvious?'

Another pause. There was the slam of a car door, and suddenly she could hear traffic noise in the background of their call. Was he actually carrying on this conversation while strolling down a busy street somewhere? Then the rushing wind of his breath filtered into her ear. 'But he's a glorified paid fuck, O'Kelly.' She could hear him struggle with the words. Every time she had reminded the Boss that they actually ran an online brothel with giant Pet carriers, he got angry at her. The Pet Shop was always something more to him. Most of the time it was something more to her too. 'Stella knows this,' he continued. 'Frankly, I was just as scared as you were that she wouldn't accept our little gift. And now, after only seeing him twice, you think she's falling for him? It doesn't make any sense. Besides,' he added as a quick afterthought. 'Tino's not the kind to fall in love.'

'I wouldn't have thought so either.' She measured her words carefully. There had never been any hiding her emotions from the Boss. He had never had to see her face to read her. 'But Stella is vulnerable for the takeover. And if you ... if we want her primed and ready for the task at hand, the one thing

60

we don't need is her thinking clouded by the stars in her eyes for one of our Pets.'

There was a series of noises that sounded like doors slamming, and suddenly the traffic sounds disappeared and the Boss's voice seemed cocooned in soft silence. Today was Monday, so he was in a hotel room in Sweden. 'Perhaps you're right.' He continued. 'Perhaps we should.... pre-empt the situation for a while.'

She felt the tension between her shoulder blades loosen noticeably. 'What did you have in mind, sir?'

'Stella's off to Portland in the morning. I can keep her there a few extra days, but not long enough to force her to cancel her weekend with Tino.'

'Perhaps we could force the issue. Cancel it for her. You know, say Tino had something come up.' O'Kelly moved to her desk and pulled up the Pet Shop website.

'I'd rather not do that.' There was the sound of running water and a rustle of cloth, and O'Kelly's stomach clenched and skittered down below her navel. It wasn't the first time the Boss had stripped for a long soak in the tub while they talked business. She suspected he'd done more than that on a few occasions when stress levels were high and they were both exhausted. It was a thought that brought back memories. It was also a thought she had endless fantasies about. At last he spoke, his voice echoing off what she suspected were bathroom tiles. 'Let's just send her another Pet.'

'Of course, sir.' O'Kelly pulled up the profiles of the male Pets, biting her tongue to keep from telling him she told him so.

'We'll send our apologies and let her have the weekend at the Pet Shop's expense, of course.'

'It's all been at the Pet Shop's expense,' she reminded him.

'Yes, but Stella doesn't know that, does she?' There was a splashing of water and the sound of waves hitting what she could imagine to be the sides of a bathtub.

Suddenly O'Kelly's pulse sped up and she was aware of the clenching in her knickers. She couldn't keep from picturing the man stretched out naked in what she imagined was a huge bathtub. Maybe he was absently playing with his cock as he spoke to her, a cock she had played with more often than she could remember back in uni. At these most intimate moments, moments that were somehow audibly acceptable to share when she would have never allowed it visually – not now anyway, now that they worked together – she indulged her fantasies, imagining him stroking his erection, cupping his balls, thinking of her.

She forced her mind back to the subject at hand. 'So, who did you have in mind? How about Dan?' Dan was a pretty-boy blond with icy blue eyes and broad, tanned shoulders. 'He's pretty popular with the ladies.'

The Boss grunted. 'Dan looks like he came straight from the pages of a bodice ripper. I can't see him and Stella together.'

'Jack?'

'A little bit too submissive for our Stella.'

'Liam?'

'I don't know.'

She rolled her eyes and shoved her hands onto her hips. 'Well who then?'

'Hmmm ...' she heard another shifting of the waters and felt her nipples tighten to press against her bra. 'How about ... How about Audrey?'

O'Kelly nearly knocked over the tepid cup of tea at her elbow. 'You want me to send Stella a woman?'

'Why not?' There was water running again, and she imagined him warming the bath, the water lapping at his thighs and buttocks.

Damn it! He wasn't making it any easier for her to concentrate. 'How about because there's absolutely no indication that she's attracted to women?'

'O'Kelly, you told me yourself all women are actually bi, and men too. Most of them just don't know it, you said. Well, it's about time Stella embraced her inner bisexual, don't you think?'

'It's more than that, sir. You always use Audrey–'

'I always use Audrey for recruiting, yes I know.'

'Well? Are you? Recruiting Stella?'

'Possibly. Depending on how things go. It occurred to me the other day that actually putting Stella through the recruitment process for the Pet Shop might be a great way to observe our unknowing protégé in action. And there's no better way to teach her the ropes.' The water stopped running and it was replaced by dripping and splashing. He was washing himself, maybe with a sponge, maybe with a soft washcloth, down along his cock, over his balls. In spite of herself, she closed her eyes, held her breath, and listened. Almost of their own accord, her hips rocked very subtly, so subtly that anyone coming in to her office would have never noticed, so subtly that the friction being created was a slow burning whisper, a hint of total combustion to come. After she got home, she told herself. After she got home.

'What do you think? O'Kelly? Are you there?'

She caught her breath. 'I'm here, sir. I think it might be a good idea.' Her pulse hammered in her throat and in her pussy.

His laugh overlaid the energetic splash of water. 'What's this, my partner actually agreeing with me? I can't honestly remember the last time that happened. O'Kelly, are you all right?'

'I'm fine, sir.' Did she sound breathless? Oh God, she hoped not.

'Are you still at the office? You are, aren't you? O'Kelly, go home, take a nice long bath, have a glass of wine, get yourself a Pet. I think you could use one. You're entitled. And stop stressing.'

'Of course, sir. Shall I make the arrangements with Audrey then?'

'Let me think about it a bit. We've got time.' The splashing crescendoed again. 'Now go home. That's an order.'

'You can't give me an order. I'm your partner.'

The splashing stopped. 'Then how about if I ask you as a friend.'

She caught her breath in a sound she knew was shamelessly audible on the phone, and she felt a lump rise to her throat. God, why was she so damned thin-skinned today?

'O'Kelly?'

She steadied herself. 'I suppose I could do it for a friend.'

She heard him release a heavy breath. 'Good. I know for a fact Liam is available tonight, and you know how much trouble he can get into if he's bored. I suggest you see to him and put him through his paces. It'll be good for both of you.'

'Oh, right. Liam.' She shook herself. 'Good idea.'

'Good night, O'Kelly.'

'Good night, sir.'

Chapter Nine

IT WASN'T STELLA'S FIRST time in the States, or the Northwest. She considered it a very good omen that her first trip for Strigida was to such a lovely place. In a lot of ways, the Western part of Oregon was like a primordial England that had been picked up by each of its corners and stretched and tugged and expanded. Then after it had been given a hearty shake to rid it of too many people, it was snapped like a puzzle piece in between Washington and California to glisten in the veil dance of wet Northwest sunlight.

There was plenty of talk about nature and the great outdoors with Vanguard. Stella had done all the appropriate research, brilliant research even, but the internet could only take her so far. On the last day of her visit, Vanguard sent her on an impromptu field trip with Bob Paris, the resident biologist, so she could actually see the site that was to be reclaimed.

She rattled down the road hermetically sealed in Bob's muddy Vanguard Land Rover. She thought it might have been green, but she wasn't willing to wipe away the grime and risk muddying her mauve pencil skirt and matching jacket to find out. The need for clothes more suited for outdoor life had not been something she'd thought about when she came to work with Strigida, but she was beginning to see the wisdom in a pair of good walking boots and clothes that could withstand the rigors of the natural world. Her lack of such attire and the fact that there had been substantial rain the night before meant it would be a drive-through sort of tour, with Bob hitting the highlights of reclamation, pointing out a few of the local birds and a couple of deer browsing at the edge of a clear-cut.

'The clear-cut will grow back on its own given time,' Bob

was saying as he pulled the Land Rover to the edge of the rutted excuse for a logging road and stopped so she could look. 'Erosion is our main concern here.' He nodded to the dark patch of heavy forest next to it. Tall conifers draped in moss and spiked with mistletoe looked like giant, pre-decorated Christmas trees. 'That patch would have met the same fate had it not been for Vincent Evanston.'

If Bob hadn't before, he certainly had her full attention now. 'Vincent Evanston? You know him?'

'Yep.' He laughed under his heavy moustache. 'Always preferred to spend his time with the birds and the beasties rather than with humans. Guess I'm a bit like that too, but then I wasn't born richer than God like Vincent. He's a strange one.'

'Then he lives around here?'

'Has all his life. Right on the other side of those trees there. Speak of the devil.' Bob raised the pair of binoculars that permanently hung around his neck then gave a confident nod. 'That's the Birdman there. He spends a lot of time in these woods when he's home.'

She fumbled with the spare pair of binoculars Vanguard had lent her, giving herself a hearty knock on the nose before she managed to get them focused. Her stomach did a flip-flop, then a pirouette. Even with her unsteady hand and the thud-thud of her heart making the scene tremble in front of her eyes, she knew she was looking at Tino, who was looking right back at her. She caught her breath 'You're sure that's Vincent Evanston?'

'Of course I'm sure. I've worked with the man often enough. Helluva naturalist.'

The butterfly dance in her stomach had moved up into her chest to do a mad mambo with her heart and suddenly she had to know. 'Excuse me.' She threw open the door. 'I'm sorry but I have to go. I really need to talk to him.'

'Wait! You can't get out there dressed like that.'

She slammed the door on Bob's objections and went slip-sliding across the road toward the man in the wood. Her kitten heels sunk in the pale mud with each step she took. On the other side of the road she found herself faced with a ditch full of fast-moving rainwater. It wasn't that wide. She could have jumped it easily enough in trainers, but she wasn't in trainers. She found purchase on a mossy rock and struggled to balance on the ball of her foot, but the rock slipped and turned beneath her sending her teetering with arms flailing before she sat down hard in the middle of the icy flow.

The gasp for breath and the high-pitched yelp barely passed her lips before he was on her, grabbing her beneath the armpits and pulling her to her feet with a heavy slurp and splosh from her skirt, which seemed to be acting like a sponge. He half dragged, half carried her to dry ground and plopped her down unceremoniously on a mossy log. His curled fingers lifted her chin until her eyes met Tino's dark gaze. 'You scared the hell out of me. Are you all right?' Tino speaking would have been shocking enough but Tino speaking with an American accent just seemed wrong somehow. She nodded, unable to reply.

He already had his BlackBerry out. 'Bob, yes she's fine. No, don't worry, I'll take care of her. Go on back to the hide.' He slapped the BlackBerry back in his pocket and turned his full attention on Stella. This time it was not concern that filled his eyes.

'What the hell were you thinking, out in the woods dressed like that?'

She was already shivering from the cold and the wet. 'Guess the great outdoors isn't my forte.' She offered an apologetic smile.

'Come on.' He grabbed her hand and pulled her to her feet. 'My pack's under those trees. Let's get you into something dry before hypothermia sets in.' But when she stumbled and nearly twisted her ankle in her now filthy mauve shoes, he cursed under his breath and lifted her as though she were weightless, causing her to gasp her surprise as he turned on his heels and headed back toward the pack.

She threw her arms around his neck and hung on tight, smelling wood smoke in his hair and on his plaid shirt, a smell that made her pussy tighten at thoughts of making love to him in the light of a campfire. They didn't have far to go, just in the protection of the trees. There he eased her down on a huge stump and thrust a steaming cup of cocoa into her hand from a flask he'd dug out of a rucksack big enough that he could have used it for a tent. 'Drink this. It'll help warm you till I can sort out something dry for you to wear.' He turned his broad back to her and began to dig through the pack.

She was trembling hard enough that is was an effort not to spill the cocoa. 'You're Tino, aren't you?' She spoke between chattering teeth.

His back stiffened slightly, then relaxed again as he continued to dig. 'I'm Vincent.'

She sat the cup down next to her and hugged her arms around her shivering body. 'I know you're Vincent, Vincent Evanston, but you're Tino. I mean, he's you, isn't he?'

He turned on her, grabbing her shoulders so quickly that she feared he would shake her. Instead, he began to chafe her arms, his dark eyes locked on hers. 'I told you, Tino's not here.'

'But I—'

He swallowed up her words in an open-mouth kiss, taking her breath away, taking away her ability to think with the heat of it, the expressive depth of it. He bit her lip as he pulled back, still holding her gaze. 'Tino's not here,' he repeated. His voice held the tiniest edge of warning. Then, as though it were business as usual, he bent and removed her shoes. 'You're lucky you didn't break an ankle in these.' He tossed them onto the ground and wiped his muddy hands on his trousers. 'Afraid I don't have an extra pair of shoes with me. Now lift your butt.'

'What?'

He nodded to a non-descript wad of clothing now sharing her stump. 'It's not elegant, but it's dry, now lift your butt. Or,' the weight of his gaze was nearly physical, causing her heart to hammer and jerk like it was trying to get closer to him, or maybe run away from him, 'if you'd rather, I can turn my back and let you do it.'

She released her breath slowly and lifted her arse off the stump, an act that in itself seemed lewd. He pushed open her jacket with warm hands and shoved up the edge of her silk blouse to unzip her skirt, exposing a swathe of her belly just above her navel. Then he curled his fingers around the waist of the skirt, catching the elastic of her knickers as well, and shimmied both down over her hips. His hands skimmed the lacy tops of her hold-ups, and for a second, she forgot about the cold. She reached out and raked her fingers through his unruly hair.

His breath caught in his chest, and he lowered his head to plant a warm kiss just below her bellybutton, lips burning on her icy skin. Then he pulled away all businesslike. 'You'll get hypothermia. You're cold.' The rush of his hot breath brushed her belly, causing gooseflesh to tiptoe up her spine.

She had little control over the trembling that gripped her body from the cold, and yet her insides squirmed with want as he inched the skirt down over her thighs leaving her hold-ups in place. 'Please,' she gasped between chattering teeth. How could she be so damn cold and so hot at the same time? 'I need ... I need ...'

'I know what you need.' His voice was tight, accented by the heavy drag of his breath, much heavier than the expended efforts demanded. His dark eyes were clouded with a cocktail of emotions too complex for her to translate in her discomfort, but there had to be some anger and maybe some concern in the mix. The second kiss chased the descent of her skirt, lightning fast and humid on the apex of her gash, searing hot against the damp chill of gooseflesh, just above the place where her clit roused itself from beneath its hood. The delicious steamy shock of it unbalanced her and she dropped back onto the stump, her bottom settling into soft moss and her elbow sending the cocoa cup clattering into the fragrant pine straw.

He dragged her skirt down and shoved at it as though it had offended him somehow until it was in a heap around her ankles. Then he eased her left leg free, lifted it so her foot rested on his shoulder splaying her crotch for his hungry gaze. 'I'm wet,' she sighed.

'You fell in a ditch.' His fingers traced a ticklish path up the inside of her thigh above the hold-ups.

She squirmed and arched her back. 'That's not what I mean.'

'I know what you mean.' His words were short, clipped. He slid a thick finger between her heavy folds causing a sharp intake of breath. Then he rose to take her mouth again, forcing her leg forward, knee bent to press her thigh against her breast, making her pussy gape like a begging bird, making her bear down into the pillow of moss. 'Please,' she gasped. 'I need ...'

He held her in his weighty gaze. 'I know what you need,' he repeated. With his free hand, he fought his trousers like they were the enemy until they were down around his hips. In her peripheral vision she could just make out his cock straining toward her. Then he pushed into her with a grunt, sending shockwaves up through her at the sudden invasion that filled her too full for comfort, yet felt way too good to be pain.

He gathered her to him and began to thrust. There was no preamble, no foreplay, just driving hungry need. She hooked her legs around him and held on for dear life, growling and grinding, feeling like she would split in two with each pounding. And yet she wanted nothing more than to live for the next thrust. It was as though her whole world had contracted to thrusting and shoving and trembling. She was freezing and burning and grasping, and he was pushing her, more quickly than she would have ever imagined, to complete overload.

The pistoning of his body raked the swell of her clit to a hard knot as he drew nearer his release. And when at last he overwhelmed her, she threw back her head and howled as her orgasm raged like fire melting ice. Only a split second later he convulsed and jerked on top of her.

For a few minutes they lay sprawled on the stump together catching their breath. Then, at last, he pulled out, and it was as though nothing had happened. Avoiding her gaze, he cleaned them both with the large blue bandana he'd been wearing around his neck, and then he tossed her a pair of grey tracksuit bottoms with a drawstring. 'Put these on. We need to get you someplace warm.' He packed up his rucksack while she struggled into the bottoms then he threw her a hooded sweatshirt. He tossed her muddy shoes into a waterproof bag and shoved it in the top of the pack, just before he hoisted it onto his back. Then he lifted her in his arms again.

'What are you doing?' she breathed. 'You can't carry me to your house.'

He nodded behind him as a dark blue jeep pulled up and parked inconspicuously by the side of the road, not far from where she had tried to cross. 'I have no intention of carrying you to my house. Ed will take you back to your hotel.'

Chapter Ten

'AND THAT'S HOW IT ended.' Stella stared out the window of the hotel into the full car park. 'He gave me a synapse-melting kiss, thrust me into the jeep with his driver and waved me off to my hotel room. He said he had urgent research.'

She heard Anne's *hmmph* on the other end of the phone.

'What? You don't believe me? I swear that's how it happened.'

'Look, Stel, honey, I don't doubt that's exactly how it happened, and you've made me so wet I'm in danger of sliding off the chair, but I just can't believe Vincent Evanston is Tino. That's ... That's just completely barking.'

There was a soft knock at the door. It was room service with her mushroom omelette and the complimentary copy of the *Oregonian*. She motioned them in with the phone still to her ear. She had spent the night at the Airport Sheraton in Portland. She'd be flying back to London in a few hours after a successful meeting with Vanguard.

She shut the door behind the server and settled into her breakfast. 'I know it sounds crazy. I keep telling myself that, but I swear, Anne, he's identical. And he knew about Tino. He knew why I pursued him into the wood. How else could he know? And why else was he so anxious to get rid of me? I mean, he would have done that before we had sex if he wasn't Tino. Don't you think?'

'Evil twin?'

'Hot twin, I'd say. Totally hot twin.' Stella poured her Earl Grey into the porcelain cup and sipped. 'Anyway, I'm seeing Tino this weekend, so maybe I can find out for sure. I mean I've had sex with both of them.'

'But you just said it was totally different.'

'I know what I said. I just don't see how there can be two people who look so absolutely the same but ... aren't. Annie? I can hear the wheels turning. What is it?'

'I don't understand why you have to know, Stella. Tino's a–'

'Prostitute, yes, I'm aware of that fact.' In spite of herself, Stella blushed at the use of the word.

'Can you really imagine why someone like Vincent Evanston, someone with his power and his resources would be moonlighting as a prostitute?'

'Tino's not a prostitute per se.' Stella contemplated. 'He's a Pet, and that's so totally different.' She picked at her omelette. 'I could have turned down a prostitute.'

There was silence on the other end of the phone.

'Annie, have you ever been with him? With Tino? I mean you work for Strigida too, and you put in as many hours as I do.'

'God no! Tino scares me.'

'Really? Why?'

Stella could hear Anne shifting the phone. 'You know why, Stella. I mean, look at the way you're obsessing.'

'I know, but I just can't help myself.' She held the phone against her shoulder and flipped open the paper.

'Stel, you know if you find out who Tino really is, if you unmask the Pet, so to speak, then he won't be Tino any more. I don't understand why you'd want to do that? Why can't you just enjoy and be satisfied?'

'It's your fault,' Stella pouted. 'You're the one who left him with me against my will in the first place.'

'Don't blame me. I only did what I was told, hon. It was the Boss's orders that you have Tino, so take it up with him next time you talk to him.'

'I just might do that. I mean it's pretty ballsy him thinking I need a ...' her voice died away in her throat, as she glanced down at the paper.

'Stella?'

On page four, she was greeted by a smiling photo of Tino!

She plopped her teacup down on the tray, slopping Earl Grey over the crisp white napkin. As she read the caption the scent of bergamot filled the air.

In an unprecedented appearance, Vincent Evanston, reclusive philanthropist, to dedicate new nature reserve near Lincoln City.

'Stella? Are you still there?'

The ceremony was this afternoon. Forgetting all about her omelette, she held the paper up to the lamp and squinted hard at the photo. The hair was styled differently. The face was shaved clean, and under the photo in small print were the words *Archive photo* again. And yet, this photo of Evanston made him look even more like Tino than the one on the news feed she'd first seen.

'Stella? What's going on?'

Stella jumped at the sound of Anne's voice, as though she had temporarily been hypnotised by the gaze of the mystery man, even through the medium of newsprint. 'Um, Anne, I'm gonna need another day here after all. I'm looking at the *Oregonian*, and, well, I ... I need another day.'

There was a gust-of-wind sigh. 'Does this have anything to do with Evanston?'

'Look, Annie, I was coming home a day early anyway, so it won't matter, right? I'll talk to you later. Bye.' She didn't wait for the torrent of questions she knew she would have no good answers for.

An hour later, Stella had rescheduled her flight, hired another car, and was speeding down Highway 18, heading back to the Oregon coast and to Lincoln City. The road atlas was open on the passenger seat and an enormous latte filled the cup holder. If she hurried, she could just make it.

It was not without considerable effort that she finally found the Fireweed Nature Reserve at the end of a not-so-well maintained gravel road that rattled her teeth and spattered the car with a fine mist of mud. She arrived to a clatter of binoculars and birding scopes. Even the journalists were dressed like adverts for L.L. Bean. She'd left Portland in a hurry. There still had been no time to shop for the great outdoors. With her clingy summer dress, showcasing cleavage and legs, Vincent would see her a mile away and have ample time to cut and run if he decided to. She hoped he wouldn't.

At the beginning of the boardwalk leading out into the marshes was a dark wooden sign with the words Fireweed Nature Reserve burnt deeply into the wood along with an artist's rendering of some tall plant covered in bright magenta flowers. She assumed it must be fireweed. At the lower corner of the sign was a stylised drawing of an owl on a branch sitting in front of a crescent moon. As she hurried up the boardwalk to the viewing platform where the dedication was to take place, her heels slid treacherously, threatening to wedge in the cracks between the boards. Tino wouldn't have cared what she wore, she reminded herself angrily.

She stumbled up the boardwalk just as the introduction finished, nearly falling against a man draped in half-a-dozen cameras.

And suddenly there was Tino, looking rugged and considerably less vulnerable in his khaki trousers and cotton shirt. He waited politely for the applause to die down, and then he spoke. 'As most of you know, I grew up not far from here.' The resonant voice and the American accent were a slap-in-the-face reminder that this was most definitely Vincent Evanston. How could Tino possibly be an American? She listened as he continued.

'My best memories are of a pair of barn owls who took up residence on our farm the year I turned 12. All that summer, my best friend and I watched those owls – even rigged up a camera and got some pretty decent photos. In fact, we were so obsessed with those birds that we started a secret club in their honour. We called ourselves the Night Owls. Those owls successfully raised five chicks that year, and I fell in love.'

He looked over his shoulder and nodded at the lake behind him. 'Places like this are important, not just because of the sanctuary they give wildlife, but because they offer all of us an opportunity to fall in love. With nature.' His gaze moved over the crowd, came to rest on her then moved on. She felt as though she had been gut punched, and yet what had she expected him to do? Forget everything and come running to her? He hadn't been all that happy to see her in the wood, and he wasn't likely to be any more happy now that she had practically stalked him here. Maybe he hoped if he ignored her, she'd go away. Surely this man couldn't be her Tino.

He continued. 'I have a reputation for being a recluse, but I'm not really.' He offered a mischievous chuckle. 'I just prefer the company of the residents of a place like this over you lot.'

To the sound of laughter and applause, he cut the red ribbon stretched across the viewing platform and stood smiling, shaking hands while cameras snapped and reporters asked questions. People adorned in binoculars and birding scopes now lined the rail of the viewing platform. The chill in the air as the damp summer sun fell below the wooded foothills made Stella's nipples ache through the ridiculously thin dress.

She was halfway back to her car, feeling stupid and self conscious, when a strong arm slipped around her waist, and a familiar scent filled her nostrils. She looked up into Tino's dark eyes.

'What are you doing here?' It still came as a shock to hear Tino speaking.

'I saw your picture in the *Oregonian*.'

'So you thought you'd just drop in.'

'You are Tino, aren't you?'

He picked up the pace. 'Tino's not here.' With his arm around her waist, he guided her away from her car to a waiting limo.

She didn't protest as he opened the door and helped her inside, sliding in next to her. Then he knocked on the privacy window and the driver took off.

'Seems a strange vehicle to bring to a nature reserve,' she said.

'You really think so? My dad made the big bucks in shipping, you know, and the Port of Portland has a reputation for murder and all kinds of intrigue so rich men can have what they want. So of course I have a limo.' He leant close and nipped her ear. 'And you just hopped right in with me, didn't you? You know what they say about accepting rides from strangers. Are you scared?'

She held his gaze. 'You're not a stranger.'

He chuckled softly and returned her gaze as though he were the king of stare-downs, then he released his breath slowly. 'Anyway, I didn't bring the limo, but you can't go back in what I came in dressed like that.'

'Then you have to be Tino, or you wouldn't have–'

He covered her mouth in an insistent kiss. 'What?' He spoke against her lips 'You think I wouldn't notice the sexy English bird distracting me from all the other birds.' He teased her lips apart, sparring with her tongue, making her insides feel like warm toffee. She was relieved to hear no anger in his voice.

She came up for breath. 'But how else would you–'

He nipped and tugged on her lip. 'Tino's not here,' he whispered against her mouth, slurring his words with the flick of his tongue. 'There's just Vincent.'

'What are you, schizo then?' she let out a little gasp as he nibbled her earlobe then the hollow of her throat.

'Didn't you take psychology 101? We all have more than one person living inside us, Stella.'

'Where are we going?' she asked, feeling suddenly disoriented as the driver turned onto the main road and picked up speed.

'Portland.'

'But my car. It's a hire, and my bags–'

He kissed her again, and his hand moved up the inside of her thigh. 'Don't worry. My people will take care of everything.'

'But I thought–' With a sharp little gasp, she suddenly forgot how to speak, as his fingers slid aside the crotch of her thong.

'Did you wear these for Tino, hoping he'd take them off with his teeth?' He raked the hood of her clit with a heavy thumb, sending a jolt of heat radiating out over her belly and down through her slit. 'Because I won't bother. I'm not here for your entertainment.'

77

'I never thought that you were,' she said, giving him an ineffective shove with the flat of her hand. But he took her mouth again, and the way his tongue invaded and withdrew and invaded again, the way his fingers teased and retreated and teased again at the very edge of her gape made her stop thinking about ... well everything, really.

He pulled away at last and held her gaze. 'We have until we get to Portland, Stella. You can waste time trying to find out about Tino or,' he slid his middle finger into her slick pout. 'You can spend that time with Vincent.' His thumb pressed tight little circles around her clit. 'It can be such a pleasant drive to Portland.'

'I don't even know Vincent,' she gasped. 'You never gave me a chance.'

'As I recall, you overwhelmed me. I wasn't prepared.'

'You were scared.'

He held her gaze. 'I didn't say that.'

'But you were. I think you were–'

He kissed her hard, and when he pulled away they were both breathless. 'Stop talking, Stella. There are lots better uses of our time.' He demonstrated by burrowing, face first, into her well-displayed cleavage, wasted on the herons and otters at the nature reserve. He shoved aside the plunge neckline and push-up bra, until her breasts tumbled over like willing conspirators into his large palms.

The seat in the limo was almost big enough for an orgy. She lost the kitten heels and her toes curled in the plush carpet as he slid a second finger into her.

'Not appropriate footwear for a nature reserve. Didn't you learn your lesson the first time?' He nodded to her shoes. Then he huffed an exaggerated groan. 'My back still hurts from piggybacking you.'

She reached out to slap him playfully, but he caught her wrist and held her in a serious gaze. 'You could have broken an ankle or worse.' He pulled her down and shifted her until she lay full length on the seat. Then he lifted her foot to his lips bathing her heel in his hot breath. 'None of this is necessary for Tino, or me. What were you thinking?' His words slurred as he ran his tongue up over her instep and suckled each toe in turn, causing her to buck against the seat as her pussy gripped his fingers in hungry nibbles.

He trailed kisses and nips and lovebites over her ankle and up the inside of her thigh while the relentless hand working her pussy never missed a beat. And when his mouth caught up with his hand, he shoved at the crotch of her thong until it was stretched uselessly over one arse cheek, leaving her splayed and twitchy and ready for the take-over. 'I wanted to taste you out there under the trees, but you were so cold. I was worried.' He didn't wait for her response, but lowered his face and lapped at her clit and suckled her labia until she was heavy and distended, still gripping his probing fingers. She heard the sound of a zipper, the swish of clothing, and he pushed into her with a groan. 'You shouldn't have come here.' He held very still, making her wait with his fullness inside her. Making her want. 'It's a complication neither of us needs.'

'But I am here now, and we can't go back,' she breathed. She tried to thrust against him.

Still he didn't move, but he let her squirm beneath him, feeling like her cunt was on fire. 'You didn't come for me. You came for Tino.' He rocked against her just enough for his body to rake her clit, and the shock of it felt like electricity jolting through her pussy. She clenched down hard on his cock.

'Please! Can't I have you both?'

'No.' He withdrew just enough to make her certain that his refusal to satisfy her would be beyond endurance. His breath was heavy, but measured, like he could go on for ever. And, dear God, she wanted him to. He held her gaze. 'You can't have both.'

And just when she was about to panic, to beg his forgiveness, to offer him anything to get him to continue, he released a long slow breath and lowered his mouth to her nipples as though they had all the time in the world. He nibbled and suckled until her nipples were tight and tender in that tetchy place between pain and pleasure. Then he raised his dark eyes, suddenly so unlike Tino's, and met her gaze. 'Do you want Vincent?'

'Yes. I want Vincent.' She sighed. 'Please.'

He released a breath she only now realised he'd been holding then gathered her to him, cupping her buttocks in his hands to push deeper into her. She raised her arse, wrapped her legs around him and dug her heels in for the ride.

He was pitiless. He battered her with exquisite force until she was almost there then he stopped, holding her so tightly that she couldn't satisfy herself, she could do nothing but yield as he kissed her until her lips felt bruised and nibbled her throat and neck until she trembled like light on the surface of water. Then he battered her again.

Just when she was certain she wouldn't survive the trip to Portland, he shifted his embrace and pulled her on top of him, nearly toppling them both onto the floor in the process. 'I'll make you come now, Stella.' His voice was raspy at the back of his throat. 'Vincent will make you come.'

Perhaps it was some magic formula, she didn't know, but with the gentle rocking of his hips like waves on a calm sea, and the stroking of his thumb against her clit, she came in whimpers and sobs. A few more thrusts and she felt him clench beneath her, and his cock spasmed inside her.

'Where are you taking me,' she asked. The streetlights indicated that they were in the suburbs of Portland.

Still naked, he knelt on the floor of the limo, wiping the wet folds of her vulva with his handkerchief. 'The airport.'

She pushed his hand away. 'I don't have a ticket, and look at me, I'm a mess.' To her irritation, she was suddenly fighting back tears.

He rose on his haunches and kissed her, cupping her cheek and pushing the hair away from her face. 'I think you look exquisite. Now hold still. I'm not finished with your pussy yet, and I'm enjoying the view.'

She felt as though she would burst as the first signs for the airport came into view. She had gone to Lincoln City for answers, but she had gotten only more questions. 'There's so much I want to ask you, Vincent.'

'Don't. Because I won't answer, and I don't want to ruin

what we've just shared.'

'Will I see you again?'

He forced a smile. 'You weren't supposed to see me in the first place.'

Panic suddenly rose in her chest. 'Will I see Tino?'

'That's up to the Pet Shop.'

The limo pulled to a stop, and the driver opened the door and helped her out. To her surprise, they weren't at the departures drop-off point, with its manic coming and going of cars, disgorging people with too much luggage and too little time. Instead they were on a darkened runway. For a second, panic rose in Stella's chest. Perhaps Vincent was schizo after all. Perhaps his intentions were more sinister than a flight back to London.

But before the thought was fully formed, he nodded above the roof of the limo. 'The plane's there.'

'Bloody hell!' Beyond the car was a sleek private jet, smartly dressed staff standing at the ready near the foot of the stairs leading to the open door.

'Come on.' He slid an arm around her. 'Your bags are already onboard, and your rental car has been returned. You'll have time to freshen up. Pilot expects a smooth flight into London.'

Then everything happened so fast. At the bottom of the stairs, he gave her a kiss that nearly sent her pussy into meltdown again. Then he turned her over to the smiling attendant, and by the time she was at the top of the stairs, the limo was already pulling away.

Chapter Eleven

O'KELLY PUNCHED THE KEYPAD of her mobile so hard it hurt her finger then she jammed the phone to her ear and paced back and forth across the carpeted floor of her bedroom.

The Boss answered after three rings. 'O'Kelly? What's wrong?' He actually sounded as though she might have woken him up. That had never happened before. It was as though the man never slept. He'd always been that way. The sound of him so vulnerable made a knot clench low in her stomach. 'Why are you calling at this hour?'

'Have you talked to Stella today?'

'No. Should I have?' She could imagine him wiping the sleep from his eyes and checking the digital read-out on the alarm clock at the side of his bed. The thought made her pulse quicken, and she was instantly wet, which miffed her considerably, since she was angry at him. She forced herself to listen as he continued. 'I did get the message that she had rearranged her schedule to stay on another day.' There was a long pause. 'O'Kelly? What is it? What's wrong?'

Jesus it was hard to be angry at him when his voice practically dripped sexy, delicious concern. She straightened her shoulders then plopped down on the edge of her bed with a huff. 'Our Stella is convinced that Tino is Vincent Evanston.'

'Really? Hmm.'

O'Kelly ground her teeth and ignored the amusement that nearly oozed from his voice. 'In fact, I'd be willing to bet she took that extra day in Oregon to pursue Evanston. He was supposed to be at some opening ceremony for a nature reserve.'

Before he could ask, she continued. 'I checked the local

82

paper online. I was shocked to find an actual photo of Vincent Evanston, and though it's not a great photo, I think she might be right, and I figured you would know.'

'Wow. What's the world coming to, Vincent Evanston seen in public making nicey-nice.'

'Just answer me straight. Is Tino Vincent Evanston?' She hated that she was always the angry one and that he always sounded like the voice of calm and reason. But in truth, he usually provoked her.

There was a long pause, so she pressed forward. 'I can't personally understand why someone like Vincent Evanston would want to be a Pet. I mean, he's such a recluse.'

'Come on, O'Kelly. You know your basic psychology. Vincent may be a recluse, but that doesn't mean Tino has to be. You've been working with the Pet Shop long enough to know exactly why it might be the outlet someone like Vincent would crave. Think about yourself, think about both of us, always in control, always in charge. Don't you sometimes wish someone would tell you what to do so you wouldn't always have to be the responsible one? Don't you ever wish you were a Pet, so you could be pampered and adored and kept safe? I do. It only makes sense that Vincent would have those same needs, and where better for a recluse to get those needs met than the Pet Shop?'

She realised she'd been holding her breath. Little droplets of perspiration slid between her breasts. Her heart bounced against her ribcage. Her voice was suddenly much less forceful, much more breathless. 'That would certainly explain why you let Tino come into the Pet Shop without going through the proper channels.'

'O'Kelly, whether or not Tino is Vincent Evanston had nothing to do with why I took him on as a Pet.'

'Why then?' The words came out before she could stop them. She had always wondered, and had never gotten a satisfactory answer.

He offered a sigh of resignation, and she heard him shift between what, no doubt, were very expensive sheets. She couldn't keep from imagining him all sleep-mussed and drowsy, sprawled across the bed with the phone to his ear. She couldn't keep from imagining herself there with him between those sheets. She pulled her attention back to the conversation. 'Well?'

There was a slow release of breath on the other end of the phone, breath that might have been ever so slightly shaky. 'We had sex.'

Of all the answers she might have guessed this wasn't one of them, and she found herself truly speechless.

'O'Kelly? Did you hear me?'

She nodded, and then remembered he couldn't see her. 'I heard you.' She gulped air, suddenly feeling the need for a lot more oxygen than what seemed to be in the room. Then she calmed herself, gripping the phone hard so her hand wouldn't shake. 'I didn't know. I didn't know that you were ...' She nodded again and tried to breathe. She felt like she'd just been gut punched. 'I mean when we were together back in uni and we ... we had sex ... Well, you seemed to like it just fine.'

'Oh, I'm not gay. I'd never been with a man before Tino, and I haven't been since.'

'You could have told me,' she breathed. 'I would have been all right with it.'

'I didn't tell you because I didn't know what to say. Vincent was my best friend all through high school. I was the weird foreign kid forced to go to a strange school in a strange place because of my father's work. Vincent was the socially awkward rich kid, always a disappointment to his father because he'd rather be out in the woods. We were both loners, and we just clicked.

'I swear to you, O'Kelly, nothing, nothing even remotely sexually ever happened between us. Oh we talked about sex like all adolescent boys do. But nothing beyond that. Then when he approached me as Tino, he broadsided me. Mind you, I hadn't seen Vincent myself in several years, and Vincent had never had anything to do with the Pet Shop. Even when we made the original bet at his birthday party, he wanted nothing to do with it. It was my idea that the money should go to Strigida. It was always my idea and he always left it to me, so you can imagine the shock. It was like he wasn't Vincent at all. Like he was someone I couldn't resist. Someone no one could have resisted. Since you'd never actually met Vincent, nor were you likely to, in the end it was easier just not to say anything, and honestly, the two are so different, it's still hard for me to believe they could be the same person.'

She let out her breath slowly. 'But they are.'

He didn't answer. He didn't have to.

'Then Tino seduced you?'

There was a long silence followed by soft laughter. 'I guess you could call it that.' His voice had that quality people's voices have when they discuss their fondest memories.

'I told him I'd hire him as a Pet if he could convincingly be my Pet for a weekend. Of course I didn't think he could. You know how much training we put our Pets through. And I told him right up front I didn't want him for sex. I just wanted to put him through his paces, you know, to show him how tough it really was.'

'But you had sex anyway.'

Another little huff of laughter. 'What I failed to figure into the equation was that I wasn't spending the weekend with my old friend, I was spending the weekend with Tino. You know Tino. Before the weekend was over, there was nothing I wanted more in the whole world than sex with him. Of course I should have known better. I mean he was my Pet, and I had to treat him like a Pet, take off his clothes, feed him, bathe him, give him permission to relieve his needs. It was my fault really. He only did what he was told.'

'How was it?' God, she sounded like an adolescent waiting to hear the juicy details after someone had been felt up. In spite of her best efforts to maintain decorum, her hand found its way up under the edge of her skirt.

The resulting laugh sounded loud, awkward, unlike the Boss. 'O'Kelly, are you looking for me to give you good wank material?'

She sputtered and fought for air. The room felt suddenly hot.

'Because I'm happy to help you out. Get out of your

clothes.'

'What?' The word came out more like a gasp.

'We used to be pretty damn good at phone sex, as I recall, and if you're gonna make me talk dirty to you about Tino, the least you can do is undress and scoot down beneath the sheets, which is where most of us are at this hour anyway. Where you should be, and you shouldn't be there alone, I might add.'

'Sir, I ... Really I shouldn't have–'

'Undress, O'Kelly. That's an order.'

'You can't order me,' she breathed, but she was already halfway out of her blouse, fumbling with the phone, which she put on speaker.

He made no response, but she thought she could hear a change in his breathing. 'You've undressed Tino. You know what that's like, how he's always horny, how he always behaves like he's just been so terribly naughty, and yet he's so completely innocent. That's what makes him so damned irresistible.'

Her own breathing accelerated. She nodded, not caring that he couldn't see her. She stepped out of her skirt then started to take off her underwear, but thought better of it for the moment. She slid in between the sheets.

'I'm amazed that you've never had him, O'Kelly, but then I've always said your fortitude is astounding. And your sense of self-preservation.'

'Oh I've wanted him, sir. More than once.'

'And you've fantasised about him.'

'Countless times.'

'Not surprising. The way he nuzzles and sniffs when he's getting to know you. And even when he already knows you, he seems to like nothing better than to have his face in your crotch or your arse. I made him sleep on the floor the first night he was with me. I let him masturbate to take the edge off.' He grunted. 'Took the edge off for him. Didn't do a damn thing to make me less horny. And I never thought I would be, you know, horny for a man. But then Tino's not just any man.

'My resolve was well on its way to being gone by breakfast, so when he nuzzled his way into my bathrobe ... Stupid of me, really, wearing a bathrobe with nothing under it, like I actually wanted him to see my cock, you know, like I was the one showing off.' There was silence on the other end of the receiver, but she could hear him breathing. She figured he was remembering it all, thinking about what it was like to have sex with Tino. At last he spoke. 'Well, I let him have what he wanted.'

'He sucked you off?' O'Kelly felt everything low in her belly grip. She was already flooding the crotch of her knickers. How many times had she fantasised about Tino? And when she wasn't fantasising about Tino, she was fantasising about the Boss. The two of them together? My God, what a heatwave!

'Tino's a big man. His mouth is deep, and I'm not small, as you know. I've never had anyone who could take me in like he did. All of me. That's how it started. Next thing I know, I'm on the floor rolling all over with him, then he's offering me his arse, his sweet, tight gripping arse, and I swear to God, O'Kelly, there was no way in hell I could refuse.'

'And it was good?' Her fingers were now well buried in the slippery slide of her pout, legs splayed wide beneath the sheets.

The groan on the other end of the phone sounded almost painful. 'Good doesn't begin to describe it. It was then I realised I had the chance to do all those secret things men think about doing with other men but never have the courage to try.'

'And you did them all?'

'With Tino, yes. Everything I could think to do. And he was so willing, so obliging, and always ready. He was so completely Tino. There was no way I could consider him anyone else, not even the man who's been my friend most of my life.'

'How did you know that he would be equally good with women? I mean, you didn't send him for me to test.' Try though she might, she couldn't keep the hurt out of her voice.

'I knew because I didn't want to send him to you, O'Kelly. I didn't want him invading your thoughts the way he did mine. You're always the clear-headed one of us. I wanted you to stay that way. Plus,' his voice got suddenly softer. 'I guess I was a little jealous.'

'What? Of sharing him with me?'

His laugh rushed through the phone. 'Don't be daft, O'Kelly, that's not what I mean, and you know it.'

In spite of the warmth his words made in her chest, she pressed on. 'But you sent him to poor unsuspecting Stella.'

'Stella's not you, and I think you don't give the girl enough credit. Now, tell me. What do you want to know about Tino and me? You've made me hard, so we'll have to deal with it, won't we?'

In spite of herself a little sigh made its way between her lips, and she could barely find her voice. But she was brave tonight, braver than she would have ever thought possible. 'You've been hard before when we've talked on the phone, and you didn't involve me.'

She heard the shifting of the sheets again. 'O'Kelly, you know as well as I do why I never involve you, so don't play coy with me. And tonight, *you* involved *me*, so I expect you to finish what you started. Are you naked?'

'Not exactly.' She peeked down under the duvet as though she had forgotten what she'd left on. 'I'm still in my underwear and hold-ups. Black lace, the lot.'

He tisk-tisked. 'A little much for daywear, don't you think?'

'As you just reminded me, it's not day. And anyway, just because I have to look professional on the outside doesn't mean I can't feel sexy underneath, does it?'

His lazy whisper of a laugh dripped sex. 'Oh my dear O'Kelly, if I had to work in the same office with you day in day out, I'm afraid I'd have a hard-on all the time. Why do you think I spend so much time away? And you still give me a hard-on.'

Surprisingly she felt his words in her chest rather than her cunt, like he'd wrapped his fingers around her heart and squeezed.

'What about you, O'Kelly? Do you ever come when we're talking business?'

'No, sir,' she stammered. 'I mean, I get wet, really wet and I want to ... But it's business, and I feel like ...'

'Like somebody has to maintain decorum. I know. You told

me when you took the job.'

It was her turn to smile.

'Well here we are at last, not in the office, neither one of us, and you brought it up, so I'm not letting you get away with it tonight. O'Kelly, if you don't have a hand in your knickers, you should get one there as quickly as possible. You are wet, aren't you?'

'Yes, sir. Very.'

'Do you think we can dispense with the "sir" bit? You made your point with that a long time ago.'

'I'd rather not, actually. It makes me hot, calling *you* sir.'

'Didn't know you felt that way or I'd have been enjoying it a lot more. Tell me about your nipples, O'Kelly'.

'Erect, sir, and my areolae too. All stippled and aching.'

'Good, good. And now you want me to tell you what Tino did to me.'

'No, sir. I want you to tell me what you would do to me. If you were here.' Her face burnt with shame even as she said it. That was their professional relationship right out the window after all these years, after all the effort to maintain neutrality. And now she was talking dirty to him on the phone just like they were back in uni again. She couldn't see any good coming from this. But before she had time to backtrack his voice filled the room. 'If I were there, O'Kelly, the very first thing I would want is to see you. All of you, so whatever underwear you've got on, hold-ups, knickers, I don't care, take them off, take them all off, then push back the sheets so nothing can interfere with my view.'

She scrambled to do as he said, finding her fingers awkward against hooks and lace in ways they hadn't since she was a groping adolescent. 'And you?' She forced the words up past her stammering heart.

'I'm already naked, O'Kelly, duvet thrown back, cock in my hand. Wishing it were your hand, or your mouth ... or your cunt. God I remember that tight cunt of yours. You have no idea how often I've had a wank to the thought of your pussy.' He spoke the words into the phone in such a way that she could almost feel the heat of his breath. 'I can't count the number of times my conversations with you have ended up with my cock in my hand. You're a cruel woman, O'Kelly, reducing me to this.'

A little whimper escaped her lips as her thumb pressed hard against her clit.

He continued. 'But you've had more restraint than I have, haven't you? You've always waited until ... Until when, O'Kelly, until at night alone in your bed, like now? Or maybe you exorcise all of that pent-up heat on a Pet? Are you thinking of my cock when Liam or Dan is sucking your full nipples or burying their tools to the hilt in your scalding pussy? Jesus, I hope so, O'Kelly. I hope so.' His voice felt like heavy syrup dripping down against her senses causing wet-hot need to ignite all over her body. She squirmed and thrust her hips.

'What I hate about the phone is that I can't smell your arousal,' he said.

A skitter of muscle memory beneath her belly recalled how excellent his sense of smell was.

'If I were there with you in the office I would always know when your pussy was hot. I would smell your sweetness. You know that I would. Even after all this time, I could never forget what your cunt smells like when it needs a cock. And if I were there in the office more often, I would always know when you were wet and swollen. I would always know when you needed my cock. And I would take such advantage that you wouldn't be able to walk straight, woman. I would have you on your desk, up against the wall, in the copy room. I would eat up all that sweetness until my balls were about to burst, until your pussy was raw and ready and sticky like toffee. Then I would push into you as deep as I could, feeling how soft and warm and wet you are, feeling how tight your cunny grips my cock. Would you wrap your legs around me, O'Kelly, climb me like a tree, clench me until I couldn't breathe?'

'Yes, sir, Like a tree.' She could barely find the breath to speak. 'Just like a tree.' She arched off the bed wriggling and straining, feeling as though there wasn't enough room in the hot tingle of her skin for the swell of her. It took her a while to sort out the sounds of them. Her breathless keening cries harmonized with the deep-chested grunts and huffs coming through the Boss's end of the phone. 'O'Kelly,' he gasped, 'I'm hard, so hard I feel like I'll shatter if I don't come soon. Jesus, I want to be inside you.'

'I want that too, Alan. I want that so badly,' she rasped just before orgasm raged over her, and the cry that forced its way through her lips left her throat raw and aching as she flooded herself and shook as though she would never stop. But only half the cry was hers. The deeper part, the part that she felt low in the base of her belly was his, like a drum beat pulsing into her until she collapsed onto the bed trembling, weak, feeling as though she were of no more substance than her sheer stockings.

'You haven't called me Alan in a long time.' His breath poured into her bed like a wind storm and she pressed the phone to her, held it close between her damp breasts, just clutching it there until at last he had the breath to speak again.

'And now, Annie, if I were there, I would kiss you, every inch of you, take into myself the taste and the scent of you well-pleasured, then I would pull you close to me and just hold you.'

'I'd like that, Alan.' She still clutched the phone to her breasts as she drifted off.

When she awoke, pale dawn was seeping through the curtains and the phone connection had been broken.

There was a text message.

Cancel Stella's weekend with Tino. Have rethought situ. It's time 2 bring her in. Make arrangements.

Chapter Twelve

ANNE SAT CURLED ON the end of Stella's sofa watching her pace. 'I can't believe you cancelled your flight and went chasing after some tree-hugging tycoon.' She handed her a tissue mid stride and Stella wiped her swollen eyes and blew her nose. 'OK, that I can believe. I can't believe he sent you back home on his private jet.'

Stella shot her a caustic look, and then she nodded toward her laptop open on the coffee table. 'Yeah, lucky me. I get home to discover my weekend with Tino has been cancelled. No explanations, no excuses, nothing, just cancelled. He's already been rescheduled with someone else, and he doesn't have another opening for months. I have no way of getting in touch with him. I'm sure Vincent had something to do with it, but I haven't heard from him either.'

'Did you really expect to? I mean you said he's a recluse.'

'Yes, but I thought maybe that wouldn't apply to me, I mean after ... everything.'

Anne poured herself a glass of wine and sipped while Stella paced. 'Well, you really can't expect him to be Tino for you now after what you know. It would never be the same. I did try to warn you.'

'Don't lecture me, all right? I get it. I don't need you to tell me what a fool I am.' Stella plopped down on the couch. 'And I don't care. I still have to see him again, Anne. I just have to.' Her eyes misted, and the empty space inside her felt vast.

'Bloody hell, Stella, be sensible. You don't even know him – whoever he is. Tino's a glorified hooker, and Vincent's a bored rich bloke who got a good shag out of you.' She waved a dismissive hand. 'Make that several good shags. And OK, maybe it was good for you too, but still. It is what it is. God, if I'd known it would cause you this much grief, I'd have told the Boss to go fuck himself when he suggested it.'

'Yeah, well, you didn't, did you? You brought Tino to my door as bold as anything and left me with him, so don't be telling me to get a grip.' She mangled the tissue she had wadded in her hand. 'Anyway, I couldn't help but notice you certainly seem to know an awful lot about the Pet Shop.'

Anne huffed a frustrated breath. 'I told you, I brought Tino to you under orders, all right? I didn't want to do it in the first place.'

'Yes, but you did. You brought him to me, and I'm assuming since there was no handler, you must have got him from somewhere. And you certainly knew all the ins and outs of taking care of Pets. You knew that he might be having a wank on my carpet if we left him alone too long. You knew that the Pet Shop kept its Pets horny. And you were quite expert at taking his clothes off, like you'd done it before, like you knew exactly what you were doing. I think you know more than you're letting on. A lot more.'

Anne toyed with her wineglass, avoiding Stella's gaze. 'You can think what you want, but it doesn't change anything, does it?' Then she tisk-tisked as Stella teared up again. 'Oh come on, Stel, this just isn't healthy. You need to let it go.'

'Please, Anne. I have to see him one more time. I just have to know. And I think you can arrange it for me.'

For a long moment, Anne held her in a gaze that would have penetrated iron then she shook her head and blew out a harsh breath. 'I'll see what I can do.' She raised a hand. 'Before you get too excited, I said I'll see. That means I'll see.' She held her friend's gaze. 'I might know a way to get you to Tino, but it may not be quite the way you had in mind. Are you OK with that?'

'Yes, of course.' Stella wiped her eyes on the mangled tissue and blew her nose. 'Anything.'

Anne studied her for a long moment then frowned. 'It's against my better judgment, way against my better judgment, but I'll see what I can do.'

Stella closed her eyes and collapsed onto the couch in a wrung-out heap. 'Oh God, Annie, thank you so much.' She caught her breath and shifted to face her friend. 'What should I do?'

'Just wait. That's all. Just wait.'

As soon as Anne left Stella pulled the computer onto her lap, entered the Pet Shop web address, and waited impatiently until a password was requested. She typed it in and found herself once again scrolling down through the bios and descriptions of Pets until she came to Tino's. Her heart somersaulted as she recalled the shy man she'd first met, the man who was unable to meet her gaze without encouragement. How could he be Vincent? How could Vincent be him? The body was the same, she would have bet money on it, but they were so different. Even the way they made love was completely different.

She clicked on Tino's diary hoping against hope that there might have been some mistake and that she would find herself slotted in next to Tino's name for this weekend. But nothing had changed. He had already been rescheduled for this weekend and for all the weekends to come for the next six months. She felt an empty ache beneath her breastbone. He should have been here with her, in her arms, in her bed. Six months was an eternity.

She Googled Vincent Evanston for the hundredth time.

He was 36 years old. He'd inherited his wealth from his father's shipping business, doubled its value in a few short years then turned everything over to his employees and disappeared, donating massive amounts of money to environmental and wildlife causes. He was nicknamed "the Birdman", and sometimes called "the Invisible Man". He was very seldom seen. In fact there was the odd rumour, from time to time, that he had been murdered, that the dubious past of the Port of Portland and its shipping industry was alive and well, and Vincent Evanston was the victim, dead and buried in a shallow grave somewhere. Nevertheless, his money was always hard at work.

Nothing she didn't already know. She poured herself

another glass of wine and paced the floor some more. Then she pulled up the Pet Shop website again. She was about to scroll to Tino's bio when her BlackBerry buzzed an incoming message. She pulled it up absently thinking it was some last-minute assignment the Boss wanted her to take care of. But when she looked at it, her hands froze and her pulse accelerated. It was a "ps" link from an unnamed Strigida email address.

With her heart in her throat, she pulled up the link and found herself back on the Pet Shop website, but in a part she had never seen before. It was entitled, *So you want to be a Pet.*

What the hell was this? She didn't want to be a Pet. She wanted to be with a Pet. A specific Pet. It was then that she noticed the letter below, which was printed in stylised copperplate. It read:

Dear Stella,

It has been brought to our attention that you may have the attributes and the interest required to become a Pet. If so, please click the Yes tab below.

'Oh you have got to be joking,' she spoke out loud into the silence. She barely gave Anne a chance to answer the phone before she launched in. 'What the hell is this? Are you having a laugh? Why would you think I wanted to be a Pet? Why? Do I seem like a, like a, like a ...'

'No you don't seem like a prostitute,' Anne filled in the blanks. 'But you said you wanted to see Tino. I told you up front my methods wouldn't be through the front door, that they might not be the way you had in mind, and you said go for it, so stop yelling at me, damn it! And who the hell are you anyway? It's good enough for Tino, it's OK for *him* to be a prostitute, but not OK for *you*, is that it?'

'I'm sorry. Look I'm sorry, all right.' Stella paced the floor looking at the webpage as though it were a problem to be solved. 'I didn't mean that. It's not that I'm too good, it's just that, well, I didn't expect this.'

'Look, how bad do you want to see Tino? That's what it

boils down to. I've already told you to let it go, but if you aren't willing to do that then, as far as I can tell, this is your only choice, unless you want to wait six months for Tino's schedule to free up.'

'But to become a Pet. I don't know what that means, Anne. I don't know what I'll have to do. And I don't know if I could ... be a Pet.'

'I don't either, Stel. If you want to see Tino, you'll have to take a chance. That's all I can tell you.'

For a long time, Stella sat and stared at the webpage after she spoke with Anne. This was so not what she'd had in mind. But neither did she want to wait for six months to see Tino again. She didn't think she *could* wait six months. And she had no way of getting in touch with Vincent. Everything she had read about him convinced her it was nothing short of a miracle that she had seen him at all, let alone twice.

She refreshed the page and stared at it until her eyes would no longer focus on the very elegant letters of what looked like a proper invitation to some very posh event. No one would have ever expected it was an invite to be a prostitute.

A Pet, she reminded herself. And a Pet was so different from a prostitute. For a long moment she tried to picture herself arriving at someone's door with a handler at her side holding the rucksack with the few things she would need for the weekend. Strangely, it wasn't as difficult as she had expected. She could imagine herself shifting from foot to foot and rubbing her legs together to create delicious friction against her weighty pout while the handler gave instructions before he left her, all horny and needy, with a total stranger. She wondered what the Pet Shop actually did to its Pets before it sent them out so that they would always arrive horny. But that was another fantasy for another time.

Absently her hand strayed under the edge of her skirt and she slouched and opened her knees to her touch. She imagined how it would feel to sit quietly on the floor, passively, while someone she'd never seen before in her life tenderly, carefully removed her clothes, maybe taking time to stroke and touch and admire her as he did so. Or maybe it wouldn't be a he at all. Maybe her keeper would be a woman. But in her mind's eye, it was a man. Then she imagined that faceless someone sitting open-legged in a comfortable chair, just like the instruction manual suggested, while she sniffed and licked and nuzzled him all over. No doubt she would make him as uncomfortable as Tino had made her in his initial efforts to get acquainted.

His cock would be pressing hard against his trousers, and she would rub her face against it, maybe even rake her teeth along it. And he would have to slap her hands away from her naked cunt, which would be slippery and open and obscenely swollen. Maybe she would misbehave so badly with her desperate need to come that he'd have to bend her over and spank her bottom until it was pink and stinging. And that would only make her pout heavier and more uncomfortable.

Then she would be so repentant, such a sorry little Pet. She'd nuzzle up next to him, sitting on the floor on her stinging bottom, with her legs splayed wide, hiding nothing from him. Then she'd place her head on his thigh as close to his cock as she could manage without getting herself in trouble again.

And then, when he felt they were well enough acquainted, when he felt his own discomfort was almost unbearable, he'd open his trousers and free himself right there in the chair, all heavy and jutting and proud of what he had to offer her. And he would see the hungry interest in her eyes, would know by her moans and grunts that she could hardly contain herself. Then he would pull her onto his lap, pausing to spread her slippery folds with nervous fingers before settling her onto him and giving a little push to slide her right down onto his cock. And she would be so hot and horny that she would grip him hard and whimper and moan with the urgency of her heat, while he fondled her tits and spoke little endearments in her ear. What a nice Pet she was, what a lovely little pussy she had, so slick, so heavy. How uncomfortable she must be, how in need of some relief. All the while his voice would get tighter, more breathless, and his shifting and grunting would become more urgent until at last he would lose control and fill her in steamy gushes.

Stella caught her breath in a little sob and shuddered against her fingers, which had pinched and stroked her to orgasm on the sofa with the laptop still balancing precariously on her thigh. When the second wave of tremors took her over, and the room was flooded with her briny sweet scent, she wiped her trembling fingers on her knickers and tapped the Yes tab at the bottom of the message.

It must always be remembered that Pets live in the moment. They are completely present to their physical needs and the needs of their keepers. They will seek out pleasure at every opportunity, and they delight most in the sharing of that pleasure with their keeper. They are prone to misbehave when they are not kept stimulated. But keep them well occupied and they will be the source of endless delight to their keepers.

Chapter Thirteen

ANNE WAS WAITING FOR her outside her office. She fell into step next to Stella. 'Well? Did you talk to him?'

'I talked to him, yes.'

'Any problems?'

'No.' Stella replied. 'He seemed fine with it. He said I'd earned a week holiday. Even offered me the company cottage in the Lake District.' She looked over her shoulder as though the Boss might have transferred himself through the speaker phone and be stood behind them listening in. 'I don't suppose you have any idea what I can expect?'

Anne shrugged. 'How the hell would I know? I just got lucky with figuring out how to get you in as a perspective Pet. No idea what happens next. Surely they must have told you something.'

Stella didn't believe Anne for a minute, but since the woman was her only connection to Tino, she wouldn't argue. 'I got an email.'

'An email?' Anne said. 'That's not very interesting, is it?'

'Well, what did you expect, dancing girls and confetti? It was just an email.'

Anne nodded, enthusiastically. 'Tell me, what did it say then?'

'It said wait at home after work Friday night. It said the Pet Shop would send someone for me. It said I should pack no bags. Bring nothing, the email said. Not even my mobile. That's all.'

'Bloody hell. Sounds vague. And intense. Are you nervous?'

Stella grunted. 'What do you think? Of course I'm nervous.

I can't believe I'm actually going to go through with this. I must be out of my mind.'

'But you will,' Anne observed. 'You will go through with it.'

It wasn't a question. She already knew the answer. And so did Stella. It wasn't just that she had to see Tino, but she had to know. And contrary to what Anne thought, it wasn't about finding out there was no Easter Bunny or no Father Christmas. It went a lot deeper than that, and she reckoned if she was about to unweave the rainbow, well she had gone too far down the road already to backtrack. And anyway, she had known almost from the beginning that she wanted more than to be slotted into Tino's diary once in awhile. As far as Vincent went, well she wanted more than a shag in a limo and an expensive plane ride. She wanted to know what the truth was, and she wanted to know why it mattered so much to her. Lest she needed to remind anyone, none of this would have happened if Strigida hadn't meddled in her private life.

The knock on the door came at precisely 8 p.m. The usual Pet arrival time, she thought. And for a second, she missed Tino terribly. She was greeted by a man and a woman dressed in the identical black suits of Pet handlers. The man carried the standard blue rucksack. 'Stella,' the woman addressed her, 'we need to come inside and you need to close the door behind us.' She raised a hand. 'And from this moment forward, you need to remain silent. Speaking from you will indicate one of two things, either that you've been a disobedient Pet, in which case you'll be appropriately punished, or that you've changed your mind and no longer wish to continue your training as a Pet. If at any point you make that decision, the decision is irrevocable. Do you understand?'

Stella nodded and stepped aside to let the couple in. The woman took her by the arm and ushered her into the lounge. The man shut and locked the door behind them, and Stella felt a cold stab of fear low in her belly.

'Sit down on the floor,' the woman commanded and Stella obeyed. She was still in her work clothes, not knowing what to expect. She hadn't been told what to wear. 'You won't be needing to dress for success this next week, love,' the woman said. Then she unbuttoned Stella's blouse, all business-like, and for some reason that made Stella blush more than if she had been seductive in her actions.

'Just let me undress you, dear. Always remember, removal of a Pet's clothing is the handler's job or your keeper's job, never yours. A Pet never interacts with her clothing.' She shoved the blouse off and handed it to the man, who now stood over them. He folded it efficiently and placed it on the coffee table.

'You have lovely breasts, Stella, darling. Won't your keepers enjoy playing with those?' The sudden shift to Pet Speak as the woman removed her bra made Stella squirm in her knickers.

'You're very lucky,' the woman said as she handed the bra to the man and unzipped Stella's skirt. 'Most Pets pay handsomely for the privilege, but someone in high places likes you and has decided you don't have to pay.'

'Pay? I thought Pets get paid, not have to pay.' The words were out before Stella could stop herself, and the resounding slap across her bare breasts startled her and stung.

'That's a warning, darling. Since you're new, I won't give you a proper punishment this time, but let it happen again and I'll have to spank your pretty little bottom, won't I?' The woman continued undressing her. 'Of course you'll have questions, Stella, and every evening you'll get a chance to write those questions down so we can answer them for you. But I see no harm in answering you now, since you didn't know. Lots of people pay a lot of money to be Pets. It's a submission thing, you know.'

'Some pay to be a Pet and some pay to take care of a Pet,' the man added.

'Now lift your little bottom for me, darling, and let me get you out of those uncomfortable clothes and into something a little more relaxed. Then, when we get you to the Pet Shop, you can be naked with all the other Pets. Would you like that, sweetheart?'

Stella's stomach twisted low and hot and nervous all at the same time. Did she really want to be naked with all the other Pets? A vision of Tino mounting her in a rough and tumble of Pets made it suddenly difficult to breathe. She lifted her arse and the woman shimmied down her skirt and her knickers in one efficient move.

'Lovely little cunny,' the man said, as the woman opened Stella's legs to work her hold-ups down over her thighs. 'And not waxed completely bare. I like a little fur, me. Like a proper Pet.'

'Don't be prejudiced, George,' the woman said. 'Some people like their Pets smooth and bare.'

The man grunted what might have been a snort of disapproval as he took the hold-ups and added them to the pile of neatly folded clothing.

'Oh goodness,' the woman said, running a hand up the inside of Stella's thigh and pressing her open further. 'Our little Petlet is already wet, and nerves be damned. Look at this, George.' She slid an efficient finger between Stella's labia causing her to catch her breath and squirm against the invading hand. 'Mmm. Wet and silky. Somebody may have to take care of her before bedtime tonight.' Then she gave Stella's pussy a little slap with the flat of her hand. 'Or maybe they'll just make her wait. Can you imagine how lovely and swollen she'd be after waiting hot and needy all night?'

George grunted his approval of the idea.

'Come, darling.' The woman was suddenly all business. 'We need to get you back to the Pet Shop and get you settled in to begin your training.'

George dug a thin mauve trench coat several sizes too big for Stella from the blue rucksack along with a pair of flip-flops, which matched perfectly. He bundled her into them and cinched the belt securely around her waist. 'It's just until we get you into the Pet carrier,' he reassured her. 'Now give me your house keys and I'll keep 'em safe until you need 'em again.'

Stella wasn't sure what she expected, but the large dog-sized pet carrier in the back of an expensive-looking black van was definitely not it. As soon as she was inside, she relinquished the trench coat and flip-flops and it was the last stitch of clothing to touch her body for the next five days.

They arrived under cover of darkness. Stella had no idea how long the journey had been nor where to. From the Pet carrier in the back of the van she could see nothing. But when she was helped from the cramped space, she could make out the shape of a large country house, a high brick wall and lots of trees. The woman, whose name she'd learnt was Audrey, fitted her with a simple leather collar then snapped a lead into the attached D-ring, which she handed to a man whose face Stella couldn't quite make out in the darkness.

The man cupped Stella's cheek in one large hand, lifted her head and turned it from side to side as though he were inspecting a horse at an auction.

Audrey moved next to her and stroked her flank. 'Stella, darling, this is your designated master. Go with him. He'll settle you in for the night. You must be exhausted, sweetheart. Get some rest. You'll have a very busy week ahead of you.'

The man said nothing to her. He turned on his heels and led her to a small annexe that might have been refurbished stables, though it was too dark to tell. He opened the door to a small room tucked in the corner between the rest of the annexe and the main house. Inside the room was bare except for an enormous pet bed that in a more normal life, she would have assumed was for a very large, very pampered dog. Under the circumstances, she was pretty sure it was for her. The man nodded to a tiny closet near the back corner, and with a blush, Stella realised it was a toilet.

'Go on,' he said. 'It's a long trip over here. You must be bursting.'

After she returned from the loo, she found him sitting on the floor next to the Pet bed with a bowl of water and platter loaded down with bits of fruit and cheese. 'Come here, darling.' He patted the pallet next to him. 'You must be hungry and thirsty after your journey.'

She dropped onto the floor beside him, and he popped a

piece of ripe mango into her mouth then wiped the dribble of juice from her chin with a flick of his thumb. 'Good?' he asked, clearly not expecting an answer. She tried to drink the way she had seen Tino do it, but ended up with more water on her than in her. At last Master lifted the bowl to her lips. 'You'll get the hang of it, Stella. But at least for tonight, if you can't manage, then you may use your hands if no handler's around to help you. It's important you don't get dehydrated.'

He fed her a couple more chunks of mango and a bit of cheese then wiped her mouth and set the tray aside. 'Now, let me look at you.' He scooted closer. 'Let me make sure you're OK to be left on your own tonight.' As he spoke, he ran his hands across her shoulders, down her arms, then onto the swell of her hips. He lingered for a moment, before he splayed them up her stomach to cup and knead her breasts, causing her to flinch slightly and gasp. He offered her an apologetic smile. 'It's all right, darling. New Pets are often a bit jumpy at having their more private bits caressed.' He brought thumbs up to rake her nipples, which were already at full attention. 'They soon get used to it, even enjoy it. It's a necessary part of learning to enjoy the pleasures offered by one's keeper.'

It didn't take all that long to get used to a man who was skilled at pleasuring a woman's tits, she thought. He was also skilled at reading the signs of arousal brought on by his fondling.

'Pets may not masturbate unless they have the specific permission of their handler or keeper. I'm told you're familiar with the Pet keepers' manual, so no doubt you know this.' He nodded toward her pallet. Once she had settled onto it, he pushed her back until she rested on her elbows. 'Therefore it's expedient for me to make you come before you go to bed. It'll relieve nervous tension and make you sleep better. Don't be embarrassed, darling. All Pets have very high libidos, and my colleagues tell me that you were in a state of arousal when you left your home. Open your legs for me. That's a girl.' He held her gaze in the dimly lit room. 'Now just relax and let me take care of you.' He dropped onto one elbow next to her and ran a heavy hand down over her belly to rest on her tightly trimmed curls.

Even in the shadow she could make out the shape of the man's erection pressing against his khaki trousers. She wasn't sure if, as a Pet, she should be tending to him or not, but it was as though he had read her mind. 'Tonight, darling you must do nothing but relax and enjoy. Tonight Master will pleasure his little Pet. There'll be lots of opportunities later for you to take care of your master.' His touch against her mons had become a caress, his index and middle finger stretching out to splay her labia before darting down between. The soft sound that escaped her lips was not unlike a contented animal, and he sighed in empathy. 'You're so slick down there and swollen, aren't you, my little darling. You must have been holding yourself tight between those lovely pussy lips for the whole long ride down here. Self control, that's a trait all Pets need to cultivate. You'll do very well here, I'm sure. Still, it must have been agony for you, you poor thing. And your little clit.' He brushed a slippery thumb over her clit and she practically bucked off the pallet. 'All distended and hard, that lovely little nib there, throbbing your need like Morse Code. SOS,' he tapped. 'SOS.' And she lifted her whole bottom off the pallet and rocked up on her heels, grunting and grinding with total loss of dignity.

'Yes, that's my little angel, just relax and let it happen. Just let Master make you come, and you'll feel so much better.' He shifted until the heel of his hand raked against the apex of her pussy, grinding and pressing against her clit. And with each rocking of her hips she slicked his palm with her juices, unbelievable juices, like the dam had broken, like the floods had come, slipping and slurping against his strokes.

'Ah, that delicious scent of wet Pet cunt,' Master sighed. 'Nothing I love more, except maybe the taste, but that's for another time, darling, that's for another time.' He positioned himself so he could hold her splayed with one hand, rubbing and tweaking her clit, and with the other he fucked her with three fingers, with her gripping and grasping and slipping and sliding over his knuckles until they were both holding their breath. Somewhere in the back of her fevered mind, it registered that he was rocking and shifting in empathy with her. When the howl of her orgasm escaped her throat and rattled the windows, it was accompanied by a series of deep-bellied grunts. He whispered breathlessly against her ear. 'You made Master come in his pants, you nasty little Pet.' He chuckled softly. 'Never mind. I won't tell, and I'm sure you won't.' Then he wiped her clean with a soft white towel, tucked her down onto the pallet beneath a warm blanket and kissed her good night. 'Sleep well, little one. You've got a busy day ahead of you tomorrow.'

'Bloody hell, it must have been heaven for you.' The Boss's eyes were glued to the monitor where the designated master pumped and stroked Stella's cunt with an experienced hand, and the sounds coming from her mouth could have very easily come from an animal on heat. At the first sight of Stella naked, he'd had to open his fly just to give his cock enough breathing room. He hadn't expected that. Though he should have; it was an age-old fantasy, the employer catching his employee naked in the midst of performing lewd acts.

He'd been at the viewings of lots of trainee Pets. Most were rather routine now. 'Often when they first arrive, new Pets are too nervous to be horny.' He chuckled and gave his cock a hard stroke. 'Of course you weren't. You were hard as a rock. But then you always are, aren't you?'

'Christ.' He sucked air in between his teeth at the sight of the master slipping three fingers into Stella's grasping pussy, as she arched up giving the camera she didn't know was there an exquisite view of her gape. In sympathy, the Boss lifted his arse to shove his walking shorts and boxers down enough to get to his balls, and the stroking became more serious. 'I hadn't expected this much heat,' he grunted. 'You should have warned me. But then you're not even supposed to be here, are you?'

He couldn't quite manage to sound angry while watching the scene unfolding between the Pet trainee and the designated master. Without taking his eyes off the monitor, he addressed his companion. 'If you need to masturbate, you have my permission, how could you not, seeing her like that. Jesus, I can see why you wanted to make room for her in your diary. I can see why you wouldn't want to schedule anyone else but her.' He half grunted a chuckle. 'Now I wonder how anyone could have ever thought her a bit prudish. I suspected all along that still waters run hot. I suspected that urg ... good Christ!'

For a long moment, the Boss couldn't speak. He was too busy grinding and shifting his bare arse cheeks against the hard metal of the chair, thrusting his cock into the delicious warm depths. Then he reached down and curled his fingers in the unruly locks of his companion's hair. 'I'll have to punish you for this, you know?' He squeezed the words out between tight lips. 'I didn't ask you to suck my cock.' He didn't speak again. He just watched the monitor and thrust forcefully into his companion's mouth as his balls approached meltdown, and the tongue on the underside of his cock tortured him blissfully.

On the monitor, Stella arched as though her back would break and howled her orgasm. The monitor captured the slippery sheen of her grasping lips as the master pulled his hand away and grunted his wad into his trousers.

And the Boss could hold back no more. Strangely it was O'Kelly's cunt he thought about just as he erupted into the greedy mouth sucking him hard. O'Kelly's cunt he hadn't seen in ages, and somehow that made his orgasm more explosive. The thought burned through him like a forest fire causing spasm after spasm of wet lust. And somewhere in the back of his heat-singed mind, he felt something hot and sticky spurt against his calves.

His fingers curled tighter into his companion's hair and he groaned. 'I can't believe you just came on my legs.' He was about to mention how much more severe such a breech would make the inevitable punishment when Tino pulled away from his cock, wiped his mouth on the back of his hand and caught his gaze with eyes not unlike a wild predator about to pounce. Then in a transformation so swift that it was dizzying, his gaze became shy, submissive just before he lowered himself and began to lick his own semen from the Boss's leg.

Suddenly the Boss was no longer sure what to do next. Maybe he'd just linger a little longer, maybe he'd take Tino back to his room for his punishment, a punishment that was already making his balls ache with the possibilities. His brain felt fevered as he watched the designated Master tuck Stella into her pallet and leave her to sleep. In the dim light the damp spot on the front of the Master's trousers appeared like a dark stain, and the Boss smiled at the thought.

His own release was already beginning to feel like a temporary fix. And, not for the first time, the Pet licking and slurping his way up the inside of the Boss's calf both disturbed and intrigued him with his strange combination of unassailable innocent lust. Not for the first time, he wondered if he should have listened to O'Kelly back when she tried to convince him that Tino was too unruly to be one of the Pet Shop's Pets.

And now, thanks to him, Tino had caught Stella's scent, and there was no denying it was a scent he liked very much indeed. The Boss had no illusions as to why Tino was suddenly interested in *his* cock after all this time. And Tino was too smart to think that he didn't know the score. O'Kelly was wise to stay clear of Tino, he thought. And he was relieved to know her wisdom had kept her safe. But even before the thought was out of his mind, he attached the leash to the Pet's collar and led him through the private passages to his room in the big house, his cock already aching for more of Tino.

Chapter Fourteen

'THIS LOVELY LITTLE DEVICE is how the Pet Shop manages to send its Pets wherever they have to go and guarantee they'll be horny when they arrive.' Audrey busied herself fitting Stella with a leather harness much like those she had seen on ponies who pulled carts. A band of leather attached to the collar connected to another strip similar to the waistband of a bra. It twisted and crisscrossed around and between Stella's breasts until they were trussed up and presented, nipples bulging like cherries atop plump Christmas puddings. Then the strap continued down over her belly, where it became soft suede, which fit snuggly between the slippery folds of her cunt. From there it continued on between her arse cheeks and up her spine to bisect the chest band again and finally connect to the back of the collar.

It was deliciously uncomfortable and sharply focused Stella's thoughts on her slickening cunt and aching nipples. 'This is your introduction to what we call "the Foreplayer". Normally you'll only wear it a few hours before we send you to be with a keeper. But we do find it to be a good training device as well. It can also be used for punishing misbehaving Pets. We just cinch it a little tighter.' Stella had no trouble believing it would be very effective in whichever capacity it was used.

Audrey nodded at one of the male Pets standing leashed to a wrought iron gate near the cobbled drive. 'Liam there is about to leave to meet a keeper for the weekend. You see how the male Foreplayer circles the balls like a cock ring, and ... there.' As Liam's handler unleashed him and led him toward a waiting van, Stella got a view of his tight round arse cheeks. 'As you can see, the male Foreplayer is also equipped with a small but very effective butt plug to aid in prostate stimulation. Quite arousing, I'm told.' She pushed Stella's hair away from her ear and stroked the side of her neck affectionately. 'Butt plugs, along with dildos of varying sizes can also be attached to the female Foreplayer too if there's a need. Do you think you would like that, darling?'

The only response Stella made was the clench of her pussy against the soft bind of leather. But Audrey giggled wickedly as though she knew exactly how Stella's body would respond.

She then stood and took Stella's lead. 'Come, darling. Time for your walk, and while we walk, I'll educate you about being a Pet, about things the Pet keeper's manual doesn't tell you, things that Pets have to know in order to be good Pets.'

The lovely grounds were awash in summer birdsong. A fountain tinkled musically at the centre of a formal garden, and the whole space was bordered by a gurgling stream overhung by willows.

On the soft moss beneath a sprawling oak tree, two Pets were curled around each other in a sinuous "69" of pleasure. Stella and Audrey passed close enough to hear the juicy sounds of their heat. 'Pike and Tika have been given permission by Master to pleasure each other.' Audrey nodded to the man who fed and masturbated Stella the night before. He stood watching the two Pets with his trousers open and his arching cock in his hand. 'Neither have keepers this weekend,' Audrey explained. 'Some Pets choose never to have keepers. They prefer just to come here and be Pets. I suspect you won't have a choice in that matter, darling, since you didn't pay.'

Though Stella would have liked to have offered a protest to Audrey's remark, she knew better. Before she could dwell on the little tinge of something not quite neutral in Audrey's voice, the woman continued. 'What you need to understand if you want to be a Pet, Stella, is that a Pet's will is always subservient to either her master, her handler or her keeper.' She pulled the leash tight and Stella stopped only a few feet from the wet oral display, now becoming quite animated. 'It's only with their permission that a Pet is allowed attention of any kind, including and most especially pleasure. Forgetting this will always result in punishment and often loss of sexual privileges, even withdrawal of affection, which for a Pet is the worst punishment of all.'

Audrey now stood very close behind Stella, almost in an embrace. She reached around with one hand to caress Stella's breasts affectionately. It was then that Stella realised Master's eyes were locked on her. She jumped as Audrey spoke against her ear. 'Would you like to have Master's nice thick cock in your wet little pussy, darling? I bet you would, wouldn't you? And I'm sure Master would like that. He looks so uncomfortable, don't you think?'

Master looked at his cock then offered Stella a slow, lazy smile. 'Seeing how much Pike is enjoying having his cock in Tika's hot mouth, I think I would prefer to have our little Pet suck me,' he said, giving Stella's bound breasts an admiring squeeze.

'Oh, very good choice, Master,' Audrey said. 'Well? Go on, dear,' she encouraged. 'Don't be shy. Master won't hurt you, and obedient Pets are always well rewarded.' She gave Stella's bum a lingering caress, then eased her fingers beneath the soft leather that pressed between Stella's arse cheeks until they brushed Stella's cunt lips ever so slightly. Her other hand was already pressing down heavily on Stella's shoulder.

Stella's nerves jangled. Her stomach knotted and suddenly the lead and harness felt like a trap. She felt exposed, on display in the centre of the garden where other Pets and minders were coming and going and looking on. By the time she allowed herself to be pushed to her knees – with both Master and Audrey offering gentle encouragement – she was trembling all over, frightened that she wouldn't be able to go through with it. 'Open your mouth, darling, that's a girl,' Audrey was saying. 'Don't be nervous. Master's very gentle with his new Pets. Just relax now. That's my darling.'

Stella closed her eyes, fighting back tears and felt Master's fingers curl in her hair, felt him ease her forward. It was a way to get to Tino, nothing more, she reminded herself just as the salty precome of Master's penis brushed her lips. So why did it feel so much like a betrayal? Maybe Tino wouldn't approve.

Maybe Tino wouldn't want her after she'd sucked someone else's cock. She shuddered, and forced herself to focus. She'd made a commitment. She would keep it. With a sob, she took the length of Master's erection into her mouth, and though he wasn't small, it seemed an easy fit after sucking Tino's heavy cock. She kept her eyes closed and concentrated on the task at hand.

'That's my girl.' Master's voice was tight with arousal, but still it was gentle, careful, as though he didn't want to frighten her. 'Oh such a lovely mouth, such a delicious tongue on Master's cock,' he crooned.

Around her she heard jostling and shuffling, as though people had drawn near to watch. She clenched her eyes shut tighter and tried to ignore the feeling of being stared at. If she had to suck off a stranger and do it for an audience, it would be easier if she could shut them all out, at least visually. Maybe they would all think she was just so involved with Master's cock that she was closing her eyes to savour the experience.

She felt Audrey kneel next to her and gently stroke her flank. 'That's such a good little Pet, sucking Master's cock so nice, just like he likes it, making him feel so hot. Such a good little Pet.' She leant in and kissed Stella's ear. 'You're making me all hot too, darling. You've made my pussy all slick and swollen just watching you. You may have to lick it for me after you're done with Master. Oh, there, there, sweetheart. Don't tremble so. It's OK if it pleasures you too. That would make Master and me even hotter. That would make all of us so happy.'

Stella's nerves were just beginning to ease. She was just beginning to focus, to think she might be able to do what was required of her, even enjoy it a little when suddenly there was scrambling and shuffling from behind, followed by a shout and a low, throaty growl.

'What the–' Audrey's voice caught in a slight yelp, and she pulled away, jostling Stella slightly as she did so. There was a collective gasp from the audience Stella had shut out, which crescendoed to a murmur, and suddenly Stella felt warm rough hands on her hips just before there was another voice, a familiar voice, tight but calm. 'It's all right. Leave him.'

There was more shuffling and more sighs and gasps. Bloody hell, was being the public entertainment a part of the training? The warm hands on her hips lifted her bottom slightly, then pulled aside the strap between her legs and replaced it with the hungry lap and press of a hot wet tongue. Pleasure broke through Stella's confusion in bright flashes of colour. She gasped and gabbled the ecstatic surprise of it against Master's cock, an effort which caused him to jerk and moan appreciatively.

Dear God, whoever was eating her cunt knew how to focus her attention. One large hand moved down over her belly to strum her clit until she moaned and whimpered around Master's surging cock. The other hand raked at her nipples, pinching and stroking until each little touch redirected painful pleasure along her overloaded nerve endings and back down to her splayed cunt, until she raised her arse like a bitch ready to be mounted.

She shifted and squirmed and raked her gape against a dance of tongue and lips while sucking on Master's cock until her cheeks ached. And yet she sucked harder, cupping his balls in her hand and kneading them in tight circular strokes. Somewhere nearby she could make out Audrey's grunts, and she knew she had a hand between her legs. But there were other grunts, other sounds of flesh against flesh, other moans of pleasure, and all of it wrapped in the rising scent of sex, a scent dominated by the familiar yeasty, desert heat scent of the one eating her cunt.

Master's grip on her hair became nearly painful. She could feel his pistoning hips straining right on the brink. She sucked harder, letting him hammer into her while her cunt buzzed, and her whole body blissed out on the mouth and the hands pleasuring her. Master bucked and grunted, and his hot semen burst against the back of her throat again and again. She nearly choked in her gasp for air as her own orgasm roared up her spine like flash fire and the strong arms that had been pleasuring her suddenly scooped her backward against a deliciously sweaty naked chest, a hard muscular body she recognised. Her eyes flew open and the words would have burst from her throat if not for the familiar hand clasping over her mouth. Through the blur of heat and emotion she glanced over her shoulder into Tino's wild, hungry eyes, just before the Boss, dressed for business in a pinstriped suit, jerked Tino's leash and pulled him off her.

The strangled cry that erupted from both their throats was animal, as another handler stepped in to help the Boss pull Tino away from her, accenting his efforts with a lash of the leather lead that resounded like a gunshot across Tino's bare arse. She suddenly realised Master had her own lead looped tightly around his fist, securing her close to his thigh. But for a second Tino held her gaze. Another lash cracked across his bottom, but he barely flinched. Instead, the tiniest hint of a smile curled the corners of his mouth before he allowed himself to be pulled away. Then Stella collapsed in a heap on the thick grass suddenly too weak to move.

'Where is she?' O'Kelly asked. 'Is she all right? What the fuck was Audrey thinking? She knows better than to allow a Pet sexual contact this early in the training – and the designated master. What an idiot! Maybe it's time we designated someone else.'

'Both Audrey and the master designate have been reprimanded, O'Kelly, and Stella's fine. I'm sure she's elated, actually, now that she's seen Tino.' The scene that had unfolded in the garden flashed through his head again. 'There's definitely no denying that the attraction is very mutual.' The Boss was surprised at how shaken he still sounded. It irritated him because if he could hear it, then no doubt, so could O'Kelly.

O'Kelly huffed into the phone.

He could almost hear her grinding her teeth to keep from saying she told him so. He pretended not to notice. 'Stella's had a bath and something to eat and she's now receiving more traditional instruction. I want to send her to be with a keeper as soon as possible. Her mind needs to be focused on something other than Tino if she's going to do us any good.'

There was a sharp pause over the phone that sounded almost like a caught breath held too long, then O'Kelly asked the question he knew she'd been dying to ask from the beginning. 'And Tino?'

'A couple of nice welts on his arse, and I wager he'll be holding his wad for the rest of the day, but otherwise he's no worse for the wear.' He forced a smile into his voice and tried to sound casual, tried to ignore his cock, heavy and tense, a prodding reminder of the wad *he'd* been holding since Tino lunged on Stella. He'd known how it would be once he gave in to Tino in the viewing room last night. He knew he would never be able to get enough. That's why he'd stayed away from him after the first time. Some addictions he just couldn't afford.

Even after being with Tino all night, even after punishing him for the unwanted seduction, punishing him until his own body dripped sweat from his efforts, until his cock felt like it would go nuclear if he couldn't bury it in Tino's lovely arse, he still wanted more. The amazing thing about Tino was that even when he yielded, his whole body still surged with hungry defiance. And in the end, as it had been before, in the fevered frenzy of a night too quickly passed, as dawn paled pink against the windows of the cottage, it had been he who had yielded to Tino, willingly, elatedly.

Though Tino always took his punishment, always took what was coming to him like a good Pet, the Boss never kidded himself about who was really in charge. It had never been an issue until now. But O'Kelly had been right all along. It became clear when Tino arched protectively over Stella, taking the lashes against his bottom like they were nothing, that for the first time in all the years he'd known Tino, there was more at stake than a physical obsession – much more.

'Did you know he was going to be there?'

O'Kelly's words forced him back to the present. He took a scorching drink of his tea and his eyes watered. 'I knew, yes. I thought the chances of them actually seeing each other were slim. But then that is why Stella agreed to the Pet training in the first place, isn't it?'

'He's not scheduled with a keeper this weekend?'

God, sometimes he wished O'Kelly were a little less tenacious. 'He's already been. One of his regulars had a Thursday and Friday off. I don't know how that slipped past us. He got back shortly after Stella arrived.' Got back and came directly to the viewing room, a viewing he shouldn't have known about, a viewing that, as a Pet he had no right to attend. He just showed up, all naked and exquisite and bristling, plopped down on the chair next to the Boss and watched Stella with the designated master. The Boss's hand moved, almost of its own volition, to rest on the bulge growing in his lap.

'You were with him when it happened?'

'Yes.' He wondered why he felt as though she were accusing him. He supposed it was his guilty conscience. 'I was taking him out for some exercise.'

Another long pause. 'There were no minders to do that?'

'He was ... with me at the time.' The Boss had never lied to O'Kelly, and he wasn't going to start now.

'I see.'

He wondered if she had to work hard to sound so neutral or if it just came naturally.

'Well, under the circumstances, I guess it was a good thing you were in the mood for some cock, then wasn't it?'

In spite of the verbal slap-down, there was some satisfaction in knowing that, yes, she did have to work hard to sound so neutral.

'O'Kelly ...' For some reason his voice felt tight in his throat. 'It was Tino.'

The pause was so long that for a second he thought she had broke the connection, then he heard her sigh. 'Yes. I know.'

Chapter Fifteen

STELLA SAW NEITHER MASTER nor Audrey the rest of the day. After her encounter with Tino she had been bathed and fed, which was good because she was ravenous. The rest of her time was taken up with basic instruction, mostly from the Pet manual, mostly stuff she already knew. She was taught by a fresh-faced, large-breasted handler called Jan, who was dressed in safari garb. She didn't seem to know the manual any better than Stella did, but she was very enthusiastic. Stella seriously doubted anyone had committed quite as much time to poring over the manual as she had. The manual always made her feel closer to Tino.

Anyway it didn't matter how knowledgeable Jan was. What mattered was that Stella had seen Tino, and she knew now that she would gladly fuck every Pet at the Pet Shop as well as the handlers and the master and anyone else she had to in order to see him again. She couldn't think about their encounter without a tight little flutter erupting in her stomach caused by his delicious half smile before he was dragged away. That smile told her she would definitely be seeing him again. Tino was an opportunist, and he would find a way to get to her.

What made the flutter in her stomach turn into a full-fledged somersault that expanded to fill her whole chest was knowing that Tino *had* found her, that he had wanted her, risked pain and punishment to be with her. His possessive embrace before he was pulled off her was the best thing she had ever felt, ever. It reassured her that she wasn't just obsessing over Tino, but there was a good chance that he just might feel the same way.

She was kept isolated through her evening meal, playing out scenarios in which Jan pretended to be her keeper for the weekend and Stella pretended to be the obedient Pet. The game continued through dinner, with the handler feeding her delicious tidbits of gourmet chicken that was definitely a far cry from kibbles. It was followed up by a sloppy, yummy pudding of tiramisu fed to her, like everything else, from the palm of the handler. It reminded her of how delicious and sloppy and sexy her meals with Tino had been. By the time they had finished, she was truly and properly horny.

After dinner she was taken out on her leash – no Foreplayer this time, just a collar. She was allowed contact with the other Pets in the garden. However, she was not allowed more than the standard getting-to-know-each-other rituals of the sniffing and licking of offered bottoms and genitals. Pet's live through their noses, the handler hadn't had to remind her as she sat back on her haunches with her legs splayed wide to allow a large Asian Pet to sniff her cunt before he offered her his bottom in turn. It didn't surprise her that Tino wasn't at the getting-acquainted soirée. He would be far too disruptive, she was certain. He would want to do a lot more to her plump little pussy than just sniff it. That thought went a long way to making the cunny she offered up for getting-acquainted sniffs slicker and more swollen. With the hot wet scent of her, she figured she would give more than a few of the males unintended hard-ons.

Some of the Pets were allowed to fuck. The handlers picked and chose who was allowed sex with whom. Stella was never quite able to figure out what the criteria were, but watching the rut did little to ease the gripping in her engorged cunt.

A dark-haired Pet who was heavily muscled and tattooed returned to Stella for another stiff and, when she leant back to allow it, his cock, which was already at full attention, surged. But before he could get more than a good sniff, Master took him by the collar and led him away. 'Not yet, Attila, give our little Stella some time to get comfortable, then maybe later you can mount her sweet pussy.' He caught Stella's gaze and offered her a smile that seemed genuine, even slightly apologetic. 'In the meantime, I see Cupcake has quite a swollen little pout. She'd be happy to service that hefty cock of yours,

I'm sure.' He led Attila, with his heavy bouncing cock, away toward a plump female rubbing herself lewdly against the seat of a garden bench.

In the evening, when she was allowed to write down her questions, as she had been promised, she asked about what had happened that morning. The handler offered her a hearty blush and a knowing smile. 'Tino happened this morning, darling. That's what happened.' Her breathless giggle made her seem even younger than she was. 'Tino's not noted for being a well-behaved Pet, and he can be very disruptive. Mind you he rarely associates with the other Pets, so that made his licking out the pussy of a Pet-in-training even more disruptive. And from the way you came, I'd say every Pet in the garden this morning envied you. Tino took quite a risk, actually, and probably got soundly punished for it afterward. Especially since he was with the Boss at the time.'

Stella's stomach did a flip-flop and she quickly scribbled on the paper, *Tino was with the Boss?*

The handler nodded. 'Strange that. The Boss usually chooses Tika or Daisy whenever he comes down on business. I didn't even know he liked men. But then it was Tino, wasn't it?' Her giggle sounded positively girlish. 'Can't tell you a whole lot about the Boss, actually. I only ever met him in person when I interviewed to be a handler, and I was very nervous, as you can imagine.' She affectionately stroked Stella's thigh. 'He seems to be in some sort of advisory position, but I'm relatively new here, and I'm told that what goes on above basic administration at the facility level is pretty hush-hush. No surprise there, I'd guess, since technically the Pet Shop doesn't exist in the real world.'

Stella was suddenly glad to have been assigned the young handler. She had the distinct impression she would have gotten far less information out of Master or Audrey, and she was learning a helluva lot more than she bargained for.

She threw caution to the wind and wrote, *Do you know who Tino is in real life?*

The handler shook her head, and her face became very serious. 'No one knows who anyone is in real life. This is the

119

Pet Shop. What's inside stays inside, and even if Pets have connections in the outside world, what happens outside stays out. In fact, it's forbidden to talk about the outside at the Pet Shop, even for those of us who aren't Pets and are allowed to talk. Surely you understand the need for secrecy. Now,' she glanced down at her watch. 'It's your bedtime, darling. You've had a rather unorthodox day, and tomorrow we'll begin preparing you for your first outing with a keeper.' She rubbed her hands together. 'Such an exciting time for a new Pet.'

She took Stella back to her room, settled her into her bed, and kissed her goodnight. She offered a little pout. 'I'm sorry, darling, but I'm only a junior handler. I'm not allowed to masturbate you. But open your legs for me and let me feel your little pussy, and if you need to be masturbated, I'll send in Master or Audrey.'

But Stella curled herself on her side and feigned being tired. Oh, she was horny all right, but she didn't need Master playing with her cunt right now. She needed to think, so for tonight, she'd just have to hold it.

When Jan left, she relaxed into her pallet and stared up at the ceiling. So the Boss had intimate connections with the Pet Shop. No wonder he could arrange so easily for her to have such a magnificent Pet as Tino. On the other hand it made no sense whatsoever that he would do so, not with Tino's reputation. And not for the benefit of a glorified executive assistant, no matter how good she was at her job.

It was a pretty safe guess that he was involved in getting her into the Pet Shop then, and Anne surely must be too. But why? Why would they do that? Why would they have brought Tino to her in the first place? Surely they didn't want to recruit her as a Pet. From what she had gathered, Pets didn't have to be recruited, they paid handsomely for the privilege – something she would have never done even if she could have afforded to.

She was still struggling to make sense of it all when the door opened. She could see a silhouette darkened against the moonlit sky before the door closed, then there were footsteps across the complaining wood floor, and the Boss knelt beside her with a leash. He clipped it into the D-ring of her collar and held her gaze. Then he stood without saying a word and she stood next to him, her legs suddenly unsteady. Was she going to have sex with him? Not that he wasn't an attractive man, but he was her boss and sex would just add another complication she didn't need. He led her out into the night, back along a narrow pavement, down a steep set of stone stairs and through a heavy wooden door.

Before she had a chance to get frightened, the Boss flipped on a light switch and a cavernous room immerged out of the shadow into details she failed to notice. Her whole attention was drawn to the pallet on the floor in the corner where Tino lay naked, blinking hard at the bright invasion on light-deprived pupils. He yawned and stretched and wiped sleep from his eyes. When he saw her, he came to his feet expectantly. As always, it was impossible for her not to notice his lovely penis, already at half-mast and rising. He laid a hand against it, not like he was about to masturbate, more like he was taking the reins of a powerful beast.

The Boss laughed quietly. 'I can almost hear your fear and anger, Stella, and I assure you there's no need for either. This is where Tino sleeps whenever he's at the Pet Shop. Not sure why he prefers the dungeon to far more luxurious places a Pet of his status could sleep. Perhaps because he spends so much time down here anyway being punished for bad behaviour, and I assure you, he gets far less than he deserves. He unhooked the leash from her collar and nodded toward the big Pet. 'Go on. If the two of you were magnets it would be easier to keep him from you.'

It was all she could do to keep from crying out his name as he scooped her into his arms. Any further slippage of speech was stopped by Tino's insistent mouth startling in its familiarity. Her throat tightened and her eyes welled as he took her face between large hands and kissed her repeatedly, ravenously, as though he would never stop. But when he did, it was because they had both become aware that the Boss was still standing there, arms folded across his chest, watching.

When they stood staring at him expectantly, he grabbed a single metal folding chair from near the door and sat down deliberately. 'Oh, I'm not leaving, if that's what you're waiting for. I did scheme to get the two of you together, that's true.' He waved a hand. 'And I expect you to do whatever nasty things your libidos drive you to, but I expect you to do them while I watch.'

He turned his gaze on Stella, whose insides suddenly twisted in a writhe of nerves. 'My dear Stella, as a Pet, you'll often be called upon by your keepers to perform sexually for them while they watch and have a wank.' He scooted the chair closer to the pallet with a loud scrape of metal on the stone floor. 'Sometimes they only do that until they get up the courage to join in the fun. Other times they really are voyeurs and get off on the watching more than the doing.

'Me, I don't need courage to join in the fun, which I may well do if I choose. But after the little incident between you two this morning, I haven't had a minute's peace imagining the fireworks that must happen when the two of you actually are allowed to fuck.' He sighed happily and settled back into the chair as though it were a comfy recliner. 'All I need now is some popcorn. Consider this a part of your training, Stella, and who better to help you with your homework than someone who's an old hand at it.' He nodded to Tino.

She expected at least an awkward moment or two while they adjusted to the idea of fucking with an audience, but Tino simply ignored the Boss's presence. He lifted her as though she were weightless and carried her back to his pallet.

For her, the world had changed drastically since the last time she was with Tino. Now she was a Pet, not a keeper, a Pet in the presence of her alpha, and she acted accordingly. She presented her bottom, raised high, so he could get acquainted with Stella the Pet. She remembered with a half smile how he had sniffed her through her clothes, then incorporated his tongue in their first getting-acquainted session, how he'd had her on the brink of a blistering orgasm by the time Anne had interrupted them. It seemed like ages ago now.

When he had sniffed and licked and taken in her scent, he pulled back and presented himself, first his bottom. She traced a gentle finger over the crisscross of the two welts from his

122

lashing this morning and heard him suck breath between his teeth as she laid a trail of kisses over his wounds. Then she turned her attention to his lovely little back-hole, which clenched and relaxed. He offered a low belly grunt as she pressed her tongue to it, raked her teeth over it, then lapped at it. She felt his buttocks tremble against her spread palms as he pressed back against her, quivering with control. Then he sat back on his haunches, legs open wide, heavy penis and tight balls displayed licentiously for her attention. The summer desert scent of him raised pungent heat to the back of her throat as she tongued and sniffed beneath his penis and nipped and suckled over the bulge of his balls, with him working hard not to hump her face, but rather to allow her to explore, to examine, to reacquaint herself with his body from a Pet's point of view.

She could smell herself as she shifted on the pallet, she could feel the fluid grip and tremble of her cunt, pouting open to invite, then clenching tight in muscle memory of gripping and yielding and gripping again on a thick penetrating cock. And this cock – Tino's cock – was exactly the cock she wanted, the cock her muscles remembered and ached for.

With a half-snarl and a grunt, Tino shifted enough to bite her raised hip, hard enough to cause a sharp intake of Tino-scented breath, hard enough to make her whimper and raise her arse higher, like a flag of surrender. And Tino was more than ready to accept that surrender. He'd had enough getting to know each other. On hands and knees he moved behind her. She opened her legs and wriggled her bottom in anticipation, then she pressed her arms and shoulders down onto the pallet to force her arse even higher. In doing so, she caught a peripheral glimpse of the Boss, who had at some point shoved down his trousers and extricated his own erection. As he stroked and cupped himself, the chair creaked softly beneath the grip and grind of his bare arse.

Then she forgot all about the Boss as the back of her neck was bathed in Tino's hot breath. His hands slid over her hips, and after a few heavy slurps with his tongue between her splayed cunt lips, an unnecessary test of her readiness, he positioned himself. With a deep upward thrust, he pushed into her, expanding her to capacity and beyond, as he always did, until pleasure pushed pain and her head spun from the buzz of being so totally and completely filled with Tino.

At first his thrusts were tentative, shallow, just enough to make her breasts bounce and jerk against her chest and her pussy grasp at him. But once he was convinced she could fully accommodate him, he rammed her full force, and she rammed back growling and grunting and arching against him. He tugged on her hair, he nipped at her neck, he howled his possession of her to any other rutting males who might be present. And she submitted to his power, taking it into herself in ravenous, slippery pussy gulps, until she collapsed beneath his weight in the heavy convulsions of an orgasm that exploded then rippled then exploded again. A split second later he stiffened and jerked and she felt his come spurting into her with each hard contraction of his penis. Almost at the same instant there was a grunt from the folding chair and the Boss stiffened and thrust his hips forward in the chair. His chest heaved, and his penis pumped squirt after viscous squirt of semen onto the dark stone floor.

Stella was used to Tino recovering quickly, but she was taken aback when the Boss stood, stripped off his clothes and joined them on the pallet. He ravaged Tino's mouth in a deep tongue kiss that took her breath away. Then he turned his attention to her, running his hand over her breasts with a cup and a knead before trailing fingers down her belly to curl over her mound and tease the hard node of her clit, making her jerk and whimper.

'You were both exquisite,' he said when he came up for air after another long exploration of Tino's mouth. 'I've never seen two Pets go at it with such raw animal lust. You've made me want to play. I'm sure you've already figured it out, Stella, darling. Tino and I are well acquainted, but you and I haven't been properly introduced.' He nodded down to his returning erection. 'I think we should get acquainted, don't you?'

The spark in Tino's eyes as she positioned herself to sniff the Boss's crotch wasn't jealousy. If she had to venture a guess, she'd say it was mischief. He offered her a smile as she lowered her face to take in the Boss's more metallic scent. The Boss was thick and heavy and uncut, his penis nestled in a veritable garden of thick curls that were slightly coppery in the bare light. With a hard intake of breath at first contact, he pulled back his foreskin revealing himself. 'You're a lovely Pet, Stella. Hard to believe you're just learning the ropes.'

Of course she wasn't doing it for him. She was doing it for Tino. Plus, she was intrigued and more than a little aroused at the thought of what the two men had got up to together last night. 'Mmm, that's nice,' the Boss groaned, as she sniffed the length of his penis down to where it bobbed against his weighty balls. 'Tino's smell is all over you, and nobody's heat smells like Tino's,' he commented. 'But when it's blended with your lust, Stella, darling,' He pushed her away and rearranged her so her bottom was raised in his face, 'well, my mouth positively waters.' She let out a little gasp of surprise as he buried his face between her splayed lips. He wasn't put off at the abundance of Tino's semen cupped there, in fact if it had been ice cream he couldn't have been more enthusiastic. 'I love the taste of Tino on you,' he said when he came up for air. 'And his cock must be awash in your flavour. Taste him for me, darling. He's hard again. Your mouth will be a welcome respite while he watches me tongue fuck your fat little pussy.'

She was happy to take Tino's offered erection into her mouth, and she did relish the taste of herself blended with him. She was half jealous of the Boss getting to taste Tino on her, and a little amazed at how much he seemed to relish the big Pet's abundant flavour. Not that she could dwell on it too much, when it was obvious the Boss's mouth clearly knew the way around a woman's pussy.

'Oh my, such a delicious cunt,' he breathed. 'I can understand why Tino couldn't wait to taste you this morning, and he must have been waiting with a stiff cock all day, waiting for me to allow him to fuck you tonight.' He shot Tino a quick glance. 'And you're needing to fuck her again, aren't you, my dear boy?'

She couldn't keep from whimpering as the Boss parted her

lips and shoved two scissoring fingers up inside her. 'And oh, she's so ready for you. Her pussy's practically sucking my fingers she needs you so badly. Come, darling,' he addressed Stella. 'Lie down on your back and open your legs wide so Tino can mount you on top, so we can see the look on your face when he puts it in you hard like you like it. That's a girl.' He helped position her, and Tino shoved her legs apart with his knees. But just as he was about to thrust into her, the Boss ran curved fingers between her pouting lips and wriggled them in until the cup of them was liberally creamed with the combination of her juices and Tino's semen. The second Tino pushed into her, the Boss began to massage their blended juices over and around the tight ring of Tino's anus.

Her first response was to squirm away in alarm, assuming Tino wouldn't want such an invasion, but after all the Boss had said, she was pretty sure she was wrong on that count. Tino cupped his hands under her arse cheeks and pulled her further onto him, holding her gaze as he did so. His eyelids fluttered and he sucked his teeth as the Boss slipped a finger into his back-hole and chuckled softly.

'Don't worry, Stella, darling, Tino's little bumhole is used to being fucked, though I daresay it's been a while since he's got it from behind while humping such a lovely cunt. I promise I'll make it good for him, love. Tino, don't you think our little fledgling Pet here would like to see what I'm doing to your lovely arsehole?' He nodded to a high stool sitting in front of a mirrored wall in one corner of the room.

Effortlessly, Tino scooped her up, still impaled, hands supporting her bottom, and deposited her on the stool facing the mirror. Her heart raced as she realised she had the perfect view of Tino's gripping pucker.

'Now, that's better, isn't it?' From somewhere the Boss produced a tube of lube, which he squirted generously on his fingers. 'Shall we continue with our little Pet's education, then, Tino?'

The view was like some close-up from a porn film as the Boss inserted not one, but two fingers into Tino's anus, and she felt in her own belly the resulting grunt and tightening of

Tino's abdominal muscles. For a second his face scrunched into a tight grimace, then his chest flared and his eyelids fluttered, and the little sigh that escaped his lips let her know just how nice it felt.

She could feel the Boss's gaze on her as Tino shifted between her legs so that the thrust of his penis stroked her deeper, and so that the hand still under her buttocks could press and wriggle at *her* bumhole. She quivered and nearly bounced off the stool as he slid his finger past the tight protective sphincter. The upward press of her body against his raked her already raw clit even harder against his pubic bone, and she gasped and dug her knuckles into his shoulders.

The Boss offered a throaty laugh. 'The problem with good sex is that someone's view is always obstructed. I'd love to see what Tino's doing to your tight little bottom, Stella, but at least I can see the results in that blissed-out look on your face, so that'll have to do, won't it? And now, I'm going to fuck your arse, Tino, just like I let you fuck mine last night.'

Suddenly Stella could barely breathe. Her body and her brain were both bordering on input overload. Far from feeling like a betrayal, the thought of the Boss all bent over, his arse presented open and begging to Tino, her Tino, made her already clenching insides skitter and let down another juicy flood. She tightened her grip around Tino, who suddenly held very still and pressed his arse back expectantly.

She watched in amazement as the Boss gave his jutting penis a liberal coating of lube with impatient strokes. Then he positioned himself and Tino pressed back further. 'That's my big boy,' the Boss crooned. 'Just relax and let me take you, let me fill that tight back-hole of yours.' With his cock fisted tight like it was a weapon, he pushed forward. Tino gave a guttural grunt and pushed back hard, his yielding pucker swallowing the Boss whole. And suddenly it was the Boss who whimpered.

It was then that Stella realised Tino's gaze was locked on her. When she pulled her attention away from the spectacle being carried out in the mirror for her benefit, he offered her the tiniest hint of a smile then dropped a hungry kiss onto her mouth. When she returned his smile, when she returned his kiss and began to breathe again, he thrust back against the Boss hard enough to make the man grunt out his breath and grab on to Tino's hips for the ride.

And a strange ride it was. At first it was almost like the Boss was vicariously fucking Stella, following each of Tino's thrusts with hard strokes, then riding Tino back until he almost dislodged himself when Tino next thrust forward. The extra weight made for extra momentum, and the press inside Stella felt like it went all the way up to the base of her brain.

Then the Boss changed the rhythm, thrusting forward when Tino thrust back. His thrusts became tight little bucks, the strain of which now showed on his pleasure-contorted face. The muscles in his arms bulged and quivered the closer he got to release. And Tino, sandwiched in between, had wriggled his middle finger deep into Stella's anus, somehow managing to keep the pressure on and maintain the perfect rhythm even with all the other stimulation avalanching in on him.

They had all three reached the point where flesh was in danger of shattering like glass, breath was only a distant memory, and the world had narrowed to their points of connection. Their breathless chase and scramble for release exploded from behind when the Boss came first, the impact of his thrust nearly knocking all of them over the stool, but Tino's legs stiffened as his own orgasm raged up through him to be met head on by Stella's.

There were screams and growls and snarls, and Stella didn't know whose belonged to whom in the pile of trembling, sweating flesh draped precariously over the stool. Then they managed to stumble back to the pallet somehow, Tino carefully lifting her so that they could maintain the connection just a little longer. On the pallet, the Boss pulled the blanket around the three of them, then they all snuggled close and slept.

Long toward morning, the Boss woke her. 'Come, Stella, darling. We need to get you back to your pallet before the handler gets worried.'

Tino was loath to let her go, pulling her tightly against him. His cock was still nestled in her pussy and she felt as though her insides had been ripped away when the Boss pulled her to her feet. 'Tino, you know she has to go. You have to go. I've been more than generous with the two of you, now don't force me to regret it.'

From somewhere he produced a towel and cleaned her pussy as best he could, then he allowed Tino a few minutes to hold her and kiss her goodbye. 'Don't look so grim, you two. There'll be other times.'

Her last sight of Tino was him standing at the open door of the dungeon watching her ascend the steps into the cool predawn light.

'He has to leave this morning, which I think is just as well,' the Boss said, when she could no longer look over her shoulder and see the big Pet. 'You need to concentrate on your training now, because you'll be with a keeper this weekend.' He raised a hand, as though he expected her to protest. 'I know it seems soon, but we wouldn't be sending you if we didn't think you were ready.' He opened the door to her room and settled her into her pallet. 'I've spoken with Jan. She knows to bathe you before you see the other Pets in the morning and to feed you well after your night's adventures.' He ran a hand along her cheek, then bent and kissed her on the mouth. 'There, you see. Everything'll be all right, and in time, you'll understand it all well enough.' He left her to sleep.

Chapter Sixteen

WITH TINO NO LONGER a constant distraction, there was little for Stella to do with the rest of her time but get on with her training. She was kept fairly isolated because she wasn't on the Pet Shop holiday package, as Jan called it, but mostly because she had a keeper who was anxious to have her for the weekend, much more quickly than a trainee Pet was normally allowed to go out.

For her final exam, she would be a Pet for a pretend keeper selected by Audrey and Master. She was to be with him through the night and until noon tomorrow. She had been told he was a man, but nothing more. She was bathed and brushed and fitted with the Foreplayer. Then she was left to wait for her handler to take her to the cottage where she would meet her keeper. It felt like she waited for ages. She was just beginning to wonder what caused the delay when the door burst open and Audrey rushed in.

'Change of plans,' she spoke between barely parted lips. Her voice was breathless, tight. 'You won't be needing the Foreplayer.'

She already had the harness half off Stella when Jan approached her with a pair of loose-fitting mauve trousers and a matching T-shirt. She was practically bouncing with excitement. 'Your real keeper has requested that you leave immediately to join him. This is so exciting.' She spoke as though she were announcing Stella's marriage.

Audrey shot the handler a warning glance before turning her attention back to Stella and hurrying her into the T-shirt. 'Your real keeper has insisted that you be sent today.' Once she had shimmied the trousers up over Stella's hips, she handed her a pen and pad. 'You'll need your passport. A handler will be arriving at your flat in about five minutes. Can you write down where it is so I can direct him to it? Good girl, now come. You've got a bit of a journey ahead of you. And don't look so frightened, darling. I promise you, all will be revealed very shortly, and everything will be just fine.' The enthusiasm in the woman's voice sounded a bit forced to Stella.

Accompanied by a black-suited handler who carried the mauve and crème rucksack someone had selected for her, she arrived at Heathrow, but not at Departures. When the handler helped her out of her carrier, it was a smartly dressed male flight attendant who took her bag, offered her his arm and led her up the steps of a private jet. On board the attendant addressed her. 'You are to relax and enjoy the flight, Ms James. I've been instructed that you have a very bad case of laryngitis and can't speak, so we'll do our best to make you comfortable. Now buckle in. We'll be underway in a few minutes.'

She could barely manage the seatbelt, she was trembling so badly. Her mind was vacillating between all the horrible things she could imagine that might happen to her once she left the safety of the UK and memories of the last time she was put aboard a private jet.

'Here, let me help you with that.' Suddenly Vincent Evanston, well turned out in Armani, clean shaven, every hair in place, knelt in front of her, laid his large hands over hers and slid the buckle into place. And she collapsed in a puddle of shakes.

'Oh for heaven sake, Stella, it's all right. There, there, now. Calm down.' He settled in next to her and slipped his arms around her. 'It's all right. What did you think, that they had sold you to the highest bidder for some despot's harem in outer bumfuck somewhere? It's just me. That's all, just me, and I promise I'll have you back in time for work on Monday.'

He tut-tutted, and his face became suddenly serious, though she could see the smile threatening to break through. 'I can only imagine how long this weekend is going to be for the mighty Stella James, a whole 48 hours bursting at the seams with so many burning questions, and not being allowed to ask any of them. You poor thing.'

The laugh that forced its way up her throat sounded pathetically like a sob. She tried to shove him away playfully, but he caught her face and landed a kiss across her lips, with just the tiniest flick of tongue to make her catch her breath. 'Don't think I'm a softie, Stella. That would be a mistake. I'll happily punish you soundly for misbehaving. How else are you going to learn to be a proper Pet?'

The pilot announced departure, and Vincent buckled in next to her. As soon as the plane was levelled at cruising altitude, and the seatbelt sign was switched off, he unbuckled himself and her, took her hand, and hurried her to the back of the plane, which was partitioned off to house a built-in bed. He motioned to the mattress. Once she was on it, he pushed her to the centre and practically tore her clothes off, with her using all the control she had not to help him. At last, when he had her naked and her clothes shoved onto the floor, she rose on her haunches to sniff and nuzzle him in the getting-acquainted ritual. But Vincent rolled on top of her and trapped her spreadeagled beneath him. 'You don't need to get to know me, Stella. You already have my scent, and I have yours.' Then he sat astraddle her and shoved and pushed his own clothes off until expensive Armani lay as casually discarded as cheap jersey.

But when he lowered himself onto her she bit him hard on the right pec just above his nipple.

'Ouch! You little devil, you!' He pinned her to the bed with his knees pressing almost painfully against her biceps and examined the bite. Then he offered a throaty chuckle. 'Marking territory are we? Well at least you had the decency not to piss on me.' His eyes sparked like fire. 'Two can play at that game though.' He dropped his full weight on her and lowered his mouth to her throat just where the bony press of the trachea gave way to the soft smooth flesh of the nape, and he bit. He bit hard enough to cause her to yelp, hard enough to make her eyes water, before his lips took over the effort, and he suckled and nibbled the soft flesh of her until she could feel the intensity of his pull all the way down to her pussy. His fingers

132

curled tightly in her hair and held her neck exposed. The other hand found its way to the nearest breast and strummed at her nipple with a rough thumb.

The sounds coming from her throat were incoherent as he brought every nerve ending in her body to tingle and rage at his attention. He forced her legs apart with his knees and dropped to rake his demanding erection against the swell and splay of her cunt. And suddenly she was struggling with every ounce of her subdued strength to position her hips to get his cock right where she needed it.

He didn't deny her. A slight shift of his hips and a grunting thrust and he was in deep and hard. He didn't bother to ease his efforts; he didn't bother to give her time to adjust to his thickness. Somehow the rough way he shoved her full made her hotter and gave her permission to play rough right back. She wrapped her legs around him and kicked like he was a bronco and she intended to break him.

He brought his arms down the side of his body and trapped her legs for damage control. Then he pulled away from her throat with another painful nip, pausing to admire his efforts. 'Now, everyone will know that you're mine,' he gasped. 'You won't even need to wear a collar.'

Jesus, she couldn't believe he'd marked her on her neck right where everyone could see, like she was some horny chav. She had to work on Monday. It was too damned hot to wear a high-necked blouse. But even as she thought about it, she had to admit she kind of liked the idea of wearing his mark so that everyone could see, so that everyone could imagine how he had fucked her, how he had subdued her, how he had made her pussy clench and gush around his thrusting cock.

She made another futile attempt to kick him, but he just held her closer and thrust harder. And it was enough. Suddenly the shaking all over her body had nothing to do with nerves as she bucked and convulsed her orgasm while he rode harder until the bed shook, and he stiffened and jerked his load into her gripping cunt. Then he collapsed on top of her.

After he'd managed to catch his breath, he pulled out, leaving a warm trail of sticky come on the inside of her thigh.

Then he cleaned himself and began to dress. He started to put on his tie, but thought better of it and tossed it on the nightstand. 'I have work to do,' he said. Then he bent and kissed her cheek. 'But you have nothing to do but lie here all wet and sticky and smelling of our sex until I get back to you.' He settled a wet kiss onto each of her nipples then pulled the blanket up over her. 'And I will get back to you before we land. I'm not nearly finished with the in-flight entertainment yet.'

She never slept on planes, and yet she did this time, deeply, peacefully. At some point in the timeless void that was airline travel, she woke to find him curled around her, naked, his hard penis nestled against her arse. One large hand curved protectively over her pubis, middle finger stretched between her folds.

'Tino?' She spoke his name from the muzzy-minded state of half-sleep, and felt his drowsy whisper against the back of her neck.

'Tino's not here. Just Vincent, and if you speak again, I'll have to spank your little bottom, won't I?' He pulled her closer.

They were already on the ground when he woke her again. He was fully dressed in jeans and a jumper looking amazingly no worse for the wear. 'Come on, woman. Let's get you dressed and out to the jeep. We still have a couple hours' drive ahead of us.'

This time there was no limo waiting and no driver. Instead the sexiest blue jeep she had ever seen was parked waiting for them on the tarmac. The top was off exposing the elegant roll bar and frame to the late afternoon sun. Vincent helped her on with a leather jacket, buckled her into the jeep then climbed into the driver's seat. 'I wanted you to enjoy the gorgeous scenery, Stel,' he said, as he cranked the engine and they headed away from the airport. 'I seldom use the limo, and besides Pets much prefer fresh air over stuffy old cars, don't they?' He spoke like he knew, she thought. And yet of course Vincent Evanston would prefer the great outdoors. He opened a cooler between the seats and pulled out two bottles of water.

'Sorry, Stel, you'll have to drink for yourself till I get you home. I don't want you dehydrating after all that fucking and the long plane ride, but I've got to drive.'

And drink she did. The whole bottle, an effort she was beginning to regret by the time they had left the city and were heading out over the Coastal Range. The bumpy scenic backroads Vincent had chosen to take them on didn't help her heavy bladder. She tried to pay attention as he chatted away about the volcanic make-up of the Pacific Northwest, and the unique ecosystems that had developed because of the volcanism of the region. And indeed it was fascinating to know that the area was long overdue for a major eruption in the Cascades, and that the Mt St Helen's eruption in 1980 might have been just the tip of the iceberg. But none of that fascinating information helped her distended bladder.

'It's one of the prettiest places on the planet,' he was saying, as he pulled to the side of the deserted road. 'And I'm looking forward to showing you some of my favourite parts of it.' He stopped the jeep, shut off the engine and turned expectant eyes on her. 'Well?'

She didn't move.

'All that water has to go somewhere, Stel.' He looked down at her hands folded protectively low over her belly, then he undid her seatbelt. 'Pee break. I could use one myself.' He undid his own seatbelt and stepped out of the jeep. She uttered a startled cry and looked away as he undid his fly.

He laughed softly. 'Oh for heaven sake, Stella, it's not like you haven't seen my cock before. Besides, Pets aren't squeamish about peeing. Guess you haven't had that lesson yet. Never mind, just turn your back and I'll turn mine.'

She would have waited if she could have, but in her desperate straits, she squatted as close to the jeep as she could and let go, hoping she wouldn't pee on her trousers, and trying desperately not to listen to Vincent happily relieving himself on the other side of the jeep.

In truth, they'd only been about ten minutes from Vincent's home, and she had the distinct impression he had made her pee in the wild on purpose. But at the first sight of The Lookout, she forgot to be angry. The Lookout was what Vincent affectionately called the big cantilevered house that was mostly glass and wood set high enough to view the Pacific Ocean in one direction while nestling against the breast of the hilly woodland in the other. Once inside, he led her across pale sandstone floors of what was mostly an open-plan house, back to a big bedroom. It showcased a glassed-in patio that led down to a protected wild garden below. The big high bed looked out over the landscape of conifers and rugged volcanic rocks and gave the distinct feeling of being in a treehouse.

Her intake of breath at the view made him blush with pride. 'My room,' he said. 'Our room while you're here.' He held her gaze. 'If you're good, I'll let you sleep in the bed with me.'

Now it was her turn to blush.

He nodded to the hardwood floor. 'Sit down and let me get you undressed. You've had an uncomfortably long time in those clothes, and I want to look at you. I would have loved to have made you ride naked in the jeep. Since I first met you that thought's given me my share of hard-ons. But alas that might have gotten us arrested, and I don't intend to spend our time together in jail.'

He knelt on the floor next to her and slipped the T-shirt off over her head, hands skimming her breasts as he did so.

'Guess the international travel and all precluded the use of the Foreplayer,' he said, as he tugged the trousers down over her raised bottom and off over her bare feet. 'But,' he placed a hand inside her knees and gently eased them apart. His eyes dropped to her exposed mons. 'I'm guessing you don't need it anyway.' He splayed her by bringing two thick fingers up over her perineum to part her heavy lips from below, folding her outward and open to his gaze. Then he caught his breath. 'Jesus, you really don't need it, do you?' She shifted her hips back to open herself further and moaned softly as he eased the two fingers up into her pout.

His eyes were locked on the cleft of her, and it made her feel deliciously nasty and swollen. 'If I had made you ride naked in the jeep, you would have left pussy prints all over the seat. I wouldn't have been able to drive for the thought of you

136

slipping and slicking all over the leather, for the smell of you all turned on and aching and needing to pee.

'And when you were done peeing, when you were back in the jeep, I would have had to fuck you while you stood holding on to the roll bar. I would have had to shove my way into all that slickness and let your pussy grip me and grind me until I made you even more slippery.'

With a little whimper, she leant forward and began licking his heavy bulge through the jeans.

His breath caught in his throat, and he let out a deep groan, curling his fingers in her hair. 'Jesus, woman, I want you all over me. I want you so bad. I've wanted you since the moment I first saw you in your silly pink shoes.' He fumbled with the buckle of his belt and then practically ripped the fly out of his jeans, shoving them down just far enough to release his cock, which practically jumped spring-loaded into her waiting mouth. But she lingered only long enough to give him a cursory lick, before she squatted over him. His big hands grasped her hips and guided her down onto his anxious penis, and he eased out a trembling sigh as she swallowed him into her cunt.

There was invisible household help who had cooked delicious food – lovely, messy, spicy Mexican food for him to feed her – followed by dark chocolate mousse with home-grown raspberries which she happily ate off his chest. There was a bathtub big enough for a pool party and delicious natural-scented bubbles rubbed and massaged all over her. There were thick towels the colour of the trees that grew outside Vincent's window. After he had lotioned every inch of her body, she followed him into the bedroom and sat quietly on the Navajo rug by the side of the bed, watching as he pulled back the duvet and slipped out of his dark terry robe. Once he was settled in and he'd turned off the lights, she waited, holding her breath.

At last she heard him sigh. 'Well?'

Silence.

'I haven't had to spank you or take away your dessert privileges, and you've made me come very effectively ... several times. So I'd say you've been a good Pet.' She heard him pat the mattress. 'Come on. Up you come.' When she sprang onto the bed next to him, he was holding back the covers. Then he settled her into a spoon position, cradled tightly against the curve of his warm body. 'Sleep well, Stel. We have a busy day ahead of us tomorrow.'

Chapter Seventeen

'SHE'S BEEN SENT WHERE?' O'Kelly catapulted upright in her bed, her grip on the phone suddenly white knuckled.

'To Oregon, the Northwest Coast, you know. To be with–'

'To be with Vincent Evanston, yes, I didn't miss that fact, believe me I didn't.'

'Didn't think you would,' the Boss replied.

O'Kelly sat on the edge of her bed and grabbed for her robe. Before she had a chance to respond, the Boss continued. 'Vincent made it very clear to the Pet Shop that he wanted Stella this weekend, and that he wouldn't take no for an answer.'

'Damn it! This could ruin everything.' She jerked the sash tight around her waist and scrubbed a hand through her hair. 'Didn't you try to stop him? Didn't you think it important enough to let me know?'

'I am letting you know. Right now.' The frustration in the Boss's voice was unusual. It got O'Kelly's full attention. 'I wasn't trying to keep it from you. By the time I found out it was already a done deal. I've just been scrambling to sort out what's going on. I didn't expect Vincent to go behind our backs and take matters into his own hands. He's never bothered before. He's never cared one way or another as long as the Pet Shop runs smoothly.'

'I can't believe this is happening. Jesus, I can't believe this is happening.' Then it suddenly occurred to her. She didn't know why she didn't think of it before. 'Were you and Vincent in cahoots sending Tino to Stella that first time?'

'O'Kelly, I–'

'Just answer my question. Were you?'

139

The heavy silence on the other end of the phone was answer enough, but she waited for it; she wanted to hear the words. She wanted him to confess. At last he spoke over a sigh that sounded almost painful. 'When I told Vincent about Stella, that we thought she was the person we'd been looking for, he insisted that Tino be sent to her. He wanted to see firsthand our choice for your replacement. He thought it would be the perfect test. I tried to talk him out of it, I did. But in the end I had no say in the matter.'

'And you couldn't be arsed to tell me, even though I supposedly run the Pet Shop.'

'I was sworn to secrecy.'

'Bullshit!' she exploded. 'You fucked the man! Twice.' She fought back angry tears, thankful he couldn't see her. She wiped her eyes fiercely with the back of her hand. 'Then the two of you pass secrets behind my back that affect my life and my career like I'm some damn pawn in your kinky little game.'

'Jesus, O'Kelly, I fucked a lot of people and didn't report back, and so did you. What are you, jealous?'

'You bastard! I don't care if you fuck each other's brains out from here to China and back every night.' She sprang up from the bed feeling like her chest would burst, fighting back the urge to hit something. 'But that you two went behind my back to send Tino to poor unsuspecting Stella.' She stabbed her index finger in the air for emphasis. 'That you two fucking went behind my back like I'm nothing more than one of the paid Pets, *that* I do care about.'

'O'Kelly, I–'

She hung up on him. Just like that, she cut him off, completely un-business-like, completely unprofessional. And if that wasn't bad enough, she buried her face in her hands and sobbed like some bloody teenager. Keeping things from her. Hadn't that been the reason she'd left him back in uni? How could she ever trust a man who kept secrets from her? Hadn't she taken this position against her better judgment? She was an intelligent woman. She should have known, but she let him get to her, just like she always did. And here she was again right back where she'd been in uni, being kept in the dark. Well, it

140

was enough. Damn it, it was enough!

She was busy packing when the Boss rang the doorbell. She knew it was him. Who else could it be in the middle of the night? She knew if she didn't let him in, he wouldn't go away until he'd woken all the neighbours. She threw open the door then turned back to her bedroom and the packing, leaving him to close it, but not before she felt his gaze take in the thin silk robe she had pulled on when he called. She found herself wishing for the protective barrier of her power suit.

He closed the door and followed her down the hall, then just stood silently in the doorway watching her fold her underwear and place it in the bag.

At last he spoke into the stretched silence. 'Where are you going?'

'On holiday. I've earned it,' she replied, relieved that she'd had time to calm herself and regain a modicum of control before he showed up. 'Then after that. Well, I don't know after that.'

'Annie, I'm sorry.'

Her modicum of control crumbled, and the room fractured through a mist of threatening tears. Did he have to call her that now? It wasn't fair him trying to defuse her anger by being sweet. He'd taken to calling her O'Kelly when she started working for Strigida. He'd done it because he was angry at her for setting the hands-off rule for their working relationship. She had retaliated by calling him "the Boss" and "sir". It had hurt at first, but it had become safe, and now he was ripping all of that away. She squared her shoulders and kept packing, kept her back to him hoping he wouldn't notice how she was shaking. 'I can't trust you, Alan. That's the truth of it. I couldn't trust you back in uni, and I can't trust you now. Nothing has really changed, has it?'

'Wait a minute, I'll admit I made a stupid mistake not telling you why I sent Tino to Stella, but what the hell does uni have to do with any of this?' He was across the floor in a heartbeat, taking her shoulders in a firm grip and forcing her to face him, oblivious to the pair of socks tightly clenched in her

141

hand. 'What the hell do you mean you couldn't trust me in uni?'

She jerked away from him with such force that she nearly fell backward onto the bed. 'Oh please, don't play innocent with me, Alan. When were you planning to tell me you were going back to the States? When were you planning to tell me about the job Vincent had offered you? Were you just going to casually call me from the airport in Portland when you got there? And all the while here's me thinking we'd be off to Manchester together like we'd planned.'

He blinked and sucked a harsh breath between his teeth. 'What the ...? Is that what this is all about? You never gave me a chance to tell you anything, in case you've forgotten. *You* were the one calling *me* from the airport in Cape Town, South fucking Africa! You just left, no explanation. No nothing, so don't go putting all this on me.'

She wiped angrily at her eyes. 'What difference did it make who called who from what airport? If our relationship didn't matter any more than that, what difference did it make?'

'Didn't matter? Jesus, Annie, how can you even say that? I didn't tell you about the plan to go to work with Vincent because there was no plan. He'd just asked me. I was thinking about it, but I had no intention of going anywhere without you, and Vincent knew that. You were an asset he'd have put to good use. Vincent may be a reclusive naturalist, but he's still his father's son where business is concerned. And it would have been good, Annie. It would have been really good whether we'd gone to the States or not. But you took the choice out of my hands, didn't you? And I didn't know why. You didn't even have the decency to tell me why.' He caught his breath in a heavy gulp and added, 'How did you know? About Vincent's job offer?'

She suddenly felt lightheaded, and the room didn't seem real. Her voice felt like it came from a long way away. 'He called when you were out.'

He took a step closer to her. 'And you didn't think it might be a good idea to discuss it with me, to ask me about it?'

She shrugged helplessly. 'He talked like it was a done deal.

He talked like it was the plan all along.'

'Well fuck, Annie! It probably was *his* plan all along. He's Vincent Evanston, for chrissake.' There was an uncomfortable silence. She didn't know what to say. She just stood next to the bed with a pair of stupid socks gripped in one hand as the reality she thought she knew disintegrated. It was the hard accusation in his eyes that held her, riveted her to the shred of reality that was the two of them arguing in her bedroom.

'I never kept anything from you, Annie. You just never trusted me enough to ask.'

In the struggle to hold it all together, to give herself space to think, she turned back to her packing.

He continued. 'I never imagined Vincent would make an appearance to Stella. I can't even remember the last time I saw the man. Tino, yes, but not Vincent. I know you tried to warn me about his feelings for her, but I just couldn't believe it. Not Vincent, not the man I knew. His fortress was unassailable. I didn't see it coming, none of it. He's never taken a Pet, you know he hasn't, not in the history of the Pet Shop. Annie, I never planned any of this, and I never meant to deceive you. Annie, damn it! Will you listen to me?'

With a sweep of his arm, he shoved the suitcase off the bed onto the floor, sending clothing cascading everywhere.

'What the hell do you think you're doing? You can't just waltz in here and—'

Before she could turn on him, he moved in close behind her and pulled her against him, holding her to his body, arms folded tightly over her ribs just below her breasts. 'I apologise for keeping the plan to send Tino to Stella from you. I was wrong. It was a stupid mistake.' His breath came hot and fast against her nape. 'But I won't apologise for something I never did, something you've held against me all these years.' The brush of his lips against her ear caused a wave of gooseflesh down over her breasts. He tightened his embrace, and she became aware of his cock pressing through his trousers against her bottom.

'I never meant to hurt you. That would be the last thing I'd ever want to do. But you haven't made it easy with all your damn rules. Still, I've kept them, Annie. I have, for you. But I never wanted them. And now, I'm breaking them, and I won't apologise for that either.' His hand shifted enough to cup her breasts and rake a thumb across her erect nipples pressing against the silk robe.

The sound that escaped her throat was wounded, needy. She tried to wriggle away, but he held her tight. His fingers worried the half knot at the belt of her robe loose, and he slid his hands inside to caress exposed belly and breast. Suddenly she couldn't get enough breath into her lungs. The groan that vibrated against her neck sounded anguished as he pulled her closer, forcing his hips forward until the growing bulge at his groin pressed tight against her arse. His caressing of her breasts was tentative at first, as though he were afraid of another escape attempt, but when she pressed into his hand, his fondlings became greedy, possessive.

It was accidental, she told herself, her shifting into his hand. She had no intention of moving, no intention of giving in to him, and yet ...

His mouth laved and nipped and suckled over her neck and onto an advancing trail of bare shoulder as he pushed the robe away with his nuzzling. His other hand trailed a ticklish path over her ribs past her navel until it moved to cup her bare mons. When he slipped fingers down to stroke her clit and press in between her labia, a little sob of a sigh escaped both of their throats. She couldn't believe her own wetness in spite of her anger, in spite of her stress.

The hand that had been cupping her breasts moved behind to grope her buttocks lightly before slipping in between her thighs. In the soundtrack of heavy breathing, she heard the zip of his fly and the slide of fabric as he manoeuvred his penis free. Impatiently, he shoved aside the back of her robe until she felt the anxious weight of him pressing between her arse cheeks. Then he took his cock in his hand and forced it downward over her perineum, to where her labia flared swollen and slick.

Instinct took over. She bent forward against the brace of his other hand pressed low on her belly and forced her hips back,

144

easing his path. And he was there, right at the entrance of her pussy, pressed up ready, as though he were leaving the decision to her. But as extra incentive, his middle and index fingers slid tightly up and down each side of her clit in a tetchy wet pinch of friction that made her hump and shift, made her cunt-hole grip and pout. And when she was pouting open and aching, he pushed into her, offering up a trembling sigh against her ear.

'Annie, I've wanted this for so long.' His words were clipped, caught tight amid his struggle to breath. His hips undulated in little circles as though he were sneaking around, as though he were still afraid she would push him away if she found out what he was up to.

And in truth, she was afraid of that too. There were so many reasons not to fuck the man she worked with, not to fuck the man who broke her heart all those years ago back in uni, the man who was so damned oblivious he didn't even know it. And yet, hadn't he just taken all those reasons away from her in just a few rushed sentences? All these years it would have taken only that much and nothing more.

Her own movements mirrored his, moving just enough to get the right friction in the right place, shifting just enough that his cock raked her exactly where she needed it. She slid one hand down to press his fingers tighter against her clit, making certain he knew she didn't want him to stop. She lifted one knee onto the bed, feeling like one of the Pets exposing herself, making her lewd gaping pussy more easily available for him to ride.

He pushed up tight into the space she had made, suddenly so enthusiastic in his efforts that he nearly shoved her forward onto the bed. A hand moved up her ribs to steady her then up to pinch and stroke and tug at her breasts.

She was trembling all over with orgasm long before she wanted to be, completely taken by surprise like a teenager with no control.

'That's what I want,' he whispered breathlessly against her nape. 'I want to make you come, Annie. I want to make you come again and again.' Then he shoved into her hard and allowed himself to come like he'd been holding it for days.

Chapter Eighteen

'THEIR NEST IS JUST behind that waterfall.' Vincent nodded to the cascade of water that the little dark bird had just flitted through. 'Dippers often find protected places behind waterfalls to raise their chicks safe from predators. The chicks should be about to fledge any time now. I'd love it if you could see that. It's amazing to watch them make their debut into the big wide world after they've been all tucked away safe and sound in their little secret hidey-hole.'

He sat with Stella's feet across his lap and busied himself removing the hiking boots he'd bought for her, checking for blisters. 'You OK, Stel? I know it's quite a little hike to get up here, but it's such a lovely place.'

She nodded and wriggled her toes happily. She'd never felt more blissed out.

'You like it here?' he asked, knowing she couldn't answer. The best she could do was smile enthusiastically and rub her bare feet along his thigh.

He curled his fingers around her foot and lifted it to his lips, pressing a kiss to the arch of it. 'I knew you would. How could you not?'

She lay back on the huge slab of rock he had found for them and let the sun's warmth wash over her. She could feel his gaze on her, and that was even warmer than the sunlight. It made her feel deliciously sexy – even more than sexy, it made her feel adored. She knew she was smiling. She could feel it. He watched her when he thought she wasn't looking, and she watched him. She didn't care if he was looking or not. She was a Pet. The rules didn't apply to her. Sometimes that was a good thing.

'Stella, my cock's hard. I need you to make me come.' She loved the bluntness of the Pet/keeper relationship. Pets were always horny, that was a given, but keepers didn't have to play coy. They just asked for what they wanted, and that usually made their Pets even hornier.

She rose to find him watching her, as she had expected. He had moved to sit on a mossy stump. His trousers were open enough to free his cock and his balls, and his heavy penis strained in the pull and stroke of his large hand. The sight of him horny made her pussy quiver with anticipation. She started to kneel in front of him, but he shook his head.

'I want to come in your pussy,' he said.

She stepped closer and allowed him to slide her trousers down over her hips. She was still barefooted, so she stepped out of them, making sure to do it in such a way that gave Vincent a good view of her plump lips. He reached between her legs and stroked her folds, then offered a lazy chuckle. 'You're slippery almost as often as I'm hard, Stel, and knowing that just makes me even harder. Turn around.' He motioned with the finger still glistening from her moisture just before he licked off the taste of her. She did as she was told. He took her by the hips and guided her back. 'I want you to sit on my lap,' he breathed.

As she squatted, he guided her, holding her cheeks apart. Then he fingered his way into her cleft to splay her fattened labia before he pulled her down and impaled her on his erection with a satisfied grunt. In response she let out a series of little animal whimpers.

'Your pussy fits me like a glove, Stel, like a tight, slippery, warm glove, and I love wearing you.' He reached around and down over her pubis. 'Your clit's always a hard little pearl all pushed out and exposed for me, ready for me to play with.' He ran fingers over her nub and she shuddered.

'You like it when I play with it, don't you?'

She whimpered again then wriggled and tightened her grip as she rocked and shifted on his thighs.

He sucked air. 'Oh God, woman, I won't last long if you keep doing that.'

She didn't care if he didn't last long. Since Vincent had taken her the first time on the plane, she was always just a stroke away from coming. Somehow he kept her there, right on the edge and squirming, and he did it with no effort at all that she could see. She clenched again and he gasped a tight laugh. 'All right then, a quickie it is. That should last us until we get back to the jeep. Maybe.' A few more strokes and she felt him spurt. The feel of his release inside her was enough to send her.

But it hadn't been enough to get them back to the jeep. He'd taken her again when they'd paused to watch a male robin mounting his female. Vincent had said something about the birds having a possible second brood, but his hand kneading her braless breasts while he spoke made concentration difficult. He had taken her from behind, her bracing herself against the rough trunk of a pine tree, trousers down around her hiking boots.

She had walked the rest of the way to the jeep with her cunt and thighs wet from their juices, looking for all practical purposes to anyone who might meet them as though she had peed herself. But the scent, the delicious rutty scent that perfumed her was a dead giveaway as to what had really happened. At the jeep, he held her back, and before she got in, he bent and removed her boots then took off her trousers and offered her a wicked smile. When she settled into the leather seat, while he belted her in, she held his gaze, opened her legs wide and squirmed enthusiastically all over the warm leather so her pout slicked the seat well.

'That's my nasty girl,' he breathed, and she could already see his cock pressing against his trousers.

She fell asleep in the jeep on the way home, and he carried her into the house and placed her gently on the bed, removing the rest of her clothes while she half dozed. 'You're still jetlagged, Stel. You lie here and rest a while.' He glanced down at his watch. 'I have a conference call in a few minutes and I'll be busy for an hour or so, then after I'm finished, we'll have some dinner, and we can play.' He cupped her breasts, dropped a quick kiss on her mouth and left her to rest.

It had been her plan to cat nap nestled in the middle of his big bed. The room was awash in the late afternoon sunlight morphing to shades of tangerine through the huge picture windows. She was still unbathed, still fragrant with the heady scent of Vincent and her together. It was such a perfect way to doze. But then she noticed the two photo albums at the bottom of the bookshelf. They were old and dog-eared. No one kept photos in albums any more, so she slipped off the bed and onto the floor.

Just as she had hoped, they were photos of Vincent's childhood. She would have recognised him anywhere, and at any age. It certainly didn't hurt that someone, probably his mother, had carefully labelled each shot. Most of the first album was of the pre-teen years, with Vincent looking too tall and too thin for his age, and with his hair as unmanageable as ever. In most of the pictures, he was with another boy, shorter, lighter haired, always perfectly combed, always looking like he couldn't wait to get into trouble. The caption beneath a photo of the two of them standing in front of a tent read: *Vincent and Alan. Crater Lake National Park.*

Throughout the entirety of the two photo albums, Vincent was always accompanied by Alan. There was a familiarity about Alan that made him feel like someone she should know. He had that sort of face, she decided. Even in their senior pictures, Alan still had that look of awkward adolescence. But by their high-school graduation photos, Vincent had grown into his body and she was certain he would have melted the heart of any girl his age. Yet there seemed to be relatively few girls. There were photos of the two looking uncomfortable, all trussed up in their tuxes next to their dates at junior and senior prom, and the odd snapshot here and there that included female companionship. But Vincent's reclusive tendencies seemed to have been already well established. Already he preferred to spend his time in the woods, a passion Alan seemed to share.

From the photos, it appeared the two were inseparable and yet their journey together seemed to end after high-school graduation. Or maybe Vincent's mother was just no longer there to take photos.

Stella leant over to check the shelves in case she had somehow missed another album.

'What are you doing?' The voice behind her was sharp, accusing, causing her to jump, as Vincent's large hand grabbed the volume away from her and pulled her to her feet. His eyes were cold, hard, and she felt a tremble in her belly that was not arousal. 'You know you're not supposed to be looking at those.'

Immediately her gaze dropped to his belt as he began to undo it, and she knew what was coming. How could she have forgotten?

Under no circumstances are Pets allowed to handle books, magazines, newspapers, computers, mobile phones or any other information device or print media. A Pet is never, without express permission, to browse, look through, or disturb in any way any of the personal belongings of her or his keeper.

Both of the above offences are to be punished severely.

Her heart raced in her throat, her palms were suddenly moist with nervous sweat. Vincent didn't take his eyes off her while he removed his belt. As it cleared the last loop, she felt more like a trapped animal than a Pet, and without thinking, she turned to run, but he caught her around the waist and pulled her close. 'I have to punish you, Stel. You know I do. You broke the rules.'

He surprised her by pushing her back onto the bed bum first. He lifted her legs together, as one would to change an infant's nappy. Then he pulled her toward him until both legs rested on his left shoulder exposing the whole of her arse at just the right angle for him to wield the belt, which he gripped tightly by both ends creating an elongated loop of leather. For a brief second the thought raced through her head that his belt was not a Pet Shop-approved spanking implement, but when the first lash came down hard against her arse, sounding like a gunshot and stinging like fire, it seemed irrelevant. She howled with rage, and struggled to keep from calling him the choice names that nearly erupted from her throat.

When the second lash came, she tried to buck away from it, but he held her tight, his face set and grim. 'Sh! Stella, Sh!' His voice sounded almost tender. 'I hate to do it, Stel, but I told you I'd discipline you, and you know the rules. We both know you do.' She could feel the rise and fall of his shoulders beneath her thighs, hear the wind of his breath racing in and out of him as he paused to examine his efforts, trailing the belt over her stinging butt, making her clench and hold herself tight, hoping that he was finished, but knowing that he wasn't.

'If you relax, sweetheart, it'll be easier for you.' And the next lash fell like fire, and she bellowed at the insult.

These were not the gentle smacks on the bottom she had issued Tino; the sting had bloomed into a full-blown inferno on her arse. And the humiliation stung even worse. She wanted to scream at him that she hadn't meant it, that she didn't deserve this, that she'd only wanted to know a little more about him. Surely that wasn't wrong. But each time the belt came down, she knew he was right. She had to be punished, and everything else went out of her mind but the sharp focus of the pain and her humiliation.

He paused again. 'Look at me, Stella.' His voice was forced, clipped between heavy breaths that seemed disproportionate to his task. 'Look at me when I punish you,' he said.

She forced herself to do as he commanded, holding his gaze as though her eyes were lasers and they could bore into his soul, make him feel what she felt.

'It hurts, sweetheart. I know it hurts. But when it's over, when you've taken your punishment, you'll understand, and you'll be a better Pet for it.'

By the time the last lash burned across her fevered bottom, she could hold back the tears no longer. She let them spill, but her gaze never wavered.

He stood over her breathing heavily, his drawn face now refracted through her tears.

She heard the clank of the buckle as he dropped the belt to the floor. She felt a stubbled kiss on the side of her thigh where it rested on his shoulder. 'Don't cry, Stel. I never wanted to

151

punish you, but you know I had to. Sh, sh, sh! It's over now. It'll be all right. It's over.'

She heard the zip of his fly and felt him shifting beneath her still raised legs. Dear God, surely he wasn't going to fuck her now! And yet as he lowered her legs from his shoulders and she winced as her sore bottom came to rest fully on the mattress, she could see he was heavily erect. The tip of his cock shimmered with precome.

'You would never have spanked Tino like that, would you?' he breathed. His face was flushed, his mouth set in a tight line.

Swallowing back tears, she tried to turn away, but he settled on the bed next to her and pulled her close.

'Perhaps you should have,' he whispered. Then he took her face in his hands and kissed her hard, kissed her until she stopped fighting him. 'Perhaps you should have spanked Tino like that,' he said again when he pulled away. He ran a hand down over her belly and slid two fingers between her labia. She gasped at the wet swell of herself against his stroking, amazed at the bloom of hunger for him that had somehow pushed its way through the rage and the pain.

He rolled onto his back and lifted her on top of him, careful of her burning bottom. Her pussy gaped for him, as it always did, hungry to be filled with him, as though he hadn't hurt her, as though he hadn't humiliated her, maybe even more so because of her punishment. And as he lifted his hips to push up into her, she trembled all over with want that made no sense to her at all. And yet it was there.

He rested a thumb against her clit and began to circle and press, and her brain practically buzzed with endorphins.

'You're my Pet, Stella. For this weekend, you're my Pet. I have to treat you as my Pet. And you have to understand. You have to understand what it means to be a Pet. And it's so much more than what the manual teaches you.'

It was crazy insane. She couldn't stop crying, but her cunt felt even more on fire than her wounded bottom. Vincent inside her. Vincent filling every part of her. That was all she could think about. That was what her world had narrowed to, and she wanted nothing else.

152

'It's all right, Stel, sweetheart,' he whispered between tight breaths. 'Let it out, darling, and you'll feel better.' His voice was heavy with tenderness she'd never heard there before. 'My naughty little Pet. You get your bottom spanked for being a bad girl, and even that makes your pussy wet. How can I possibly resist you?'

He held her there, rocking gently, thumb caressing her clit to its own heavy erection. He watched her, fondling her with a gaze so hungry it burned over her skin and flayed her to the depths until she was sure she could come just from his gaze. And she was so close, so fucking close.

But just when she was about to slip over the delirious precipice he'd led her to, he held her hips, held her very still on his cock. 'Hold it, Stella, make it last. Hold your heat. I don't want you to come yet.'

She squirmed and mumbled something incoherent. Pets don't speak, and in truth she felt as though she had totally forgotten how. And as he held her there, unable to move, her tears became tears of frustration.

'Sh, Stel, sh! Just hold it there, tight in your little cunt. Hold it for me.' Then he slid his hands down and gave her stinging arse cheeks a hard knead, hard enough to make her gasp and cringe. The cringe tightened her grip on his cock and made him groan in reply.

'Ah! There, you see? You feel it, don't you?' He gave another squeeze, and she saw red and would have bucked off him, had she not been so deeply impaled.

He held her unmoving, frustrated and aching, while he suckled his middle finger until it glistened with his saliva. Then, still holding her, he pushed and wriggled it into her back grip, causing her to pull a deep breath. With the other hand he squeezed her arse cheek in warning. 'Don't come, not yet. Hold it.'

She breathed in shallow little pants, trying to hold still against the invasion of her arsehole that only made the buzz in her cunt feel more urgent. Vincent's hands were large, his fingers thick, and the one up her anus felt nearly as big as his cock. It made her want to squirm and thrust against it like a cock. And yet at the same time it made her want to be still, like she was holding something in her that shouldn't be there – and yet something she didn't want to let go of.

'Relax for me.' His voice was calm, focused. 'Good girl, now push out. That's it.' She felt him manoeuvre his hand to catch the gush of her pussy juices from where his cock penetrated her. Then the well-lubricated second finger slipped into her tight hole, and this time she did squirm with the discomfort of it.

'Sh! Hold still for me, Stel, sweetheart, just a little bit longer then you can come and it'll be so good.' As the second finger slipped past her back opening to join the first, the sound that escaped her mouth was somewhere between a growl and a cry. He no longer prevented her from moving. Instead he now returned to circling her distended clit with the thumb of his other hand while the two fingers in her back-hole began to scissor ever so slightly, ever deeper inside her. Until at last they were able to reach forward just enough to stroke the thin wall of her rectum that separated them from his cock. He sighed his satisfaction, and she held her breath. For a second neither of them moved, everything felt suspended, heavy, like syrup too thick to pour. Then, with his gaze locked on her face, he began to stroke and press, and she felt the pressure of his stroking against his cock. The shudder of breath that ran up through him told her he did too.

'Now, Stel,' he forced the words out over a tightly held breath, and for the first time, she became aware that she wasn't the only one struggling to hold back the flood. 'Now we'll come together.' Then he began to thrust beneath her, somehow managing to keep his rhythm perfectly timed in both her stuffed holes and still press upward with his pubic bone enough to rake her clit with each thrust. The cocktail of feelings rushing through her dwarfed the pain of the spanking. She fucked him with anger and shame and lust and hurt and pain and need and other things she had no name for. She rode him down hard into the mattress in spite of the pulling stretch of her anus, in spite of the burning of her arse cheeks. And he took it, all of it. And when she passed the point of no return and

154

shuddered as though she would break apart into a thousand tiny pieces, he came in tremors that shook the bed, that shook his body, that shook her to the core. Then he pulled her down against his chest and smothered her face and throat and shoulders in breathless hungry kisses.

They never did get around to a real meal, but it didn't much matter. Sometime in the hours before dawn, she woke to find him standing naked in front of the sliding window and she thought how beautiful he was standing there bathed in moonlight, but the thought barely surfaced above consciousness before she slept again.

In the morning, she awoke to find Vincent gone and a smiling female handler waiting to bathe her. 'I'm sorry, Stella, darling, but Mr Evanston got called away unexpectedly. He's asked me to apologise to you for his untimely departure and to see that you get safely to the airport and back home to London.' In the gut-punch of emotions that followed, Stella couldn't keep from thinking about Audrey saying that withdrawal of affection was the worst punishment of all for a Pet.

Chapter Nineteen

THE PAIN IN HER bottom was lessening by the time she returned to work on Monday. The one in her heart, however, hadn't diminished at all. She wanted to believe – desperately wanted to believe – that Vincent really had been called away unexpectedly, but she didn't. If that had been the case, he would have at least woke her up to say goodbye.

According to the manual, punishment never resulted in a rift between the Pet and the keeper, but rather it was a bonding experience. She wouldn't have believed it had she not felt it for herself. If it were possible, the sex had been even better after Vincent had spanked her, and she was sure that there had been an openness between them that hadn't been there before. In fact, when they fell asleep in each other's arms, she felt closer to him than she had ever felt to anyone. And yet in the morning he had been gone. In the end there was no denying the pathetic truth. No matter what rubbish the manual spouted about bonding, she had still been nothing more than a glorified prostitute.

During the week, she had been busy with even more work than usual, for which she couldn't have been more grateful. Working to the point of exhaustion helped keep her mind off Vincent, off wondering why he had left. Most of her week was spent in research at remote sites, which also kept her blessedly free of Anne's unwelcome questions. Though strangely, Anne hadn't called, and her phone conversations with the Boss had been completely Strigida-focused with no mention of the Pet Shop or her ruined weekend with Vincent. There would be a confrontation, she was sure of that, but at the moment she just didn't have the heart for it. Maybe Anne already knew what had happened between her and Vincent and had the decency not to humiliate her further by prying.

It was Friday before Stella actually had a day in the office. Anne was always there by 8.30 a.m., but by nine o'clock she was still the only one at her desk. She was just beginning to get worried at 9.30 a.m. when the door opened and Anne entered with the Boss at her side.

There was a blush on the woman's cheeks that Stella hadn't seen before. A surreptitious look passed between Anne and the Boss, resulting in a hurried, if unnecessary straightening of jackets and collars, as though they'd just been caught having a quickie in the copy room. It was enough to tell Stella all she needed to know. The two had been together as sure as they were standing there, and the smile that passed between them said it was no one-night stand. Stella offered a shocked nod as they both greeted her. She had never suspected that they were more than just business associates.

'Stella, could I speak with you, if you've got a minute,' the Boss was saying as she jerked her attention back to business as usual.

She grabbed the Vanguard folder and followed him, wondering what the hell was going on as Anne headed off to her desk actually humming.

Inside the Boss's office, Stella barley got seated before he spoke. 'So, you've had your first weekend with a keeper.' He didn't bother with any preamble or any explanation as to why he was at the Pet Shop fucking Tino up the arse. Clearly he didn't consider it her business.

'Yes, sir.'

His smile was effusive, 'Then why so glum?'

She felt her face burning, felt the lump growing in her throat at the thought of waking up to find Vincent gone. 'It's just that ...' She looked down at her hands folded over the file in her lap. 'I don't think I did very well.'

'Nonsense!' He waved his hand as though he were about to conduct an orchestra. 'I have it on the highest authority that Mr Evanston was extremely pleased with you, extremely pleased.'

For a brief moment there was a flutter of hope in her chest, but then she reminded herself that of course Vincent would want to spare her any embarrassment. His praise of her didn't cost him anything, and didn't commit him to anything either.

The Boss didn't wait for her response. 'You're free to go home at noon today.' He looked down at his watch. 'A handler will be picking you up at six to take you to your next keeper.'

Stella felt heat flash up her throat and neck accompanied by a sudden wave of dizziness. 'So it's official then, I'm a prostitute now.' The words were out before she could stop them.

The Boss looked as though he'd been slapped, but he recovered quickly. 'You're a Pet, Stella. That's a far cry from a prostitute.' He held her gaze until she looked away. 'And your training isn't finished.' He rose and came around his desk to stand in front of her. He settled a curled finger beneath her chin and lifted her face so their eyes met. 'Besides, we both know what your motives are, and they have nothing to do with prostitution.'

She pulled away and lowered her eyes, fearing she might cry, wanting to tell him that she was pretty sure that motivation was no longer a valid one. She was pretty sure that this coming weekend all she would be was just a glorified prostitute, and she wasn't at all sure she could pull it off. But she said nothing.

He reached out his hand again and stroked her cheek then returned to his desk. 'Noon, Stella, then if you're not gone, I will physically escort you to the nearest taxi stand, are we clear?'

'Yes, sir.'

'Good. I expect you to go home and get some rest so you can actually enjoy the weekend. Are we clear?'

'Yes, sir.'

'Good.' He nodded to the door. 'Then send in Annie, if you would.'

She didn't miss the fact that, for the first time she could remember, he called his secretary by her first name.

'It's not bad enough they saddle me with Tino, now I get his female counterpart.' The familiar handler in his black suit pushed his way in and started tugging at Stella's clothes. 'Do I have "Torture me" written across my forehead? Is it bad karma? I swear I don't know what I did to deserve you two.'

She tried to shove his hands away. 'Look, I just can't do this. I'm just not cut out for the Pet Shop. I was told if I spoke to a handler it would mean one thing, that I wanted out, and, well, I want out, all right?'

'Bullshit! Of course you can do it, and it's not all right, now get out of your clothes and stop talking or I'll have to spank your arse, and don't think I won't do it. Fuckin' hell, first Tino, then you, and now both of you. They don't pay me enough for this.'

Suddenly she stopped fighting him, and he continued with the disrobing. 'Did you say Tino? Tino's with you.'

'I'm speaking English, aren't I?' He gave her a resounding smack across the arse he'd just bared and shoved the trench coat at her. 'Get into this, and you'd better manage to at least act horny 'cause I don't have time to strap you into the Foreplayer.' He smacked her bottom again, then wrestled her into the coat and jerked the sash tight. 'Now let's go unless you want both your arses spanked by your keeper for being late. Tino might like that just fine, but I'm not sure how your tender little bum would hold up.'

She was trembling so hard by the time she got to the van that the handler had to help her. He had taken the trench coat and practically shoved her into the large pet carrier before she realised she was sharing it with Tino, who scooped her to him in a tight embrace. The delicious scent of the big Pet filled her nostrils, made her cunt clench and her pulse race. But it was Vincent's scent too. Her nose couldn't be fooled now, no matter how differently the two of them behaved. And the clench in her cunt was followed quickly by an even harder clench in her heart and a knotting in her stomach as she thought of waking up to find him gone. What the fuck kind of game was he playing at?

With a growl that sounded too wild to belong to a Pet, she shoved her way out of his arms and elbowed him in the stomach generating enough momentum, even in the confined space, to make him grunt. The look of hurt on his face made her even more angry. How dare he be hurt? She wasn't the one who ran away, and she'd had just about enough of this emotional bait and switch. When he reached for her again, she bit him, hard. He sucked air and flinched. She wasn't certain, but she thought he might have actually had to wrestle back a curse.

She shoved her way to the far corner of the carrier, banging her head on the side as the van took off. The handler, who stayed in the back with the Pets, pounded on the top of the cage, misunderstanding what was going on.

'Tino, you keep your cock to yourself, you hear me? If I see any sign of spunk, or smell it, I'll tell your keeper to tie your pecker in a knot and make you hold it all weekend, don't think I won't.'

Not if hell freezes over will he find any spunk, Stella thought. At least not any having to do with her. She could see Tino's pulse pounding against his throat. His chest rose and fell like he would hyperventilate. And he was hard. He was always hard, damn him!

She pressed her cheek to the side of the pet carrier and tried to ignore the way his gaze bore into her, tried to ignore the press of their legs, which was unavoidable in the tight space. And the smell of him. My God, how could she ignore the smell of him? She dreamt of his scent. She masturbated to thoughts of his scent, and here she was trapped with it, and aching for it, and still so furious she could barely breathe. She wanted to yell and scream at him, she wanted to hit him with her fists, she wanted to know why, why he had left her. Instead she sat with her back pressed as tightly to the slats of the carrier as possible and tried to ignore him.

The next time he reached for her, she slapped him, slapped him hard enough to make her hand sting.

'What the hell are you two up to?' The handler rattled the pet carrier again. 'If I have to drag you both out and wear the spanker out on your bottoms, don't think I won't. Now knock it off.'

Stella pulled herself as far into the corner as she could get and tried to ignore the smell of Tino's arousal, made even more obvious by his erection bobbing against his thigh, the thigh he made no effort to pull out of her space. She shoved at him. But he didn't budge. She tried to turn her back on him as much as she could, but he pushed in still closer, not allowing her to ignore him.

He kept pushing at her and pushing at her until she kicked at him, which was useless with bare feet in such tight quarters. But he took the opportunity to pounce, nearly upsetting the pet carrier. The handler cursed and uttered a string of threats, most of which Stella didn't hear because she was fighting to keep from being pinned under Tino.

The van screeched to a halt with both pets being shoved by the momentum to the front of the carrier. Then the carrier door flew open and Tino was wrestled out by the handler and the driver. 'Goddamn it, I said knock it off!' The handler shoved Tino into the seat next to his, clamped his hands into cuffs attached to the side of the van, then snapped an equally attached short lead into the D-ring of his collar. Satisfied that the Pet would cause no further problems, he stormed out of the van and Stella could hear him shouting into his mobile something about all hell breaking loose.

Tino ignored it all, as though nothing else in the world had his attention but her. His gaze was now unreadable, a little more like Vincent, but then how the hell could she tell who he was playing at. The van driver stepped out to have a smoke, and she took advantage. 'You left me, you son of a bitch. You left me without telling me why.'

She swallowed the last word as the door to the van burst open and the handler shoved his way back in to sit down next to Tino. 'Lucky for you two miscreants the Professor assures me he'll have no trouble handling misbehaving Pets. I think he rather likes the idea. The thought of you two being soundly disciplined definitely warms the cockles of my heart.'

The driver got in and started the engine and they were off again. This time the look on Tino's face was utterly wounded, a look she couldn't bear. She closed her eyes, fighting back tears.

Chapter Twenty

'PERFECT, RIGHT ON TIME as always. And, oh, just look at them. Such a lovely pair they are.' The man who stood at the door to welcome the handler and his two Pets – now clothed in their typical outdoor attire and hopefully not looking too much worse for the wear – was middle-aged, tall and lean and not hard to look at with his intelligent eyes and thick mop of dark hair.

An archaeologist, the handler had informed them as he'd dressed them, a man way too busy for a relationship, and too kinky for most anyway. He always arranged to have Pets in pairs. He didn't care what sex they were. When celebrating his last successful dig, the handler informed them, he'd had three Pets, and they all rode back in their pet carriers sitting very carefully. 'Has a heavy hand, that one,' the handler had said. 'And just what you two deserve. Tino's arse has calluses from the spankings he's taken, but Stella,' he gave a wicked little laugh, 'well, I'll try to remember to bring a cushion for your tender little bum on the ride home.'

With a strange knot of emotion tightening her chest, Stella recalled the Boss saying Tino stayed in the dungeon because he was always getting punished, and Vincent had said after spanking her that maybe she should spank Tino harder. Was that why he left, because she didn't spank Tino hard enough? She was still thinking about spanking Tino when the keeper shooed the handler away and motioned the two Pets into his lounge.

'Shall we undress our beautiful little bitch first, Tino?'

Stella's gut tightened at the use of the word, bitch. She'd never liked it when men used what she considered derogatory

162

terms for women. But then the man added, 'I specifically asked for a bitch on heat, ready for you to service, Tino. Though I hear she's a feisty one, one you may have to fight for. All the better, I say. Oh it's always so very exciting how the rutting ritual plays itself out.' She was reminded once again that they were, after all, Pets, and a bitch on heat was exactly what she was playing at. As she sat down on the floor and lifted her arms for Professor to take off her top, she tried to ignore Tino's ravenous stare.

Tino paid no attention to their keeper. He had eyes only for Stella, as the keeper removed her trousers and continued his running commentary of how hot and horny this little bitch was. All the while the keeper stripped Stella, Tino scooted closer and closer to her. As the trousers came down, he moved in for a sniff and a lick of her exposed pussy, but before she could stop herself, she shoved him back, landing a kick on the inside of his thigh that made him growl as she crab-walked away from him.

The keeper chuckled gleefully. 'Looks like you've got your work cut out for you, big boy. I wager she'll warm up to you though.' He pushed Stella's legs open. 'You see, she needs your cock badly. She'll come around when she's horny enough then she'll be raising that lovely fanny to you, begging you to mount her.'

Stella fought down the blush that rose to her face. He made her feel like some kind of breeding stock thinking only with her cunt. And to her humiliation, she knew he was right; she was wet, desperately wet for Tino, and that made her even more furious.

Professor left Stella to watch while he set to work removing Tino's clothes. 'Oh yes, you'll want him soon enough, Stella, darling. He's enough to drench that little pussy of yours and make your girlie lips swell with heat. He ran his hand down Tino's chest then began to tug his trousers off over his hips, freeing his cock, which arched lewdly in Stella's direction.

When Tino was naked, he lunged for Stella, but Professor grabbed his collar and held him. 'Not so fast, Tino. You'll get her when I say you can have her. And that isn't going to

happen until she gets acquainted with me. You know the rules.'
He turned his attention to Stella. 'Tino is already well
acquainted with me, darling, and you will be too before the
weekend's over.' He sat down in an over-stuffed chair and
opened his legs. Stella positioned herself to sniff and caress
and lick, but not without making sure Tino had a perfect view
of her gape, a fact that made her even more furious. She wasn't
a cock tease, and this kind of behaviour was no solution for her
anger.

Professor was heavily erect through his trousers, and he
smelled piquant, like good clean male sweat.

*We recommend that keepers use no soap, shower gel or
deodorant in their last shower before they meet their Pet.
Smells of perfume only confuse the Pets' finely honed sense of
smell and makes it more difficult for them to get to know their
keepers, which means the keeper will have to wait longer
before initiating sexual contact.*

Even as she sniffed Professor, his scent was overshadowed by
Tino's scent, which was all over her body after their tussle in
the van.

'I smell your little pussy, Stella, dear,' Professor said,
cupping her breasts as though he were mentally weighing them.
'You're such a horny little girl, aren't you? I don't think the
Pet Shop has ever sent me two more outrageously horny Pets
than you two. Would you like to suck my cock for me, darling?
Wouldn't that be a good way of getting to know Professor?' He
was already undoing his fly. She sat back on her haunches
between his legs, heart racing, suddenly struggling to breathe.
This was it, then. No matter what the Boss said, she was a
prostitute, and she was a prostitute because she had chosen to
be one in order to chase down a man who left her without
saying why. Well, she got what she asked for, didn't she? And
this man in front of her, none of it was his fault. He was just a
keeper, and he had, no doubt, paid handsomely for her services.

'Come, darling, don't be shy.' He manoeuvred his cock free
enough to give her easy access. 'You can see I'm ready for

you.'

His cock was large, almost as large as Tino's. He offered it to her as though it were the special treat he knew she'd been waiting for, as though he fully expected appreciation for such a delicious offering. 'Come on, Stella, dear, be a good Pet and make Professor come.'

She took a deep breath. It was time she stopped whinging and just got on with it. She gave his balls a stroke and tried to give him her coyest Pet look, but just as she was about to take him in her mouth, Tino tackled her from behind, dragged her away from Professor, rolled her onto her back and straddled her. Before she could do more than yelp her surprise, Professor had Tino by the collar and physically dragged him off her.

He caught Tino off guard, jerking him back on his haunches. Then he pressed a knee into his ribs, which in conjunction with the stranglehold on his collar, was enough to subdue him. The force with which he manhandled the big Pet took Stella's breath away.

She was surprised at the soft chuckle that passed the handler's relaxed lips. 'You want her that badly, do you, Tino? Mmm, and I sense a little jealousy from you, don't I? Never sensed that from you before. Very poor form to interrupt our little bitch when she's about to suck her keeper's cock. But then males in rut are often poorly behaved, and they're not very rational, are they? Always thinking with their cocks. Oh, this is going to be such an interesting weekend.' He tisk-tisked. 'You'll get her in time. Maybe. But not now you won't. Now you know what you'll get, don't you, Tino?'

She had seen it before, she had seen Tino hang his head like a bad little Pet and turn his bottom toward his keeper to be punished for misbehaving. When it had been her doing the punishing, her pulse had raced and her pussy had practically gushed, but what she felt as Professor redid his straining fly and pulled his belt free from his trousers in nearly the same way Vincent had done, was much more visceral, much more closely linked to fear. But not so close that she didn't still feel it in her pussy.

'If first impressions are any indication,' Professor was

saying, 'I think our sexy little bitch would love nothing better than to watch you take your punishment, don't you agree, Tino? I get the distinct impression she feels you deserve punishing at least as much as I do, so perhaps I'll punish you for both of us. Yes. I think that's exactly what I'll do.' He stepped closer and ran the edge of the belt up between Tino's arse cheeks, making him clench.

Professor motioned to a heavy oak coffee table in front of the sofa. Tino moved to bend over the table, bracing himself with his arms stiff against it and his legs wide apart. As he did so, he shot a surreptitious glance over his shoulder at Stella.

'Perhaps once she's seen you properly punished with your arse cheeks all red and burning, she'll be a little more receptive to your cock, Tino.' He tut-tutted. 'My goodness, one can only imagine what you've done to her to make a bitch with such an obviously needy little cunny fight you like a wildcat.'

The first lash with the belt split the air with an invasive crack. Tino flinched and sucked oxygen, but Stella cried out.

Professor raised his hand to Stella without looking at her. 'It's all right, my darling. Believe me, Tino's arse can take it, and he bloody well deserves it, I'm sure we both agree. Now you just sit back and watch, my sweet little bitch, while I punish our naughty, rutting stud here.'

Strange that she should feel a sense of camaraderie with this man, strange that the sense of dread and fear she felt should be mingled with so many other feelings, and somewhere in that mix was righteous anger. But who'd have thought righteous anger could be so arousing? She surprised herself at the very thought, and when the next lash came loud and vicious, leaving an angry red mark across Tino's beautiful bottom, the wet, squirmy buzz in her cunt was shocking. In spite of the taut nerves that almost made her stomach hurt, she found herself inching closer as the next lash came. Then Professor paused to run a hand, almost tenderly, along the crimson striping now marring Tino's pale bottom.

'Come here, my little bitch, I know you want a closer look. I can feel your tension, your arousal. Clear across the room I can feel it.' He beckoned to Stella without looking at her. He motioned her to sit on the floor next to where Tino bent over the coffee table. To her astonishment, Tino was as hard as ever. 'Cup his balls, darling,' Professor commanded. 'Go on. It's all right. There, you see? You feel how heavy he is, how badly he wants to come. Now take his cock in your mouth. Don't be afraid. You've done nothing wrong.'

She did as she was told.

'As deep as you can. Go on. That's my girl, now suck him.'

This time Tino cried out, and a shudder passed up through his spine. He lifted a hand to her head and curled his fingers in her hair, but Professor knocked his hand away.

'That's enough, Stella. We're not ready to let him come just yet, are we?'

She pulled away trembling so hard she practically fell backward on her butt.

'You see how aroused he is, Stella, darling. You see how badly he needs to come, even with me punishing him.' Then he turned his attention to Tino and reached forward to tenderly cup his tight jaw. 'But he won't come. He won't come until he's been fully punished for all his bad behaviour. He knows how much sweeter it'll be then, darling. Oh, he knows, don't you, Tino?'

Tino's lovely face was already red and perspiring from the hard lashes, and as the keeper landed another, she flinched in sympathy, but found herself unable to take her eyes off his cock, the way it surged, the way the tip already glistened with precome. How could what was so obviously painful to him arouse him so? How could it make her so hot? And why did she want to participate in something that only a few days ago she would have thought totally perverted?

She caught Professor's gaze between lashes of the belt and rose to sit open legged on the sofa just in front of Tino, just beyond his reach. The keeper's wicked chuckle told her he approved. She held his gaze for a moment longer before sliding her fingers down between her legs to caress and fondle her cunt. With her other hand she stroked and pinched her nipples to aching heavy points.

'I see you understand fully, little one,' Professor spoke in a voice that was thick with his own arousal. 'Go on then. You have my permission to play with your wet little quinny. And, Tino, you watch her. If you look away, you'll make your punishment even worse, and you know I'm not talking about my belt.'

She sat on the sofa spread wide. Along with the cracking of the belt and the noisy intake of oxygen, the wet squelch of her fingers joined the soundtrack as they shoved in and out of her creamy gash and raked rhythmically over her clit.

'Her eyes, Tino,' Professor barked. 'Look at her eyes, don't look at her cunt. You know what she's doing with her cunt, and you know it doesn't involve you. You look her in the eyes, and you don't look away until I say.'

Tino obeyed, but not before the next lash scrunched his face in pain, and something more than pain, something that made Stella want to run away, on the one hand, and on the other hand it made her crazy horny. She felt like the burning in her cunt could easily outstrip that in Tino's bottom if she didn't get some relief soon. She squirmed and bounced on the couch, unable to believe she could even think of being aroused when Tino was in pain, but she was. She held his gaze, pouring all her anger, all her frustration, all of the other things that were too complicated for words into that gaze, as though she could send it all straight to his brain, straight to his soul and make him hurt like she had hurt when he left her.

She didn't know how many lashes he'd had, but silent stoicism had given way to deep-chested grunts and groans that vibrated up through her and made her ache and hurt and want. Finally, with the last hard lash, he cried out; they cried out together. As his knees buckled, she was half over the coffee table toward him before the keeper stopped her.

'Not yet, Stella. I'm not finished with him yet.' He dropped the belt and unzipped his trousers to release his own straining erection. But as she started to sink to her knees in front of him, he shook his head. 'It was Tino who interrupted my oral pleasure, darling, therefore it's Tino who must make amends before he can mount you.' He held her gaze. 'That is if he has expiated his bad behaviour enough to be worthy of your cunt.

If not, then I shall take care of you myself, darling, while he watches.'

He seated himself on the coffee table in front of Tino, who offered her a quick glance then took Professor's cock deep into his mouth, an act which made the keeper groan and hitch his breath, an act which made her cunt grasp hungrily.

'Tino is never more exquisite than when he's contrite, penitent, well punished, with his bottom burning like fire. Feel it, my little bitch, feel how hot it is.'

The growl that escaped Tino's throat was leonine as she laid a hand on his burning arse, noticing how his buttocks contracted beneath her touch, how his anus gripped to a tight little knot of muscle. She couldn't resist. She couldn't resist the heat radiating off his lovely red backside, nor the delicious view between his thighs of his tight balls and jutting penis. She lowered her head and ran her tongue from the top of his left thigh all the way up over his clenching arse cheek, and did the same to the other one, feeling the resulting shudder move up his spine.

'Ah, there, you see, Tino,' Professor spoke between efforts to breathe. 'I think she's forgiven you.'

She licked every inch of his scorched bottom, at first only with careful, tentative licks. Then she graduated to wide flat presses of her tongue, and finally little circular lavings that ended in tight suckling kisses until he thrust back against her in rhythm with his fellating of Professor's cock. Professor's hands were curled in Tino's hair. His eyes were locked on Stella, whose tongue bath of Tino's wounded arse could end nowhere else but in a tense dance and thrust against his pucker. His shivers and tremors resulted in a warning from Professor for him to hold his load. It was a warning Stella knew was unnecessary. Tino would hold his load as long as he had to, as long as it took for him to be able to mount her and empty himself into her cunt. It was a privilege she reckoned he had earned.

Just then Professor caught a harsh breath and bit back a curse. 'I'm coming now, Tino, swallow down my wad like a good boy. Oh Jesus, that's it!' A few more grunts and thrusts and Tino pulled away wiping his mouth on the back of his hand.

Once Professor could breathe enough to speak, he turned his attention to her. 'You may have him now, Stella, if he's earned your forgiveness. He's ready for you.'

This time, as Tino turned to her, he waited, holding her gaze expectantly, waited for her wishes. He was a Pet, they were both Pets, and suddenly her mind was full of how it was for them the first time. She lowered herself onto hands and knees and raised her bottom to him, legs open, pussy slippery and gaping. He practically fell on top of her, scooping her to him. The smell of him was different, spicier, more urgent – if smell could be more urgent. And he pushed into her more urgently. He slid between her labia up to the grudging clench of her opening, which yielded to the delicious pressure of him, yielded completely until he totally filled her. The high-voltage thrum in her clit practically ignited as he slipped a hand down to tweak her. That he had enough concentration left to give a thought to her pleasure after what he had endured amazed her.

He bit the back of her neck and tugged her hair back hard, and she let him. She let him possess her, mount her, rut with her.

Professor shed his clothes and came to sit on the floor next to them, positioning himself so he could easily cup and caress Stella's breasts or finger Tino's gripping anus if he chose. And he did choose. 'That's my darlings. That's my lovelies. Now everything's OK. Now you can fuck, my horny little Pets. Oh I'm sure you must both be so terribly uncomfortable. Now you can have your bitch, Tino, and she'll accept you and let you make her feel better too. Oh so lovely! Oh so good.'

Suddenly all circuits overloaded and Stella bucked back against Tino and screamed her orgasm until her throat was raw, shaking and convulsing her loss of control. He responded by shoving his own release up in her so far that she swore she could feel him coming just beneath her heart.

'Oh yes, my darlings, that's it, come for Professor, come for your keeper, let me see how hard you can come.' There was a sharp, tight grunt and a warm spurt of the keeper's semen against the side of Stella's breasts and up over Tino's arched back. Then they all collapsed in a slippery, sweaty, sated heap.

That night when they had feasted on sea bass, had several more serious romps on the lounge floor, and had been well bathed, Tino curled around Stella in the very large pet bed at the foot of the Professor's big four-poster. As she snuggled down tightly against the slow even rise and fall of his chest, Stella remembered Vincent saying, after he'd spanked her, that being a Pet was so much more than what was in the manual. There was no denying, he'd got that right.

Chapter Twenty-one

STELLA WAS AMAZED HOW fast the weekend past, and how much she actually liked Professor. When he said his goodbyes to her and Tino and sent them on their way with the surly handler, it was with very affectionate kisses and caresses, affectionate enough to leave her wet and Tino visibly hard through his thin trousers. And Tino – being Tino – made no effort to hide his full package, nor was he subtle about rubbing it against her bottom while they waited for the handler to open the back of the van.

Inside, the handler stripped them, completely ignoring Tino's erection. Probably a routine sight for him, Stella thought, as he shooed them into the Pet carrier together. It wasn't that routine for her, though, and despite the very long sweaty romp they had barely managed to get showered and dressed from before the handler showed up, she was hungry for him again.

The handler chuckled as Tino arranged himself to sit carefully inside the carrier. 'Got your arse spanked good, did you? No doubt you deserved it. What about you, Stella?' He patted her bottom gently and, when she didn't flinch, he smiled knowingly. 'Guess our good Professor had other plans for you. Wanted to watch you fuck Tino's brains out, did he? Has kinky tastes, that one.'

Stella couldn't keep from smiling, wondering just exactly how the handler would know about Professor's kinky tastes. Once he had them settled, he buckled himself into the seat at the side and gave the driver the go-ahead, then he picked up his rumpled copy of *The Sun* and began to read.

The driver hadn't gone more than a couple of blocks when

Tino shifted himself with tight little grunts and sighs that rumbled deep in his chest. She moved to accommodate him, assuming his arse was hurting and he was trying to get comfortable. He nuzzled and pushed at her until she lay curled on her side, but instead of tucking in against her body in his favourite spoon position, he lay down facing her with his forehead pressed to her upper thighs. He shoved and nuzzled and nipped until she opened her legs for him. Then he scooted in to rest his head on her bottom thigh. He wriggled and twisted until his face was only millimetres away from her cunt. She tried to push him away, not wanting him to get another spanking and not wanting one herself, but when he gave her heavy clit a deep, suckling kiss that made her already trembling pussy shudder, she figured the crime was worth the punishment.

He made deep thrusting forays with the flat of his tongue between the swollen pout of her labia, working his way from the tight stretch of her perineum forward to the hard press of her clit, pulling at it, nursing on it as though it were a nipple ready to let down sweet milk, and she was letting down all right. Her pussy was drenched and fragrant with the want of him. His hand, pressed to the small of her back, pulled her still closer until the shape of his lovely stubbled face, right down to the solid jut of his chin and the sweep of his jaw raked her with tetchy, ticklish caresses.

His straining cock brushed her cheek, silky smooth hardness demanding attention. It was a demand she couldn't refuse. She palmed his tender buttocks to pull him close and felt him flinch, but the flinch was lost in a shudder and a groan that vibrated deliciously against her inner lips as she took his penis into her mouth and cupped the cool heft of his balls, massaging the bulge of them with tight circlings of her thumb.

It was heaven. It was absolute heaven, caught in the time warp that was making love to Tino. She shifted and writhed and rubbed at his face with her receptive, grasping cunt marking him with her scent. And when they were finished, he would carry her smell, carry the weight of her desire as surely as if she had collared him and bound him to her. And she would take his semen in her mouth, swallow it down to her centre, and perhaps she would rub some of it across her breasts and dabble it on her pulse points and carry his scent as a reminder to anyone who should wonder that she was his, and he had marked her as such.

She was completely lost in the feel of him on her body, when he shifted. Without pulling away from his lapping at her pussy, he rose and lifted one leg over her until he straddled her face. Then he positioned himself above the O of her open mouth and lowered his hips until she could just make out the clench of his anus on her horizon as she took his cock back between her lips. She ran splayed hands up the sides of his tensing thighs and onto his hips to control his downward thrusting. He cupped her arse cheeks to bring her still closer to the wild thrust and lave of his tongue dance, the rake of bared teeth and the tug of his pursed lips.

It was as she shifted to accommodate him that she caught the handler's eyes above the edge of his paper. She paused in her ministering to Tino's cock only for the briefest moment. Of course he had to know what they were up to. Tino had long since ceased any efforts to be quiet, and she wasn't doing a very good job of keeping her own passions under wraps. But it didn't matter. He could pull Tino off her if he wanted. He could punish them both, but he surely couldn't expect them to ignore their animal nature in such close quarters when they were both so tight with need. They had done their duty for the weekend; surely they deserved this much.

As though he had read her mind, the handler lowered his eyes once again to the paper like he had seen nothing.

Tino's thrusts became stiff and tense. She pulled on the length of him until her jaw ached, and yet her mouth was on autopilot. Her brain had completely relocated itself to the building tension within her pelvic girdle. They were close, both so close. Surely her grip on his arse must be painful, but he was too far gone to notice. She could barely move her hips the way he had her cupped to him, the way his face was burrowed against her pout. And yet, she could move just enough. Her body threatened to break bones with the violence of the orgasm that raged up through her, that caused her to pull even harder on him, hard enough that his hips jerked and his cock unloaded its fullness in the back of her throat.

When they were done coming, he rearranged himself, pulled her tight against the curve of his body and they slept.

Stella was surprised to find herself at the Pet Shop rather than her own home as she expected. Audrey met her at the van. They watched the handler lead Tino away, grumbling under his breath about his bad karma and misbehaving Pets. Tino kept pulling against the lead, glancing over his shoulder at Stella. When at last he was out of sight, Audrey spoke. 'After you're bathed and dressed, the Boss and Ms O'Kelly are here to see you.'

A half an hour later, with Stella dressed in the clean clothes of a Pet about to go to a keeper, Audrey escorted her from the annexe to the main house, a place she had not been allowed access to during her training. The handler led her through the long, dark-panelled hallways to a conservatory full of exotic plants and comfortable rattan furniture. On a sofa that looked out onto the grounds behind the house sat the Boss and Anne O'Kelly. On the coffee table in front of them was a tray with a steaming pot of tea, a plate of sandwiches and another of cakes.

'Stella, darling,' the Boss greeted her with a kiss on each cheek and Anne followed suit. 'We hear Professor was very pleased with you and Tino this weekend. Congratulations on a job well done, dear.'

She couldn't keep from blushing. How hard was it to allow herself to be endlessly fucked and fondled by Tino while another man watched and wanked? Thoughts of the weekend were enough to cause her pussy to tingle in spite of being very well satisfied.

'Please, sit.' Anne said. 'And have something to eat. You must be famished.' Anne poured tea and they both made a pretence of eating, but Stella made no pretence at all. She was starving, and Pets never got too concerned with proper tea-time etiquette.

'You probably wonder why we had you brought here rather

than sending you home, Stella.' The Boss made no effort to explain what he assumed she was intelligent enough to have already figured out, that he and Anne were both involved in the running of the Pet Shop.

There was a long pause before Stella realised she was expected to respond. She was amazed how easy it was to get used to not speaking. She swallowed a mouthful of smoked salmon and cucumber sandwich without chewing. 'Yes. I do,' she replied dutifully, her voice sounding strange in her ears after two days of not using it.

'Anne and I agree that you've more than exceeded our expectations in your work at Strigida. Vanguard, as well as the other organisations you've had contact with on Strigida's behalf are singing your praises. But ...'

'But that's not why we want to talk to you.' Anne took over. 'We hired you knowing full well you'd do a great job at Strigida, just as I'm sure you knew you would, but what you may not know is all the parameters you're being judged according to and why.'

The Boss took over again. 'We suspected when we hired you that you had other gifts, latent gifts that even you might not know about, gifts that could do Strigida a lot more good in other ways than you working as my assistant. I don't have to tell you how important the work Strigida does is. You've worked with us long enough to know some of the significant environmental projects we've funded and to know how much those projects cost to bring to completion. But no company's resources are limitless. Mind you, with careful management, Strigida has had the capital to finance a lot of environmentally worthy causes for a good number of years.' He waved a hand as though he were batting away an insect. 'I'm not telling you anything that isn't already on the Strigida website.' He held her gaze. 'But there are things that aren't on that website, Stella, things that you should know. In recent years that capital has increased drastically allowing Strigida to take on projects of a much larger magnitude. That increase in funds has come from one source. It's a surprising source, actually, one no one ever imagined would generate such a cash cow. The Pet Shop.'

'What?' Stella burnt her tongue on a mouthful of tea.

Anne offered her a tolerant smile. 'I know it's hard to believe, and an amazing story actually. It all came about by accident.' She glanced at the Boss as though expecting him to corroborate her story. 'It happened on a drunken bet, but the money from the bet was pledged for a major project Strigida was working on at the time. The discussion, I believe, had something to do with man's responsibility toward his animal cousins. Someone brought up the fact that we could hardly expect humans to take care of their wild cousins when they didn't even take proper care of their own pets. And one thing led to another. Anyway, in the end a bet was made, a bet that certain people, people who had no shortage of funds at their disposal couldn't resist.

'The wager was that they couldn't live like animals – like pets totally dependent on their keepers – for a whole weekend. It went further to predict that their keepers would not be able to take proper care of them for a weekend. The sociology of the whole idea was fascinating, as you can imagine, and the concept too intriguing not to try – especially when money was no object.

'The rules and regulations were all drawn up, the Pets and keepers all designated, and the experiment took place over a long Easter weekend.' She chuckled and sipped her tea. 'You won't find that story on the Pet Shop website, though I certainly think it should be. As for the sex part of the story, well surely you can see how one thing leads to another when you keep naked humans around the house, naked humans who need bathing and feeding and grooming. Anyway the proceeds from the weekend fattened Strigida coffers, and the bet and the accompanying experiment became gossip, sort of an underground cult, and more and more people wanted to have a Pet of their own for a night or a weekend. They were all willing to pay handsomely for the privilege, all willing to keep it discrete so the service could continue.'

'But that's not where the real money comes from,' the Boss joined in. 'The real money comes from people, wealthy people mostly, who want to *be* Pets. They don't necessarily want to be with a keeper, though a surprising number of them do. But some just want to be Pets, you know, to be pampered and loved and cared for, to be told what to do and not have to worry about any responsibilities. Remember, many of these are very powerful people, people used to being in control, but longing to let someone else take charge for a little while. Of course, by the time the apparatus to make all this happen was set in place, sex was a major component. The Pet Shop Pets wanted a relaxed, comfortable atmosphere where sex would be as natural and open as it is for animals, but they also wanted the pleasures afforded very pampered pets. Voilà! The Pet Shop was born.'

Anne continued. 'For some the Pet Shop is their summer home, for others it's a weekend retreat. There are even a few that have taken up permanent residence here at the Pet Shop. And those who want to be Pets without having to service a keeper pay handsomely for the privilege, very handsomely indeed. In a way, it's like buying in to a very expensive, very exclusive timeshare. And that's where the serious money comes from.' She sipped her tea absently. 'That and good investments, of course.'

'I don't see what any of this has to do with me,' Stella said. 'I'm not a paying Pet.'

'It has everything to do with you precisely because you're not a paying Pet,' the Boss said. 'Eight years ago when I could see the Pet Shop's potential, I realised I wouldn't be able to run both Strigida and the Pet Shop, so I hired Anne to take over and build the Pet Shop as a business.' He offered her a confidential smile. 'A very unorthodox business, of course, and one we've had to manage very discretely. But under Anne's control, the Pet Shop has grown and thrived. In fact, it's grown so much, and the demand has become so large, that we're planning to open a North American branch. Since Anne has been in on the ground floor with the UK Pet Shop, who better to be in charge of setting up its North American sister shop.'

'That being the case,' Anne said, 'we need someone to take over the UK Pet Shop when I leave.'

There was a pregnant pause, and Stella nearly dropped her teacup. 'And you want me to do it?'

They both smiled and nodded.

Before she could respond, the Boss spoke. 'You would continue on at Strigida, as Anne has, in the guise of my executive secretary, but all of your responsibilities would be at the Pet Shop. If you take us up on our offer, your salary will be double what it is now at Strigida with a very hefty benefits package, not the least of which includes unlimited access to any of the keeper-trained Pets.'

Stella's salary at Strigida was substantial. The thought of doubling it left her breathless. As for access to the Pets, well, there was only one Pet she wanted access to, and she wasn't quite sure why the thought of being able to have Tino at her command whenever she wanted him didn't quite feel right.

Stella suddenly forgot about how hungry she was. 'So all of this has been a test? And offering me Tino in the beginning?'

'Tino was available,' the Boss said. 'And we figured if you would accept our gift, and if you could handle Tino, then you were definitely the right choice for the position. And all of your interaction with the Pet Shop so far has done nothing but confirm you as our choice.'

Silence stretched between them. Outside in the garden an owl trilled. The Boss's cup clinked as he sat it back on the saucer. 'Well? What do you think?'

Stella remembered to breathe. 'Just because I can be a Pet doesn't mean I can run the Pet Shop.'

'Of course not, hon,' Anne said. 'It was other skills, skills you've demonstrated at Strigida that convinced us you could run the Pet Shop. The fact that you have Pet experience, and can handle tough Pets so well, that means you'll understand the inner workings of what makes the Pet Shop such a special place in a way I've never been able to. And frankly, your lack of family who might cause a conflict of interest, along with your noted reputation among your previous employers for being a workaholic were factors in our choice as well.'

'As for taking the reins of the Pet Shop,' the Boss said, 'of course we'll see to your training. You'll be working with the best people, and we'll make sure that you're not left on your own until you're ready.'

'I'm flattered that you're considering me.' Stella wasn't sure that she actually was flattered, but her default was always polite business mode. She took a deep breath, wiped suddenly sweaty palms on her trousers and continued. 'This is too much for me to take in right now. I didn't expect this, and I need to think about it.'

'Of course, of course.' The Boss offered a reassuring smile. 'We didn't expect an answer tonight. We know it's a big decision, and an important one.'

Anne leant so far forward that her arse was nearly off the sofa. 'What we need to know is that you're considering it, Stel.' Suddenly she sounded like Stella's friend again. She reached out, took Stella's hand and squeezed. 'We need to know that it's a position you could see yourself in.'

Stella nodded, suddenly finding it difficult to speak. 'It is. Of course, but–'

'But you're exhausted, hungry, and you need some space to think.' The Boss spoke as though he'd read her mind. 'We understand completely. When you get home, you'll find a new password in your email. It'll allow you access to areas of the Pet Shop website that will answer some of your questions and perhaps help you with your decision. Then we'd like to bring you back here tomorrow afternoon to show you around the place, give you a feel for it – from a non-Pet perspective, of course – and answer any questions you may have. There'll be dinner and a chance to meet a few of the more senior handlers.' He made a gesture around the conservatory. 'A room's been prepared for you here in the cottage for the night if you'd like, and a limo will take you back to London in the morning.' He held her gaze. 'I'm sorry to say Tino won't be here to share your bed. He's been called away to other responsibilities.' She didn't miss the visible tension in Anne's shoulders at the mention of Tino sharing her bed. 'So if you prefer to go home, there's a limo waiting to take you back. Of course you won't be expected in the office tomorrow. After all, it's our fault that you're getting home late, and you'll be expected here later in the day.'

Feeling strangely disconnected, Stella chose the latter.

'I don't like her connection to Tino and Vincent. We could lose her if she finds out Vincent's involvement.' Anne spoke as the limo pulled away taking Stella back to London. 'God, I told you from the beginning we shouldn't have sent her Tino.'

'And I told you, I had no more choice in sending her Tino than you did. The decision wasn't mine to make.'

'Lots of decisions don't seem to be yours to make any more, or mine, and that's a part of what bothers me.'

'Annie, darling, Vincent wants Stella to take over the Pet Shop too, remember? That's why he sent her Tino.'

'He did want her to take over the Pet Shop.' Anne shivered and pulled the light cardigan she wore tight around her to ward off a chill that had nothing to do with the weather. 'But that was before he started wanting her for other things, and those other things have nothing whatsoever to do with business, we both know that. Whatever the relationship is between the two of them, it's a complication that frightens me, Alan, a complication that could ruin all our plans.'

He slipped an arm around her and caressed the nape of her neck. 'Are you so anxious to get away from me, Annie?'

She shrugged free of him. 'Don't do this, Alan. Don't make me the villain. This has always been the plan. It's a part of why I wanted to keep our relationship on a business level.' She turned on her heels and headed back toward the big house, but he caught her by the arm.

'Things change, Annie. Plans change.' He pulled her close and kissed her. When he released her, he offered a tight smile. 'Don't worry about Vincent. I'll talk to him. I'm sure he doesn't want Stella to know about his involvement in our plan any more than you do.'

'Oh I'm sure he doesn't want her to know either. In fact he probably wants her to know even less than I do. I'm just not sure his reasons are still the same as ours. In fact, every time the two of them are together, I'm less and less sure, especially when I see how little control we actually have over the situation.'

As Alan led her upstairs to the suite they would share for

the night, Anne found herself wondering about his reasons as well. As he undressed her and explored her, as that familiar feeling of euphoria, the feeling she only had when she was with him, expanded in her chest and filled every cell in her body, for a brief second, just before he entered her, just before he filled her until she was too full to think of anything but him, she doubted her own reasons.

Chapter Twenty-two

STELLA WOULD HAVE NOTICED him standing there if she hadn't still been ruminating over the Boss and Anne's proposal to run the Pet Shop as she climbed the stairs to her flat. She had just dug the keys out of her pocket when she stopped short and uttered a little cry.

Standing by her door with his arms folded tightly across his chest was Vincent. He was dressed in jeans and a light cotton shirt. In spite of the fact that he was well scrubbed, the stubble was gone from his chin and his hair was almost manageable, he breathed as though he had been running a marathon. His gaze was hard. His mouth set in a tight line. 'What took you so long?'

'The driver took the scenic route.' Actually, she didn't know what route the driver took because the windows of the limo had been especially darkened to prevent VIP Pets from seeing where they were. She tried to smile, but she could feel her lips twitch at one corner.

She fumbled with the keys then dropped them, but he caught them before they hit the floor and handed them back to her, moving close behind her like an impatient shadow waiting as she struggled with the lock. He was close enough that she could feel the body heat radiating off him.

'I wasn't expecting you,' she breathed. She was furious at herself that she was nervous; even more furious that it was so totally obvious.

He placed his hand over hers and steadied her. The key slid home and the door opened. 'Tino didn't get nearly enough of you this weekend,' he whispered against her ear.

'Tino's not here.' She shrugged him off and went inside

with him right behind her.

She barely managed to shut the door before he pinned her against it and kissed her hard, his tongue slipping between her lips and making itself at home like it owned the place. And her tongue was a willing welcome party. He didn't bother to pull away as he spoke, just pressed his words into her mouth with little nips and darts. 'Do you have a problem with that?'

'What?' she replied, nibbling at his lip. 'That Tino takes the punishment and you get the rewards?' She lowered her hands to his denim-covered arse cheeks and gave them a hard knead, hard enough to make him suck a pained breath. 'Why should I have a problem with that?'

He let out a low, wicked chuckle and rubbed against her until she could feel the press of his heavy penis through the tight stretch of his jeans. 'I promise I'll share with him, 50-50 just like I shared his sore ass.' He reached to pull her T-shirt off over her head but she slapped his hands away and sidestepped.

'I'm not your Pet tonight, Vincent. I take my own clothes off.' She wrestled the shirt off but as he reached for her breasts, she shrugged away and nodded for him to take his off too.

With hands that were suddenly awkward, he fumbled at the buttons. He cursed under his breath then finally gave up and yanked the shirt over his head.

'And the jeans, take them off too.' She was already stepping out of her standard Pet Shop-issue trousers. 'I want you naked and gagging for it just like Tino.'

'I promise you,' he said shoving his jeans and boxers down to his ankles in one swift move, nearly tripping himself in his efforts to step out of them, 'Tino couldn't possibly want you more than I do right now.' He reached for her again, but she stepped back, and he cursed out loud.

'When you come to me in my home and you share my bed then you stay until I say you can leave. Are we clear?'

'Crystal. You'll have to chase me out with a broom.' He set her on fire standing there naked, head unbowed, cock thrust in front of him at full attention, large hands clenched at his side. And his arse, she thought, his lovely arse was still aching from

Tino's spanking. He was shockingly unlike Tino, couldn't be less like Tino if he tried. She wondered if he did try, but she wondered only for the briefest of seconds before she launched herself at him mouth first.

He cupped her arse and lifted her onto him as though she weighed nothing. There was no fumbling, no shifting for position. His cock knew the way, and her pussy yielded to his press with slippery eagerness.

He manoeuvred until her back was against the slightly rough press of the wall, then he thrust hard, raking upward against her pubis and over her distended clit until she gasped. 'Tino left me with the taste of you on my tongue,' he said. 'And my whole body smelt of your sex. I couldn't stand it. I couldn't go back home without more of you.' Then he stopped talking, and if she closed her eyes and listened to the way he grunted, the way he growled, the way he caught his breath, Tino and Vincent were the same, both there, both pounding her cunt relentlessly, and Vincent was no less of an animal than Tino.

She grabbed him by the hair and pulled his mouth to hers biting and tonguing her way closer to his breath. Her body thrust to meet his with pounding and scraping of flesh, and in the press her clit felt nearly as big as his cock and as desperate to come. The wall abraded her shoulders and her coccyx. She locked her heels around his waist and squeezed to get still closer to the imminent explosion. And when it happened he jerked and clawed at her hips. She banged her head on the wall as heat seared through her, flashing white-hot and shimmering then collapsing in on itself to ever-more gentle tremors around his jerking cock.

As he pulled away and settled her on her feet, leaving her at the peril of her wobbly legs, she cupped a hand against her vulva and pressed until her palm was drenched in their combined juices, then, holding his gaze, she wiped it up over her belly and onto her aching breasts.

He half growled as he inhaled their blended scent, nostrils flared, lips parted, taking the smell of them into the back of his throat like she'd seen cats do. Then he slid his hand between her legs and followed suit until his chest and belly glistened with a sheen of their heat.

With a series of nips and kisses and playful shoves more Pet-like than she'd actually intended, she pushed him onto the couch and forced his legs apart. Then she straddled one leg at a time, pressing her labia wide, undulating, grinding, rubbing her wet cunt up and down the length of each thigh, delighting in the way his cock already squirmed and jerked in response to her marking him.

And suddenly she was as anxious to taste as she was to mark. She knelt between his spread legs and took in his scent, licked her way up the inside of his thigh until she could flick the tip of her tongue over the pliant skin cupping his balls. Then she worked her way up below his penis to the place that smelt yeasty and urgent.

He ground against her and curled his fingers in her hair. 'Thought you weren't my Pet tonight.' He forced the words up through his tight chest.

She rubbed her face against his balls, feeling his tentative gasp of protectiveness. 'Not all animals are Pets.' She worked her way beneath his balls teasing and tonguing back toward the grip of his anus. He lifted his feet onto the coffee table on either side of her and pressed up, sucking air at the extra pressure on his sore bottom as she moved her hands beneath to cup him and spread him until he was completely exposed to her. His back-hole clenched and relaxed as she pressed a tentative finger to it then he released a low belly grunt as she pushed at it with the tensed tip of her tongue. 'Jesus, Stel, that feels good.'

'Do you like being fucked in there?' she asked, spitting on her fingers and easing one into his grudging tightness.

'I do,' he breathed. 'Does that bother you?'

'It intrigues me, turns me on, actually.'

'What about you?' he asked. 'Do you like being fucked back there?'

'Never actually been.' She was surprised to feel the heat of a blush.

He pulled away, and there was a tangle of arms and legs and

something bony hitting the edge of the coffee table before he settled onto the sofa with her on top of him. Then he ran a hand around to caress her back-hole. 'Would you like to?'

Her stomach did a nervous flip-flop. 'You're so big. Do you think we could?'

He held her gaze with a look that was slightly frightening, but mostly sexy. Then it softened to something almost tender. 'We can stop whenever you want. Just say the word.' He offered her his delicious smile. 'After all, as you reminded me, you're not my Pet at the moment.'

She led him into the bedroom. Better that she was in the place she felt most comfortable for the first time, he said. He asked for her vibrator, which he laid on the nightstand where he could reach it, along with a bottle of lube then he settled into a spoon position and lifted her upper thigh so that her leg was bent at the knee and her foot rested on the mattress giving him easy access. When he had her positioned like he wanted her, he reached down over her belly, slipped his fingers into her cunt, and began to stroke. 'We'll use your own juices at first,' he chuckled softly, 'and mine, of course, but when I push into you, I want you as slippery as possible, so we'll use lots of lube. OK, Stel?'

She nodded, already feeling the swell of his cock pressing against her bottom. 'And the vibrator?' her voice sounded breathless, a little more frightened than she wanted it to be.

He kissed her ear. 'I've only got one cock. What else are we going to fill your pussy with?'

For a time he caressed and fondled, stroking her heavy breasts, giving her clit an occasional tweak, kissing and nuzzling her neck. When she had relaxed into his cuddling, he probed her pussy until his fingers were slick with their juices, then he easily slid a middle finger into her anus. She tensed and caught her breath and felt her pussy gush in response to the invasion.

'All right?' he asked, stroking a nipple in reassurance with his other hand.

She nodded and pressed back against him.

By the time he inserted the second finger and had begun to

scissor and thrust, she was feeling uncomfortably full and yet desperately wanting more. By the time he had reached for the lube and hinted at a third finger, both of his hands were engaged in the back door business. 'Stel, sweetheart,' his voice was tight with arousal, and though she couldn't see his cock, she could feel the press of it against her arse cheek when he moved just right. 'Play with your pussy for me. I want you right at the edge when I push into you. That's it,' he sighed as she slid two fingers into her gape and began to thumb her hard clit. 'That's my girl.'

He needn't have worried about her level of arousal, the very thought of what he was doing, what he was about to do, the tight full feeling in her anus, the forward press against the back wall of her vagina had her well buzzing with arousal slightly tinged in fear.

'Now relax, sweetheart, just relax and let me ease my cock in slowly.' His voice was barely more than a tight whisper against the back of her shoulders. Then she felt his warm breath on her bottom and she knew he was looking at her lewdly gaping backside, positioning himself just right to fill her. That in itself was almost enough to make her come. She felt one large hand holding her buttocks apart then she felt the press of the slick head of his penis against her worried pucker. 'You're nice and dilated. Are you ready for me, sweetheart?'

She whimpered and nodded, fingers resting tight against her clit, suddenly forgetting the task at hand as she concentrated on the slight shifting of his hips that pushed him forward forcing her open with a slow, but relentless press.

'That's it, that's my Stel. You're doing so well, your hole is so ready for me, and I need to fuck you there so badly.'

She felt as though her pelvic girdle were being pried apart from the bottom up, and yet the more intense the pressure and the push in her anus the more her pussy gushed against her fingers, the more the buzz of arousal was amplified.

She moaned and gasped against the insistent invasion of her impaler. 'I want you to fuck me back there, Vincent. I want you to fill me full.' Then she took a deep breath and shoved back onto his cock as hard as she could. The sound from her

188

throat was animal, pain and pleasure splitting her apart.

It was Vincent holding her hips kissing her shoulder that brought her back. 'Sh! Stel, Sh. I'm in now. I'm in. Relax, that's my girl, just relax, and get used to it.' Then he reached for the vibrator, first pressing with gentle strokes on a low setting just at the parting of her labia and up almost to the base of her clit. Then he turned up the setting and pushed in deeper until she could feel the press of it on the thin wall that separated the fair-sized vibrator from the large cock up her arse.

She hadn't realised it, but he had let her initiate the thrusting, and she wasn't quite certain when she overcame the fear of being split in two and began to slowly move against him, but thrusting she was, and he was thrusting too, gently at first, but building in depth and momentum until he felt confident she could accommodate him.

His timing was exquisite, his coordination perfect as he manoeuvred the vibrator to rake deliciously against her g-spot in perfect rhythm to his thrust in her arse. At first she had lain very still, moving nothing but her hips and that only marginally, but as Vincent turned up the vibrator and as she grew used to the delicious, uncomfortable fullness, thrusting became writhing, and writhing became squirming and wallowing over the bed.

'I can't hold back much longer, Stel,' he gasped. 'I have to come.' And as though her own orgasm were voice activated by him, she came in a tidal wave that crashed and pounded inside her until she was certain she would break apart, barely aware at the back of her mind of the warm spurt of Vincent's semen up into her nether-hole.

Later in the bath, she let him clean her gently with a terry washcloth. 'Hopefully you won't be too sore tomorrow.' He smiled up at her. 'I could barely walk after my first time.' He held her gaze. 'But then you know I like it rough sometimes.' She thought she saw a tinge of a blush crawl up his cheek.

'Then do I need to learn to be rough?'

He laughed softly. 'After the way you put Tino in his place this past weekend, I think you already know how to be rough when it suits you.' He soaped her breasts, bringing her nipples to white foamy peaks.

'Do you like it better with men?' she asked.

'Not better, no. But I like it well enough,' he shrugged. 'Or Tino does at least. Vincent's never really been with a man.'

'Vincent's the voyeur and Tino's the exhibitionist?'

'Something like that. Tino always wants to be in the thick of it, but I've always experienced the world through binoculars. It's safer that way.'

'Is that why you keep them separate, Vincent and Tino? Because it's safer?'

'Not sure I could cope with both of them at once.'

'So you opt for safe.' She scooted close to him and began to wash his cock. 'Except with me.'

He released a sigh of pleasure at her touch. 'You're definitely not what I'd call safe.'

She soaped the length of him, struck again by the fact that he never seemed all that far away from a hard-on. 'Is that why you left me?' She sounded matter-of-fact enough, but she felt her chin quiver slightly at the thought of waking up to find him gone. Her stomach clenched.

For a long time he didn't speak, only watched her ministrations to his cock. At last he sighed and forced the words past the straight line of his lips. 'You called out in the night while you were asleep.' He avoided her gaze. 'You called out and it was just so overwhelming.'

She gave him a rough stroke with the washcloth. 'For fuck sake, Vincent, I was asleep! If I called out for Tino, it meant nothing. Besides, Tino is really–'

He laid a wet finger across her lips to silence her. 'You didn't call out for Tino, Stel.'

'I didn't?'

He shook his head, moving his hand to smooth a stray strand of hair behind her ear. 'You called out for me. You called out for Vincent.' Before she could regain enough balance to reply, he continued rapidly. 'If you had called out for Tino, that would have been OK. I could have handled that. I would have understood that. Why wouldn't you call out for

Tino? Everyone calls out for Tino. But you called out for me. No one's ever called out for me and that was ...'

'You were scared.'

He nodded. 'Terrified.'

Suddenly her throat felt tight and she found herself way too close to tears for comfort. 'What the hell did you think I was going to do, tie you up in the basement and keep you as my love slave?'

He raised a damp eyebrow. 'I hadn't thought about that. That wouldn't have been so bad.'

She covered her mouth and fought back a sob of a laugh. 'You're an idiot, Vincent Evanston, a total idiot. I don't even have a basement.'

Chapter Twenty-three

WHEN STELLA WOKE UP she was once again alone in the bed, but the delicious smell coming from the kitchen reassured her that she wasn't alone in the house. She shoved her way into her robe and shuffled down the hall to find Vincent standing bare-chested over the cooker scrambling eggs. He smiled up at her. 'I was going to bring you breakfast in bed, but since you're up, maybe we could just have it on the kitchen floor.' When she came to his side, he pulled her into a grope of an embrace and kissed her, running his hand underneath the robe to caress her bottom. 'Little back-hole not too sore, I hope.'

She wriggled against his hand. 'Every time I sit down today, I'll have a tender spot for you. Why are you up so early?' she asked, pulling some plates from the cupboard. The clock on the wall read 6.40 a.m.

'I have a meeting today, and I've got to get back to the hotel and get changed so I don't look like I've been having wild messy sex all night.' He gave her a hungry look. 'Wouldn't want to make anyone jealous, would I?' He turned his attention back to the eggs. 'Anyway, I figured you'd be up for an early start at Strigida. Can't imagine you not being the first one into the office.'

'Usually I am.' She shoved bread into the toaster. 'But I had a little meeting at the Pet Shop with the Boss and Anne O'Kelly last night after Tino left.'

'Oh?' Suddenly she had his full attention.

'You didn't miss out on any hot group sex if that's what you're worried about.'

He offered a half smile. 'I was hardly lacking in the hot sex department, if you recall. So what was this meeting about, or is it none of my business?'

She buttered the toast. 'Believe it or not, they want me to take over the running of the Pet Shop. I'm meeting them back over there later today so they can show me around properly, from a perspective other than that of a Pet, I mean.' She nodded to the plates on the counter next to him. 'Unless you like your eggs burnt, I think those are done.'

He tipped the eggs into the plates and the two sat down at the table. She was half finished with hers before she noticed he wasn't eating.

'What is it? What's the matter?'

'Do you want to run the Pet Shop? I mean, I got the impression that you really loved your work at Strigida.'

She spoke around a mouthful of toast. 'To be honest, since I got home last night, I've had other things on my mind.' She threw a wicked glance at his lap. 'But it's a fabulous opportunity really. Great pay, great benefits. I could have Tino whenever I wanted him.'

He didn't smile. 'You can already have Tino whenever you want him.'

Her heart did a little skitter against her ribs at his words, but she stayed on topic. 'Don't you think it's a great opportunity?'

He laid the fork down on his plate and took her hand. 'It's a great opportunity if it's what you want to do, but I'd imagine it would be a very demanding job.'

'I'm not afraid of demanding jobs.' She curled her fingers around his. 'I wasn't planning on making the decision today anyway, Vincent. I mean it's such a huge change for me. Surely you know I'd not make a decision like that without considering it very carefully.'

'Good. That's all I ask.' He shovelled an enormous forkful of egg into his mouth and chewed with gusto, suddenly very much reminding her of Tino.

His BlackBerry rang just as they were finishing the meal. He apologised and excused himself. She caught a mention of reclaiming habitat and something about a salt marsh before he disappeared into the back of the flat.

She cleared the table and was standing at the sink washing

up when he came back into the room. 'Everything all right?' she said without looking up.

'Never better.' He moved behind her and ran a warm hand inside her robe, forcing it open, causing her to jump and give them both a good dousing as she dropped a heavy plate into the suds. 'Do your nipples always get this hard when you do the dishes?' he asked, nibbling on her nape as he stroked and cupped her breasts until she could feel her pussy quiver.

She caught her breath and smiled. 'Only when someone gropes my tits and presses a very large hard-on against my crack.'

'I'm going to be away from you for hours. You don't want to send me off with a full load in my balls, do you?'

'Then you're coming back?' The butterflies in her stomach danced double-time.

'For tonight, yes. If you'll have me. Then I'll have to go back home in the morning.' He slid his hand up under her robe to fondle her arse cheeks.

'I suppose I could stand another night with you, though I may not be able to walk in the morning.'

'There are lots of things we can do that won't involve your little wounded asshole, Stel.' He ran a finger teasingly along her cleft. 'Of course if you really want me to fuck you back there again,' he nibbled her earlobe, 'then I guess you'll just have to suffer the consequences.' Instinctively she opened her legs and thrust her hips back to offer him easy access to her cunt, already wet and gaping for him.

He slid his fingers between her labia in a probing caress. 'Is there any place that feels as good as your slippery pussy? You're so creamy and swollen that I'd almost think you sat there through breakfast rubbing your slick pussy all over that chair. Are you a stealth masturbator, Stel? I bet you are. I bet you can come any time you want to and nobody's ever the wiser unless they slip their hands down into your little lace panties and feel how wet you are.'

She wriggled back onto his fingers, thinking about masturbating at the office after her first time with Tino. 'You can go check the chair if you want, see if it's wet, see if it

194

smells like my cunt.'

'Mmm. I suppose I could, but I think I'd rather just stay right here with your sexy bottom all bared and hot and open to show off how swollen you are, how ready you are for my cock.' He slicked her stiffening clit with her abundant juices and stroked it to a hard little nib with his thumb.

She heard him unzip his fly and wriggle his jeans down over his hips. 'Afraid I wouldn't be much good in my meetings carrying around such a heavy load for you.' He slid his cock between her legs and stroked her with it, slapped her pout with it, made her squirm all over for want of it. Then he shoved into her with a grunt, forcing her forward over the sink, her robe open enough for her bare breasts to graze the white peaks of dish soap, their dance and sway making little wavelets in the water as he began to thrust.

'I need to come, Stel, and I can feel how much you need to.' His fingers strummed her clit and she bucked and wriggled back against him with the intense shockwaves of pleasure spreading outward from her cunt until her legs trembled with the weight of her arousal.

It didn't take long. It didn't need to. After all, they were just re-establishing territory and strengthening bonds. Animals did it all the time.

'So you've done it then, you've offered her the position?' Vincent walked next to Alan in pristine khakis and a long-sleeve cotton shirt. It was the first time in a very long time Alan had seen him in clothes. On the one hand it seemed strange, and yet it brought back memories of tromping through the woods together when they were little more than boys, memories of watching pileated woodpecker nests for hours, memories of watching a northern harrier quarter the fields, memories of keeping detailed accounts of the insects they found every morning under the cook's potted pepper plants. Memories that no one could have ever imagined would lead the two of them to where they were now, to having shared each other's bodies nearly as casually as they'd shared each other's soft drinks or sandwiches back when they were young.

Alan forced himself back to the present. 'Anne and I made the offer last night. We felt it was time. Of course we don't expect an answer right away. It's not a decision to be taken lightly and, as I'm sure you well know, Stella never makes a decision lightly.'

Vincent's lips curled in a private smile, one Alan was certain wasn't intended for him. 'You were with her last night, weren't you? Not Tino, but Vincent.'

The smile spread from his lips and lit his eyes and changed the countenance of his whole face. Suddenly it was less severe, more relaxed. But it still had nothing to do with Alan. 'How could I be in London and not want to be with her?'

They were walking along a path that offered lovely strolls through a woodland of predominantly beech that surrounded the Pet Shop. It offered privacy for the Pet Shop as well as privacy for Pets who wanted to have a little space away from the group activities. Alan brought Vincent here partly because he knew no one would appreciate it more, but mostly because he wanted to keep their meeting a secret.

It was a lovely day and any other time, Vincent being who he was, would be lost in deep appreciation for the chorus of birdsong and the variegated blanket of woodland flowers. Alan knew only too well that his distraction wasn't a good sign. He figured he might as well press the issue and end the suspense. He forced a chuckle. 'Anne's worried that you'll tell Stella about your relationship to the Pet Shop.' It was a lie, but he couldn't very well say what Anne really feared, what he feared.

'Why would I do that?'

'Oh, I'm sure you wouldn't,' Alan waved away a couple of gnats. 'But you've got to understand, Anne's dreamt about opening the North American Pet Shop for a long time. She just doesn't want anything to go wrong. And frankly, you showing up unexpectedly here of all places makes me a bit nervous too, Vincent.' There it was, honesty at last, and suddenly Alan felt like the friend he used to be.

Vincent turned to face him and offered that half-smile that always put people at ease. Well most of the time anyway. He rested a large hand against an ancient beech tree, and in spite of everything, Alan's cock squirmed in his trousers with other memories more recent, more complicated than watching hawks quarter the fields, but any thought of arousal fled when Vincent spoke.

'Alan, I know I promised Anne the North American Pet Shop, and that's a promise I have no intention of breaking, but I don't want Stella running the Pet Shop here. You'll have to find someone else.'

It was only after Vincent left that Stella checked her email. Sure enough the password she had been promised was there. As difficult as it was, she forced herself to concentrate on something other than Vincent, something other than his scent still all over her body, something other than the fact she would sleep in his arms again tonight. On a lark, she went into Tino's profile. His diary was full, like always, and yet Vincent had said she could have Tino whenever she wanted him. With Vincent here, she felt smugly possessive of both her boys.

Viewing the website served only to make her restless, and she found herself wondering how much she could really learn from just looking at a computer monitor. And yes, she knew she would be shown around by Anne and the Boss this evening, but would they really tell her what she wanted to know when they had their own agenda? She didn't even know what she wanted to know, but she was very aware that because they had plans for her, when the Boss and Anne had arranged for her to be a Pet, they had purposefully isolated her from other Pets and kept her experiences of the Pet life limited.

One of the helpful bits of information she found on the website was a selection of phone numbers. The numbers were only prefaced by initials, so Stella had no real way of knowing who she was getting. She took a chance and picked one.

'This is Jan,' came the voice at the other end of the phone and Stella recognised immediately the young handler who had been responsible for her after the debacle with Audrey and Master.

'Hi, Jan, this is Stella, Stella James. I have a favour to ask you.'

Chapter Twenty-four

IT WASN'T THE SURLY handler who came to collect Stella, but Jan herself, in a small white van barely big enough to be considered a van at all. She had stripped her and tucked her into a Pet carrier exactly as though she were going to be with a keeper.

One of the important pieces of information gleaned from her more complete access to the website was a list of rules that didn't apply to the Pet/keeper relationship, but rather to the Pet/Pet Shop relationship. And one of those rules stated that all Pets had access to the Pet Shop at any time. Even non-paying Pets, Pets who mainly serviced keepers, had open access when they had free time. For obvious reasons, none of them knew the actual location of the Pet Shop, however, so transport was always provided.

When they arrived at the Pet Shop, Jan helped her out of the carrier and attached the leash to her collar. She patted the small pad and pen that protruded from the pocket of her khaki blazer. 'I'll carry these, and whenever you have a question just touch my arm and I'll give them to you.' She gently tugged the lead. 'Come on now, bath time is just about over and since it's a nice day, most of the Pets will be congregating in the garden.' She offered a girlish giggle. 'This kind of weather makes them all horny, so I imagine there'll be lots of mounting going on, and no doubt, the sight of you will raise a few cocks.'

As they walked into the courtyard, a few Pets were beginning to exit the bathhouse with a mix of handlers. 'Audrey and Master know you're coming early to hang out, and they've said I may allow you to have sex with any of the Pets, if you wish. Handlers, you may also have sex with if they agree. Can't imagine any of them refusing you.' She blushed her lovely little blush. 'I'd offer myself, but I'm not allowed to have sex with any of the Pets for another month yet. I do apologise.'

The woman was such a delight. Stella could imagine it would be lovely to fondle those heavy breasts and explore what was hidden beneath well-pressed khaki. Her own innocence often startled her in comparison to Vincent's experience. She'd never been with a woman. She hadn't been with that many men. There had never been time. No doubt she would take a female Pet at some point if she took the position being offered. She didn't know if Anne had, but she felt like it was probably an experience she would need.

They rounded the corner, which led past a small grotto surrounded by hebes and heavily-laden montanas which vined and clung to several weeping birch that provided extra privacy. There on a bench sat Audrey, khaki shorts down around her ankles, legs open wide. A lovely olive-skinned male with a heavily riveted collar squatted in front of her, his face buried in her cunt. She looked up and offered a wicked smile. 'You're here, Stella, darling, just in time to help us out. Vigo has a lovely tongue, and I can't wait to ride his horny cock, but he can't lick my pussy and play with my titties at the same time. Her gaze raked up and down Stella's body and caused a tetchy tremor below her belly. Come help me out, sweetheart.'

Stella shot Jan a quick look. The handler responded with a shrug. And Stella suddenly realised because she was here without the knowledge of the Boss or Anne, the kid gloves were off. There was no one to insulate her. The tremor in her belly grew exponentially with the addition of nervous tension, as she stepped forward.

'Behind me, darling,' Audrey breathed. 'Stand behind me. I love it when someone fondles my tits from behind.'

As she moved to obey, she noticed the gaze of the big Pet between Audrey's legs followed her. Audrey swiftly dispatched with her buttons and opened the lacy pink front-loader to give Stella access.

As she moved her fingers down over Audrey's shoulders

and under the cups, down around the outer edges of the handler's small, firm breasts, Audrey sucked in a harsh breath. 'Goodness, Stella, your little hands are cold. Are you nervous? Don't be sweetheart, you're a Pet. You're here to have a good time.'

That wasn't exactly true, but then if Stella really wanted the Pet experience without being hedged in safety, this was her chance. She took a deep breath and slipped her hands under to cup Audrey's breasts along each side. Then she scooped them into her hands so that the easy weight of them rested in the curve of her palms and her thumbs and forefingers were free to stroke and pinch the jut and press of Audrey's nipples.

As she did so, Audrey gulped a little sigh of a breath, 'Oh, that's nice, darling, you know how to play with a girl's tits, don't you? I bet you play with your own lovely boobies all the time. I would if they were mine.' She arched up and ran a hand along Stella's bare breast and Stella gasped. 'Oh goodness, hon, you are high strung today, aren't you? Do you need to come, darling? Of course you do. Jan, play with her pussy, would you?'

'But, Audrey, I'm not–'

'Oh for heaven's sake, Jan, I know you're not allowed. It's a stupid rule, and we're going to ignore it. Besides, I'm guessing your pussy is just as slippery as Stella's is. Admit it, you're dying to know what she feels like, what she tastes like. And besides, I'm sure our Stella needs the relief.'

The junior handler released an uneasy sigh and moved close to Stella. Her hand rested briefly on the small of Stella's back. Stella pressed back against her touch, shifting her hips, opening her stance until she was sure the woman could make out the heavy folds of her cunt. The little hitch in the handler's breath told her she was right.

'She has a lovely pussy, doesn't she, Jan? Come on, bring her around here in front now so I can see too, that's it, right here in front of me. I have a feeling watching the two of you will do me a lot more good than having my titties played with. Right there, sit down.' She motioned to a grassy spot right in front of the bench and slightly to one side where her view wasn't obscured by the Pet licking her pussy. 'Now, Jan, undo your top. I'm sure Stella must want to see that lovely rack of yours as much as I do.'

Stella could see the younger woman's hands trembling as she shoved out of the blazer and opened her blouse.

'Good girl, Jan,' Audrey's voice was laboured with arousal; her fingers were curled tight in the thick dark hair of the Pet between her legs. 'Now let Stella take care of the rest like a good little Pet.'

With nerves of her own, Stella nuzzled and shoved her way into the heavy lace bra, which supported large weighty tits that bounced and swayed with the ease characteristic only of silicone-free breasts. With anxious hands, the young handler reached behind to unhook and release herself fully into Stella's nuzzling.

Stella could tell by the shifting of her hips that Jan needed her own pussy fondled. Instinctively she began to nuzzle and nip her way down the tensing muscles of Jan's tight abs toward the delicious female scent emanating from between the woman's thighs. Jan quickly got the message and fumbled to undo her shorts. She'd barely got them over her hips before Stella continued to shove and press her way down, feeling almost as though she had been infused with a little of Tino's hungry spirit. She suddenly wanted nothing so badly as to taste the handler's femaleness and compare it to her own. It was high time she found out what another woman felt like.

Audrey injected a breathy giggle. 'Oh my, our little Pet isn't as timid as we thought, is she? She's hungry for your pussy, Jan, do let her have it. You know how curious Pets are. Besides you'll feel better once she's given you a good licking and made you come.'

Stella pushed and shoved and tugged with her teeth until she had created a path straight to Jan's lovely smooth pussy. Her lips were heavy and deep blood-engorged red, glistening with the patina of her growing need. Stella extended her tongue for what had been meant to be a tentative taste. But as Jan wriggled her bottom and spread herself a little wider, Stella got a view of the tantalising opening between those splayed lips and the tentative taste became a pearl dive straight to the centre. The handler practically bounced off the ground as Stella ploughed a deep, delicious gouge with her tongue, all the way up to the distended press of her clit. She gave it a hearty suck, and the woman erupted into an orgasm that shook her all over, made her heavy breasts quiver and dance.

'Oh goodness, Stella,' Audrey sighed. 'I think your mouth is going to be very popular around here.' Vigo pulled away enough for her to scoot off the bench to join the pussy party in the grass. There she stretched on her back and motioned for Vigo, who wriggled his way between her legs and pushed into her with a guttural grunt. 'Ah, that's a good boy, Vigo.' She snapped her fingers. 'Come here, Stella, that's a girl, come squat over my face now and let me take care of your hot little fanny. You must be about to explode.'

Stella obeyed, positioning herself so that her whole gash settled against the long, deep lavings of Audrey's very skilled tongue, hoping she wouldn't drown the woman in her flood of heat.

And as if by intuition, the rest sorted itself out. Vigo manoeuvred until he was on his knees and Audrey's legs were around his waist to keep the connection. Jan, who seemed to be a quick learner, lost her clothes and eased herself in between the big Pet and Stella allowing Stella to pay homage to her exquisitely soft breasts while Vigo tongued her cunt in the build-up for round two.

The group orgasm that followed not far behind toppled them all in a pile of Pets and handlers kissing and groping and caressing as they caught their breath. As Stella settled against the soft pillowing of Jan's breasts, still stroking a mesmerising nipple, she reckoned she could understand Tino's attraction to the place.

Chapter Twenty-five

'WELL, I HADN'T EXPECTED that, though I must say it was rather nice.' Jan chuckled softly. 'It was something I was looking forward to when my probationary period was over, you know, something I've fantasised about. And I have to say, my fantasies didn't come close to the reality.' Jan had just bathed Stella and herself, which had turned out to be quite a touchy-feely experience, and Stella could no longer say she hadn't known the pleasure of a woman. Jan was tucking in her shirt, smiling happily in the mirror at the reflection of Stella who stood next to her in nothing but a collar and leash. 'And you're all bathed and ready for your meeting with the Boss and Ms O'Kelly when the time comes. Now, shall I answer some of those questions for you?'

Jan dug into her pocket then patted herself down. 'Uh-oh, I think I must have lost the pen while we were all having sex. It must have fallen out of my pocket.' Her cheeks brightened and she offered an apologetic smile. 'Never mind. We'll find another one in the office.' She led Stella away from the annexe and into a side door of the big house over which there was a sign that read, *Office. No Pets allowed.*

'It's all right, don't worry,' Jan said, when she saw Stella staring at the sign. 'Pets can come in if they're with a handler and on a leash. You've read the manual. You know that Pets aren't allowed to interact with any form of media. That's why the office is off limits. Anyway you're not exactly here as a Pet at the moment, are you?'

Stella followed her inside and watched as she shuffled through the top drawer of a small hard wood desk buried under a huge computer monitor. The handler nodded to the screen.

'We keep track of all the Pets on this, you know, who's here, who's not, and if they're not, are they with a keeper or living their other life. Alan had the programme specially designed by some company in America, some company on the West Coast, I think.'

'Alan?'

'You know? The Boss? Alan Boswell. It's hard for me to think of him as anything but Alan. That's how I was introduced to him when he recruited me.'

A. Boswell, "The Boss" was Alan. Stella hadn't known that.

Jan offered a conspiratorial smile. 'I'm sure they're going to show you this anyway, so let's just see what some of our Pets are up to. Most won't be with keepers in the middle of the week, though a few always are. You know how wild work schedules are these days.' She typed in Liam. 'Looks like he's in the real world at the moment, but he'll be with a keeper this weekend. Let's see, Daisy's here on holiday, so she'll be with the other Pets in the garden.' She pointed to a door at the back of the office with a big *Do not enter* sign. 'We have CCTV here, so we could go in there and find out exactly where Daisy is, though very few of us have access to it.'

She turned her attention back to the monitor and flipped down through the list of Pets given alphabetically almost like a roll call. 'This is very helpful, as you can imagine, when we need to know who's here and who can be available if a keeper wants a last-minute Pet. The names flash red if the Pet is here and–'

Stella pulled her hand away as Tino's name came into view flashing red.

Jan chuckled. 'Oh he's here all right. A bit of a surprise to all of us, but he's not staying. He's back into the real world in a little while, sorry, Stella.' She leant in close and half whispered, 'Audrey saw him come in. She was gobsmacked. She'd never seen him in clothes before. She said Alan wasn't very happy about it. They went off somewhere to talk.' She tapped the keys and closed the programme. 'Tino's always in trouble though. Don't know what he's thinking showing up here in civvies.'

The handler's words suddenly sounded a long way away beyond the sudden flutter of wings in Stella's ears as the monitor faded to black, then blinked and pulled up a woodland scene that could have been shot on the Pet Shop grounds. That she ignored. It was the stylised logo of an owl perched against a crescent moon in the lower left-hand corner that caught her attention. It was barely noticeable amid the profusion of bluebells, but once her eyes locked on it, she saw nothing else.

Trying to keep her hands steady, she thrust a finger at the symbol.

Jan nodded. 'Oh, it's the Night Owl symbol. I think it has something to do with some company in America. Not sure though.'

But Stella was sure. Suddenly she was deadly sure of everything and sure of so much more than she wanted to know. With a trembling hand she grabbed up a pen and scribbled on the edge of the blotter pad. *I need to get dressed now. I know all I need to.* She barely laid the pen down when she heard familiar voices in the hall behind her.

'We don't want her to find you're here when she arrives. It's already–' The Boss's words died in his throat as his gaze came to rest on Stella. At his right shoulder stood Anne. Right behind them stood Vincent frozen mid-stride, as they all were, as though the sight of her had turned them to stone.

She squeezed Jan's hand and did the totally forbidden for a Pet. She spoke. 'Please wait for me outside.'

The flustered handler did as she was told, squeezing by the three who still stood unmoving in the doorway. When she was outside the three came in. Vincent closed the door behind them.

For a long time no one spoke. It took Stella a few seconds to be certain she wasn't going to cry or scream or pass out. She longed to linger there in the silence before someone opened their mouth and her world was destroyed, but she knew it was already far too late for that. At last she lifted her eyes to Vincent. 'You own the Pet Shop, don't you?'

He swallowed hard, and his voice was low, raspy. But he held her gaze. 'How did you find out?'

She nodded to the monitor. 'The Night Owl symbol. The

story you told at the wildlife reserve in Lincoln City. And it was on the sign at the refuge. It wasn't hard to figure it out.

'I should be flattered, I guess.' She bit back tears and grabbed onto the desk fearing her legs would give under her. 'I mean I must be really something that you, all three of you, felt you had to manipulate me and lie to me, to get me to take this position, even get me fucked, and so well fucked at that,' she struggled with the phrase. 'Though I suppose it doesn't say too much for what you think of my intelligence, does it?' She bit her lip hard to regain control.

'Stella, please,' the Boss stepped forward and reached for her. 'You have to understand, no one ever meant–'

She shrugged away from him and stepped back until her butt was pressed against the desk. 'You're Alan, aren't you? The friend from the photo albums. I recognise you now. I can't believe I didn't see the resemblance before.'

He nodded. 'We've been friends for a long time, Vincent and I.'

She turned her attention to Anne. 'I'm very sorry that your promotion to Pet Shop North America will have to be delayed, but I can't take the position. I like what you've done here, though. The Pets are great, and the money couldn't go to a better cause. I wish you all the best.' Before Anne could speak, she continued. 'Also I resign my position at Strigida. I won't be back. There'll be no two weeks' notice. I'm sure you can understand under the circumstances. I'm sorry for that. I've enjoyed the work very much. If you'll excuse me now, I have to go.'

She pushed past the Boss and Anne, but Vincent wouldn't budge. 'Don't do this, Stella.' His voice was low, husky. 'You need to let me explain.' He grabbed her arm, but she jerked away and in doing so lost all semblance of control.

'I don't *need* to let you do anything. Did you really think I was that desperate for money, for sex? I didn't ask for any of this.' She made a sweeping gesture with her hand. 'And I sure as hell didn't see it coming. You've made a fool of me. Well done. All of you.' She fought back a sob. 'I really didn't see it coming.' She pushed past Vincent and jerked the door open, and when he started after she turned on him. 'Don't follow me. I don't want to see you again.'

In the hallway, her view of Jan was already splintered by tears. From somewhere the handler had managed a trench coat. She removed the leash and carefully wrapped the coat around Stella's shoulders. 'Come on. I know a more private way to the van. I'll take you home.'

Chapter Twenty-six

IT WAS LATE WHEN he arrived. He was the only Pet who knew the way to the Pet Shop, and he came and went as he pleased. He did own the place, after all, a thing he half-cursed himself for after losing Stella. And yet, it was so often the place where he sought comfort, he could hardly imagine not having it to escape to now and then. He had been to Stella's flat again, but she still wasn't there. The woman who cleaned for her told him she hadn't been home in a while. No, she still didn't know where Stella was, but she thought perhaps Stella might be considering leasing the place out.

There was nowhere he wouldn't eventually find her, he kept telling himself. He was a powerful man. He had boundless resources. And yet the more time passed without him finding her, the more time passed without him doing everything in his power to make it right, the more worried he became that maybe she never really felt for him what he felt for her. Maybe he was never more to her than a Pet Shop fuck. On the good days he didn't believe that. On the bad days he wasn't sure. He wasn't sure of anything without her. The fear of his feelings for her was nothing compared to his fear of losing her. He wouldn't allow that to happen. He couldn't.

He didn't turn on the light. He knew the place well enough he didn't need to. He found his pallet on the floor of the dungeon and stretched out in the darkness. He closed his eyes and remembered Alan bringing Stella to him here. He remembered waking from a deep sleep to find her, like a dream, standing there backlit by the moonlight before Alan shut the door. The feel of her, the taste of her, her scent, they were all so much more visceral than just the thought process of memory. How could he have let this happen?

In the dark behind his eyelids he let the moving picture images of her stir him; the feel of her against his body when she slept, the sound of her laughter, the determined sound of her silence when she was his Pet. He laid his hand against his heavy cock and ran a fist along its length, amazed once again to find that the weight in his heart was much heavier than what settled against his groin.

He heard the heavy door open on its aged hinges, heard the click of the light switch, and the darkness behind his eyelids bloomed, but he didn't move. He just continued to stroke his erection. He heard the footsteps across the stone floor and felt the weight and the warmth of a body settle onto the edge of his pallet. He could tell by the scent it was Alan.

'I saw you come in,' his friend said. 'You all right?'

'I stopped by her flat, just in case. She's still not there.'

'I know. Anne went by yesterday. We're both at a loss as to where she might go. She has no family, and we've never heard her speak of any close friends.'

For a long moment the seamless silence stretched between them. The two had always been comfortable in their silence. Their shared passion for exploring nature had made silence an essential quality in their friendship.

At last Vincent spoke, though it was more thinking out loud really. 'I can't believe she's evaded me this long. Maybe she really does hate me. I couldn't blame her if she did.'

'Don't be ridiculous. She doesn't hate you. If she hated you, she wouldn't have bothered. What we did hurt her,' Alan said. 'We humiliated her. It wasn't what we intended, but she doesn't know that.'

'And we can't tell her when we don't know where she is, can we?'

'We'll find her. And when we do we'll make it right.' Alan reached out and laid a hand on Vincent's belly causing him to flinch. He ignored the flinch and moved his fingers down over Vincent's, which were still curled around his erection.

'Don't.' Vincent tensed and tried to push him away.

But he got a stinging slap for his efforts.

209

His eyes flew open and he found himself caught in Alan's serious gaze. He wore a look that he reserved for the Pet Shop. 'I should spank your arse, punish you properly. Who the hell do you think you are coming to this place and running your gob? When you're here, you're a Pet, remember? And Pets don't talk.'

Vincent lay back on the pallet thinking that the transformation the Pet Shop wrought on his friend was nearly as big as the one it worked on him. Alan stroked Vincent's penis almost as though it were his own, but his eyes never left Vincent's face. When he was certain Vincent wouldn't fight him, he released a long slow breath. 'There now. That's better, isn't it? I can forgive your outburst this time. Pets in distress are known to lash out.' He leant forward and placed a warm kiss low on Vincent's belly then sat back up. 'But a good handler knows that sometimes Pets need comfort of the most basic kind, and they give that comfort. They do what they can to make their Pets feel better.' He pulled away long enough to slip out of his clothes then he settled in next to Tino, and it *was* Tino who came into his arms buried his head in his chest and howled his agony.

'Sh! Tino, sh! It'll be all right. We'll find Stella, and we'll make her understand, I promise you, now let me take care of you. Let me make you feel better.' His hand found its way to Tino's erection again, lingering to cup and caress the weight of his balls before stroking his length. He trailed kisses down Tino's neck and throat, pausing to run the press of his tongue in tight circles around each of Tino's nipples. 'There, that's it, relax for me, let me take care of you. You'll feel better after you come.' He gave Tino's balls a firm squeeze, firm enough to make him flinch. 'You can't rest when you're so full you're ready to explode. And you need to rest.' He ran the tip of his thumb over the droplet of precome seeping from the end of Tino's cock and spread it and stroked it over the head. Tino sighed and shifted against his hand.

He moved his lips from the nibbed points of Tino's nipples down his belly, dropping a kiss and a thrust of his tongue into Tino's navel, caressing the dark mat of pubic curls with ticklish fingertips until Tino caught his breath in tight, measured sips. For the briefest second, he raised his eyes to Tino's then he lowered his mouth onto Tino's cock, cheek muscles tight, lips pursed for a slippery slide down the length of him until his breath stirred hair and raised gooseflesh. The hard muscles below Tino's navel clenched and trembled at Alan's tight slick pull.

Alan's throat was deep and his control exquisite. He knew what felt good to another man. Tino reached to stroke his hair, and felt the vibration of his sigh down his cock, all the way to his pubic bone.

It was comfort, nothing more, and yet that was everything at the moment. At some point in the back of his darkened mind, he could feel Alan shifting and rocking against the pallet, but when he reached for him, Alan pushed his hand away. 'Not tonight. Tonight the handler comforts the Pet.'

He curled both hands in Alan's hair and pulled him still closer, but the man took him, every inch of him, taking Tino's tight thrusts and tonguing the underside of his cock with hard, muscular strokes that made Tino writhe and arch up off the pallet unable to hold still, unable to control whatever it was in him that raged full-force to relief, any kind of relief. And the relief Alan offered, like always, was without strings.

He came with a cry that rattled the rafters and stiffened his spine. Alan held him fast and swallowed down spurt after spurt of his semen until he was spent and glistening with a thin sheen of sweat. Then Alan wiped his mouth on his hand and slid up next to him. 'I'm sorry, mate,' he breathed. 'I came on your pallet.' Tino could feel his friend's sticky penis pressed against his hip. He pulled him close and kissed him, and found blessed relief in sleep. In the morning, he left early and caught a plane back to Portland.

It had been almost two weeks when the phone call came. He'd spent the day with his lawyers who were in negotiations with the Collins Company lawyers to save the Bear Grass Corridor. They had worked out a brilliant win-win solution and he'd gone home aching to tell Stella, knowing she would have approved, wishing desperately he could share such a major victory with her.

Instead, he'd had Maria pack him a sandwich and a thermos of coffee, and he spent the evening photographing a family of great horned owls who had successfully raised four chicks, all of whom were busy branching in a sprawling fir tree. It was balm for the soul and the best he could hope for at the moment.

It was late when he returned home. He'd just showered and settled in with a glass of wine to look at the shots he'd gotten when the phone rang. It was Alan.

'Vincent, we've found her.'

Suddenly Vincent couldn't breathe. He felt like his heart would explode. His fingers ached from his death grip on the phone.

Alan continued. 'The cleaning lady just called to say Stella asked her to pick up some groceries. She'll be home the day after tomorrow. Apparently she's been somewhere in the Outer Hebrides volunteering for an RSPB bird count.'

Vincent smiled in spite of himself remembering the woman in the muddy pink heels and pencil skirt who had chased into the woods after him that first time they met. And suddenly the weight of his need for her felt like it would crush him. 'I'm on my way,' came his breathless reply.

Chapter Twenty-seven

STELLA COULDN'T REMEMBER EVER being so tired. She had been wet and cold and miserable for the biggest part of a month, which had helped keep her mind off of what really hurt. It had been a friend of Bob Paris's from Vanguard who had put her on to the position. She knew precious little about seabirds when she left London, and now she knew more than she supposed she'd ever need to know, but not nearly as much as she'd have liked. It was an adventure that had kept her from falling apart, but now it was time to go home and pick up the pieces, if there were any left to pick up.

She was completely shattered after the train delays, then there was the struggle to get a taxi in the pouring rain and the long crawl through city traffic. Being home was off to a rough start, she thought as she dragged her bag up the stairs to her flat. She was about halfway up when suddenly Vincent stood beside her, and she knew she must still be dozing in the train, dreaming the dream she'd had so often since that horrible day at the Pet Shop. He said nothing, only turned and carried her luggage the rest of the way up for her.

At the door, when she tried to speak, he placed a warm finger over her lips. 'Before you say anything, I'm not leaving unless you call the police to come and drag me away.' Surely it was a dream then. Only in a dream would he say the very thing she needed to hear.

And again she was struggling to unlock the door. It was like déjà vu as he placed his hand over hers and helped her with it.

Inside she stood in the middle of the floor in the lounge not quite knowing what to do until he took her hand and led her down the hall to the bathroom. Everything seemed so real, even the smell of the geranium bubbles, as he drew a bath then undressed her and helped her in. He settled a kiss on her cheek and stood. 'I'll be in the kitchen if you need me.'

She must have dozed some more, and then she was dreaming again. He was standing over her with a fluffy towel and the flat smelt like an Italian restaurant. She couldn't remember ever having olfactory dreams before. It was nice though.

When she stepped out, he dried her, gently, carefully, like she was his Pet. 'I've made spaghetti bolognese.' He offered that delicious half smile. 'Contrary to popular belief, it's not the only thing men know how to make, but you didn't have the stuff for enchiladas.' He eased her into her thick terry robe and guided her to the table.

She remembered eating. In fact she remembered him feeding her as though she were a child. And the food was so tasty. She couldn't remember tasting in dreams before either. Then he carried her to bed and settled her into the soft, clean sheets. And suddenly she really was like a child, clutching at him, begging him not to leave her, terrified she'd wake up from the dream and he would have never been there at all. But he settled in next to her, nestling her into a spoon position, holding her close. And she had slept.

It was the sun filtering through the gauze curtains that woke her. But she didn't open her eyes immediately. She often tried to linger in the dream as long as possible, to put off the cold awakening to life without her boys, to hang on to the last vestiges of their warmth before she was forced to wake up alone.

And it had been such a delicious happy-ever-after dream. Audrey was taking over the Pet Shop, and well suited for it, so it seemed. Vincent had fed her bolognese and chatted on endlessly so unlike the silent brooding man she'd come to love. Anne and Alan would start the North American Pet Shop together. They were head over heels, in case she hadn't figured that out. Strigida UK, well he'd run it himself for a while. It was time he took a bit more of a hands-on approach, and Strigida was doing good things. Besides, he had ulterior motives for wanting to stay in the UK. He'd seemed a bit shy, a bit hopeful when he'd told her that, so much like Tino wanting her approval, that in the dream, she had pulled him to her across the corner of the table and given him a hard bolognese-flavoured kiss between blubbering sobs. Such a dream. Such a delicious dream. She so didn't want to wake up from it.

But something was coaxing her up from the dream world, refusing to let her bask in its sweetness. She tried to brush it away from her ear. But it was persistent. This time it pressed soft and humid against her nape, and the waking world wedged its way in with the awareness of a warm hard body pressed against hers, and parts of that body were very hard, indeed. Perhaps it was a dream within a dream. Oh dear God, she really didn't want to wake up. She'd missed having Vincent inside her so desperately, even the thought forced a sob from her lungs.

'Stel? Stella, are you all right?'

Her eyes popped open, and she was suddenly fully into the waking world with her heart pounding and her chest heaving for breath. She jerked up, nearly hitting him in the chin with her head before he could settle her back onto the pillows. Then he lifted himself on one elbow and held her in a concerned gaze.

'You're here,' she breathed. 'I'm not dreaming. Vincent? Tino?' For the first time ever she couldn't really tell who she was with.

He offered a sleep-kissed smile and nodded. 'It's no dream, Stel. We're both here, Tino and I, and we're not going anywhere.'

'Then last night, the bath, the dinner, you saying you're ...' She couldn't bring herself to repeat what he'd said lest she jinx it.

'That I'm staying here,' he pushed a strand of hair behind her ear, 'No dream, all real, even the bolognese stains on your white robe.' His laugh was warm and tactile. 'I've never seen anyone so tired and still functioning.' He shrugged. 'Well, sort of functioning.'

'Then you came to bed with me, and you just cuddled me,

and I just slept.' Her eyes welled. 'All night long, I just slept. I'm sorry, it must have been so frustrating for you.'

His gaze softened. 'Stella, I'm a Pet. I know how to hold my wad, and my cock was the least of my concerns last night.'

She turned into his arms with a sob, and he pulled her closer. 'Sweetheart, I'm so, so sorry. It was never my intention to hurt you. You have to believe me.' He pulled away enough to look into her eyes. 'I never dreamt I'd fall in love with you. That wasn't a part of the plan, not something I'd factored into the equation. But I did, hopelessly, helplessly. At first I thought it was just a Tino thing. Tino lives from his heart, from his emotions – Vincent doesn't. But then when I arranged to meet you, I knew I was as head over heels as he was. That's when I began to suspect I couldn't keep Vincent and Tino separate any more, not with you marching right in and boldly proclaiming that you wanted us both.'

'Wait a minute. You arranged to meet me?'

'Yeah, you know in the woods in your cute little shoes and that oh-so sexy but totally inappropriate skirt.' He offered her a wicked smile. 'That was all a set-up, an arrangement I'd made with Bob Paris. Afterwards, after you pursued me to Lincoln City, I panicked. It was absolutely my plan that neither Tino nor I would see you again. I cancelled your weekend with him, and I knew you didn't know how to get in touch with me.' He released his breath slowly. 'But I couldn't stay away from you, and when I found out Alan and Anne were bringing you in to the Pet Shop and that they had used Tino as an excuse to get you there, well, by that time I would have moved heaven and hell to see you again.' He placed a soft kiss on her shoulder. 'You see what crazy things you make me do?'

The thought settled so warm and full in her chest that she thought she'd burst from it. 'How did you know I was coming home?'

'I do have a few resources, Stel. Did you think I wouldn't rip everything apart and turn it upside down to find out where you were, what your plans were. Anne and Alan have been helping, though I have to admit, none of us would have thought to look for you with the seabirds in the Outer Hebrides. Stella.'

216

He lifted her hand to his lips and planted a lingering kiss on her knuckles. 'None of us ever meant to hurt you. Ever. We all love you and respect you. We wanted you to be a part of what we're building, and I ended up wanting a whole lot more than that. But you have to believe our intentions were always for the best.'

'This isn't a dream then?'

'Nope. All real. He gave her a little poke in the hip with his insistent erection then raked a thumb over her nipple, which had somehow managed to peek out over the edge of the duvet. 'All of it.'

She giggled softly. 'I'm so glad to know I wasn't dreaming that.' She reached down and stroked his cock.

He slipped a hand between her legs and wriggled two fingers to spread her labia, and she felt his cock surge. 'It must have been a very good dream,' he said, feeling her wetness.

'The best.' She wriggled closer to him and nodded down to where she awkwardly fondled his cock. 'And he was the star.'

'Oh he likes that.' He offered her a wicked chuckle and raked the pad of his thumb across her clit causing her to grip at his fingers, which wriggled and pushed deeper and deeper into her cunt. She shifted her hips and rocked against him catching the salt marsh scent of herself mingled with the familiar blend of sleep and perspiration and spicy, yeasty maleness that made her hot all over. She whimpered softly at another rake of her clit. 'Please,' she breathed, giving his penis a hard squeeze, making an effort to turn her body toward it.

But he held her tight. 'You're not ready. I'll hurt you if I push into you now.' He settled a long slow kiss onto her lips and spoke breathlessly against her mouth. 'You were so impatient the first time Tino made love to you, and he hurt you. You have no idea how much he regretted hurting you.'

She groaned her frustration, but he kissed her again and ran a quick tongue across her hard pallet. 'Trust me, Stel, I'll make the journey worth the wait. My cock may be the star of your dream, but the rest of me's not bad either. And when I push into your pussy I want it sopping and gaping and ready to devour me whole. Now stop struggling and let me get you there.' He dropped a tight kiss onto each nipple before he slid down her belly with his tongue leading the way. Instinctively she opened her legs wider and bent her knees as her pussy clenched and pouted in anticipation.

He splayed her with two fingers and ran his tongue up the length of her gash in deep, probing strokes, bringing his whole mouth to rake up over her apex and concentrate the full force of a hard, suckling tongue-kiss onto her straining clit.

She bucked and gabbled and arched, curling hard fingers into the rumple of his hair wondering if she'd even survive the first assault.

When he pulled away she felt the hot humidity of his driving breath against her slit. 'My God, Stel, I'd forgotten just how much I love the taste of you.' His fingers went back to probing and stretching her while he caught his breath, then he took her again, mouth first, face deep like he would tongue and nibble and eat a path all the way up to her heart.

As he cupped his hands beneath her arse to pull her closer, the press and probe of alternating middle fingers teased at her anus, and her cries became deep-bellied animal sounds that would not have been out of place in Vincent's wood. When the first orgasm hit with riptide force, she growled and arched up to meet it, wrapping her legs around his shoulders and digging her heels in with each ecstatic wave of heat.

When the wild celebration between her hips had settled to aftershocks, he crawled up the length of her body, smelling of her pleasure, his face glistening with her lust. 'I think you're ready now,' he breathed. A slight shifting of his hips and his cock pushed home, spreading her, pushing at her, splaying her until she felt like every inch of her body was completely full of Vincent. And Tino was there too. There was a blending of the two she'd never experienced until today. Vincent had always kept them separate, and neither had ever been complete without the other.

She could feel the tension building in him until his rhythmic undulations had become hard, desperate hammering that telegraphed the intensity of his own need all the way up her spine and into her head. There it was translated into a drunken, delicious buzz that overloaded circuits and totally scoured her brain of any thought other than the wild, raging animal between her legs. Not a Pet. Not even close. She hung on tight, hammering him back until her muscles ached, until the world around them imploded down to their joining point then flashed bright in feral, brain-melting heat. As they fought their way deep into the mattress in a tangle of sweating arms and legs and knotted sheets, the thought flashed through her head that surely this had to be a dream. Surely nothing this good could exist in the real world. Consciousness drifted in and out of a haze of heat. The sunbeams lengthened across the duvet, and her breath slowed to the relaxed in and out of bliss. Then the warm body on top of her shifted slightly to the side, enough to give her breathing room, and Vincent brushed a stubbled kiss against her cheek.

'I love you, Stella James.' His voice was tight, thick with emotion. 'Vincent Valentino Evanston III loves you totally and completely and unreservedly.'

She hugged him to her, his cock still deep inside her, his heart hammering against her own. 'I get both of you, then?'

He dropped another kiss onto her parted lips. 'You get both of us, the whole enchilada quirks and flaws and all.'

It was the sob of laughter that erupted from her throat that made her aware of the tears in her eyes. She wiped them away, took his face in her hands and held him so he couldn't look away. 'Good, because I love you both with all my heart, and I could never give up either one of you, flaws, quirks and all.'

THE END

Also by K D Grace

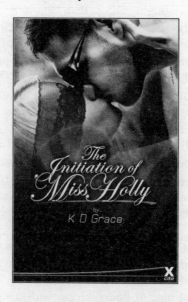

Sex with a mysterious stranger aboard a train leads Rita Holly to an initiation into the exclusive and secretive Mount club. Sophisticated and deviant rituals await Rita, as do the endless intrigues and power struggles deep within the heart of the organization.

ISBN 9781907016431   £7.99